The Devil's Disciple

ROCKY BARILLA

Rosquete
Press

Cover and book design by Eileen Jurkovich © 2015

Interior angel figures by Rocky Barilla

Library of Congress Control Number: 2014920717

ISBN: 978-0-9904851-2-4

Other work by Rocky Barilla:

A Taste of Honey

2014
Second Place, 2015 International Latino Book Awards Winning
Author for Fantasy Fiction

Forthcoming work by Rocky Barilla:

Ay to Zi

Published by Rosquete Press
All works are or will be available as Kindle or
CreateSpace Editions on Amazon.com

DEDICATIONS

This book is dedicated to my friends whose families
were part of the 12 million Holocaust victims.
May we and future generations learn from
the inhumane atrocities of the present and the past.
May we treat one another with respect and love.

"Thou shall not kill"

Exodus 20:2-17, Exodus 34:12-26, and Deuteronomy 5:6-21

"And do not take any human being's life - that God willed
to be sacred - other than in the pursuit of justice."

Qur'an, 17:33

"Thou shall not kill any living thing."

First Precept of Buddhism

"Ahimsa means not to injure any creature by thought,
word or deed. True ahimsa should mean a complete
freedom from ill-will and anger and hate,
and an overflowing love for all."

Mahatma Gandhi

"Love thy neighbor as thyself"'

Mark 12:31, Matthew 22:39

CONTENTS

ACKNOWLEDGEMENTS

I want to thank all my family, friends, and colleagues who afforded me tremendous support and love while I wrote my books. This is especially true for my wife, Dolores, who is my teammate and partner in everything we do. She has also assisted in the laborious editing of this work. Why did I write this book? To be honest, it was more of an epiphany than an act of creation.

As a teenager, I read a lot. I went through the different stages of juvenile reading e.g., The Hardy Boys and Nancy Drew. However there was a brief period, for whatever reason, when I read prisoner of war books: The U.S. Civil War and Andersonville and the march to Bataan. I was shocked, but I kept reading about these atrocious events. I get the same feeling when I watch *Breaking Bad* on television. I was just drawn to it.

Later on in college I had a friend in Los Angeles who had an Arabic father who was a doctor and a Jewish mother. This was in October of 1967. The Six-Day War broke out between Israel and the Arab Middle East. The family was distraught. They just prayed for peace in the region. They taught me that there is always more than one version of the truth. This was quite different from the absolute right and wrong indoctrination I had grown up with.

I recall an experience I had in grammar school during the Joseph McCarthy/Richard Nixon era and the anti-Communist movement in the United States. One day our teacher instructed us to go home and ask our parents, "Which is better: capitalism or communism?" Was the teacher asking us to spy on our fathers and mothers or was she conducting a social experiment? Hmm?

Well, the next day, all the students came back in favor of capitalism, except one. My father at this time had not gone to college; he would later go to college at night. He had been a music major in high school. When I asked him the question for the homework assignment, he gave me the most intelligent and memorable response that I have ever heard and that I have always tried to learn from. He said, "There are good and bad points for each system." Hmm?

In grad school, I tried to sort out why the United States was involved in the Vietnam War. To this day, I still really don't know.

As I have been an avid reader throughout the years, I have found that the settings of many novels have revolved around wars. What a hostile species we are! Most of our wars have been about power, religion, sex, racism, or economic advantage. A few about clothing. Some about pastries. I don't think any wars have been fought over rock-and-roll. Most conflicts have not only involved killing, but also torture, rape, mutilation, slavery, medical experimentation, humiliation, etc. They have not only involved combatants, but also civilian women, children, grandchildren, the handicapped, and the elderly. Religious factions have enslaved indigenous peoples in order to adorn European churches with gold. African tribes have sold neighboring clans to European slave traders. Semitic cousins have fought one another because their God is better.

Moreover, another lesson that I have learned in life is that just because something is legal, that doesn't not make it necessarily moral or right. Legal fictions pervade our society.

I think this will be the subject of a future work.

This segues back to our daughter Carmen Cave (Ph.D. Stanford) who did the critical editing and fact checking of this manuscript. She is now attending law school and will be quite the attorney.

A special friend, Eileen Jurkovich, created the wonderful cover and did the formatting.

Muchísimas gracias to the fantastic blog, Dunheim: Punto Misterio where I discovered horrific photos of the Holocaust [http://dunheim.blogspot.mx].

Also, special thanks for sharing goes to Stephanie Sara Sucher who in 1986 gave me an inscribed manuscript of *"Horse and Wagon"* [Ponce Press 1985], that shares a personal experience of the Holocaust.

Let us learn from history.

PART I - MÉLANGE

CHAPTER 1

VIN OU BIÈRE

Friday, November 25, 1921, Vienna

The black eagle emblazoned beer stein clanked against the clear wine glass as their liquids splashed onto the old wooden table.

"Prost, Professor," toasted the thick, squatty man with heavy jowls.

"And to you, my friend Maxi," grinned his bald, even more corpulent companion.

The Schubert Stube was overflowing with post-operatic performance patrons. The alcohol was flowing and the grease from the kitchen offset the pungency of the thick cigarette smoke that hung over the dozen or so tables in the cramped dining room.

"Thank you for inviting me to see *Faust* this evening," Maximilian Thimig chimed obsequiously. This square-faced, beady-eyed, and hooked nose speaker was wearing a long black jacket that looked like it had been handed down from an older brother. His black hair was unkempt and he contrasted greatly with Professor Mayr.

"You are more than welcome, Maxi. What better way to spend a Friday night after a long week with those students?"

Hugo Mayr was a professor of mathematics at the University of Vienna. This 44 year old was proficient in German, Hungarian, Russian, Italian, and French. He had a passion for opera and the arts, and a disdain for commoners. He reached into his forest green evening coat and pulled out his cigarette case. With his wormy fingers he extracted a cigarette and lit it. After two puckered puffs, he added, "The tickets were given to the university by the Cultural Affairs Council. They were gratis."

A voluptuous bar wench with ruddy cheeks came by and took their food orders. Mayr ordered another stein of beer and Thimig a glass of a sweet Tokaji wine. Maxi Thimig leaned back in his wooden chair. He was the Art Director of the Theatre of Vienna. He also often wrote critical reviews of the operas. His opinions were rarely flattering. He thought that the actors and actresses received too much attention for just being good looking. However, his friend Hugo saw the critiques as merely a release for Maxi's misplaced witticisms or manifestations of pseudo-intellectual superiority.

"I thought that Siébel seemed rather flat," Thimig proffered impishly.

"Are you talking about the voice or the chest, Maxi?" both men snickered.

"These days, who can distinguish the boys from the girls and vice versa?" the sycophant laughed.

The steaming goulash soup was placed in front of Thimig while the potato soup was given to Mayr.

"Bring us some spoons," Mayr bellowed at the buxom wench. "And more bread."

The two went on, remarking about the high points of *Faust* and the low points. Professor Hugo Mayr mechanically played with the signet ring on his left pinkie, a finger that resembled a Viennese sausage, as he suggested, "Maybe you should hire the performers for one of your plays since singing is not their forté."

Thimig gave an obsequious bow.

The bar wench brought two forks and bread.

"I said spoons, you miserable woman!" roared Mayr. "And be quick about it!"

There was giggling in a far, dark corner of the bar. It appeared that a middle-aged man with thick brown sideburns was indecently groping a young strumpet.

The spoons miraculously appeared in front of Mayr and Thimig. The professor was not happy that his soup had gotten cold. He slurped up his potato soup in a hurried manner.

"Where do these people come from, Maxi?" said Hugo. "And when are they going back?" They both laughed.

Their two orders of wiener schnitzel arrived steaming hot and overflowing with fried potatoes. Each man took his knife and fork and began to eat. Their conversation slackened.

Spittle ran from Mayr's mouth as he chewed and waved his knife, "I don't know how those French even write such works." They went back to talking about opera.

Thimig's head bobbed in agreement as he forked food into his mouth.

The bar maiden came by and collected the dirty dishes. Mayr ordered another beer and this time his commensal opera critic took a coffee.

A swift movement of cold air rushed by the two. Several young men whisked themselves out the door into the inclement weather. The opening of the door had given all the patrons a chill that froze their bones.

"Umm!" grunted the professor.

"What's the matter?"

"I am fairly certainly that those ragamuffins who bolted out of here were students of mine."

"By the way, how are your math students, professor?"

"Imbeciles! All imbeciles!"

"Do you have a problem with them relaxing and enjoying themselves, Hugo?"

"They should be studying! I gave them a homework assignment for the weekend that they should be working on. On Monday they will give a million excuses why they could not complete their assignment," he pounded his mutton fist on the table. His manner was huffy and puffy.

"Was it a difficult assignment?"

"Not really. But these youngsters are lazy and undisciplined," Mayr's frown then turned into a smirk. "But I fixed them."

"What do you mean, professor?"

"The task was to calculate π to the hundredth place."

"My God! That's next to impossible!"

"Not really. It just takes time and one has to check and recheck his work."

"I'm glad that I am not taking your class, professor. Aren't you afraid that there will be collusion among the boys?"

"That's the beauty of the assignment. I naturally assume that they are going to cheat."

"You would tolerate that?"

"For the devil of it! I left a counterfeit solution in the library! I am certain that they will copy this false calculation."

"If they turn in the fraudulent solution, will you report them to the dean?"

"The dean is an imbecile. He doesn't deserve that position. I should hold it. But mind you, I don't have such a rich father-in-law who magnanimously donates thousands and thousands of kronen to the university," he sneered sardonically. "That worthless sophist would simply give out the platitude 'that boys will be boys.' Hmm."

"They will go unpunished?"

"No, I will not accuse them or punish them for this transgression right now."

"That's mighty Christian of you."

"However, I will fail them at end of the term. Not for the scam, but for their contempt. Thinking they could disrespect me and get away with it." The professor ground his cigarette butt into the tabletop.

CHAPTER 2

FLYING ON A JET PLANE

Saturday, June 8, 1974, Santiago, Chile

Andrés was struggling to wedge his worn-out, tan leather briefcase into the airplane's overhead bin. He was competing with three winter coats and a bright pink paper bag filled with foodstuffs. He removed his multicolored muffler and plopped it down on the patterned middle seat on the starboard side of the aircraft. He was in the first row of the economy class abutting the bulkhead.

Most of the passengers were speaking Spanish on this direct flight from Santiago, Chile, to San Francisco. Andrés Miramón was traveling alone back home to the Bay Area where he would soon begin his senior year at the University of San Francisco.

"Excuse me, sir," interrupted the airline hostess whose smile highlighted her cranberry uniform. He had felt her light tap on his left shoulder. Andrés was not used to talking to designer clad models either in real life or in Fantasyland. He was just a poor student who was doing his junior year abroad at the University of Valparaiso. Everyone he knew wore blue jeans: the boys, the girls, and the faculty.

He looked at her and his eyes dropped. He was embarrassed. Had he sat in the wrong seat or failed to follow some Chilean authoritarian protocol? "Yes?" he murmured in a deferential tone.

"Would you be so kind as to move to another seat?" her dark brown eyes and raven black hair mesmerized this poor soul.

"Do I need to move my things?" he said in a respectful tone, thinking about his recent struggle with the demons in the overhead bin.

She affirmed that he would have to do it, with a double blinking of her false eyelashes and an ivory grin. He almost swooned. Never in his life had such a lovely lady paid so much attention to him. *She is giving me the totally foxy lady treatment*, he mentally sighed.

"There is a group that needs to keep their family together and we need this seat. Do you mind?"

Andrés was acting like a babbling boy on his first date to the prom. His heart was beating rapidly. Beads of sweat started to form on his brow.

The handle of his briefcase snagged a mothball-smelling, long charcoal grey coat. Unfortunately, one of the sleeves flew in the face of an elderly lady who had purplish grey hair and a large mole on her cheek. She shrieked. He apologized profusely and somehow managed to restore the errant coat back to its original home.

The stewardess put her right hand on his left shoulder and directed him forward. Her light touch seemed to warm his entire body and brand his heart. The two skirted around feet blocking the aisles, avoided newspapers spread open across the leather seats, and escaped a mother with two screaming children.

"Do you mind sitting here?" she inquired with the grin of a Cheshire cat.

The airline goddess had moved him into First Class. Never in his wildest dreams would he have believed this, especially after having to fight the airline when he checked in his old vinyl suitcase a few hours earlier. Dirty clothes should weigh the same as clean clothes, more or less. No way was his bag overweight!

He felt the black leather seat. So cool!

"Would like something to drink before we take off?"

He was too excited to respond verbally and shook his head no. He pulled open the overhead bin and there was enough empty space to house a corpse. The flight attendant disappeared.

After settling into his seat, Andrés closed his eyes and was soon breathing deeply. He inhaled, trying to relax. Moments later they were ascending into the air. He couldn't see out of the starboard window. His seating companion was snoring loudly under a thin navy blue wool airline blanket. It looked like the large, elderly man had a rubber inflatable pillow under his neck.

He turned his head to look across the aisle to the left. There was a girl and an elderly man sitting there. He still could not see the skies through the port side portals either. He closed his eyes.

A cold beer was brought to him after the plane reached 39,000 feet. Another airline hostess had served him a fancy assortment of cheeses, grapes, and crackers. Andrés was not accustomed to this type of food or this kind of attention. He fiddled with the seat and finally it reclined. This was better than his old dorm bed. He started to doze off.

"Excuse me, sir," someone softly said to him. *The goddess is back!* He thought.

It was the girl from across the aisle. While she was cute, she was not in the va-va-vroom class of the stewardess. Andrés gave her a polite smile.

"Could you please help me get a box down?" she pointed with a sleek forefinger upwards. A white and blue polka dot silk scarf knotted under her neck framed her diamond shaped face. She wore an eggshell white wool sweater over a long silver-grey skirt.

Cavalierly, he arose from his seat after unbuckling the belt. He reached up and opened the bin. He asked which box it was. She replied that it was the heavy cardboard box with the name "Schmidt" written all over the exterior with a green permanent marker.

He leaned over her as he placed the box at the elderly gentleman's feet. The teenage girl smiled and she thanked him. The older man was wearing a plaid shirt under his tweed coat. There was a silver-tipped cane leaning against the window side of his seat. Andrés assumed that the older man was her grandfather. The girl kept staring at Andrés and finally gave him a courteous half-bow.

About a half hour later, the tantalizing beef bourguignon dish, adorned with champignons and pearl onions, overwhelmed him. He washed this tasty plate down with some Chilean cabernet sauvignon. For dessert, the soufflé drowned in Grand Marnier was the coup de grace. Andrés had never had this decadent an experience in San Francisco. Maybe it was because he was a poor student.

"Sir," a small hand touched him on his left forearm.

My goddess is back! He perked up. He opened his eyes and looked upwards. Instead he realized that again it was that annoying girl from across the aisle. Although he was sorely disappointed at not seeing his airline siren, he feigned a friendly smile toward the young interloper.

"I hope that I am not rude," the youngster now spoke to him again in an English that had a Castilian accent laced with a slight guttural inflection, "but would you like my father's dessert. He can't eat it. It hasn't been touched."

Andrés had assumed that the elderly gentleman was the young girl's grandfather. The heavy elderly man was bald and had the face of a million wrinkles. He had a long white beard. The young man knew as a starving student he should never say no to food, especially such a gourmet treat. He would have to tell his classmates about the twitchin' Grand Marnier soufflés and flying first class. He assented.

The girl suggested that the two of them exchange seats to make it easier for Andrés to facilitate the passing on of the dessert. Andrés placed the book that he was reading in the seat pouch in front of him and stood up. He was relieved to stand up. The girl did likewise.

"This is my father, Johann Schmidt," she gestured with her hand. "And I am Astrid."

"Pleasure to meet you, sir, I'm Andrés María Miramón," he extended his hand, bowed his head, and shook the older gentleman's hand.

"Please, take this," Schmidt pointed to his dessert. "Save me from this decadence." The old man chuckled.

Andrés did not need to be asked twice. He grabbed the silver spoon and dug into the center of the delight. He did not realize that the daughter had snuck off to the restroom for a few minutes.

A hostess came by and offered them coffee. Both said yes. Andrés helped the gentleman fix his coffee with a little cream and sugar. It appeared that elderly man had emphysema or some other type of breathing difficulty.

"Do you speak English and Spanish?" asked the elder.

"English for sure," replied Andrés politely. "My Spanish needs a lot of work."

The old man smiled, "They say that it takes a lifetime to learn a language."

They made small talk about the weather. How strange it was to go from winter to summer in less than 24 hours.

The auburn haired young girl returned and stood by Andrés' side waiting for him to return to his own seat. Andrés was oblivious to this, but the father saved the awkward situation.

"Young man, Astrid is going to start the university in September."

Andrés turned his head to the right. "Awesome," he tried to get up but was buckled in. "Sorry."

Astrid tried not to giggle, but she couldn't help it. He apologized again and then laughed too.

"Overdosed on sugar," he said as he tried to regain his composure. "I'm buzzed on the caffeine too."

"I am sorry. I do not understand 'buzzed'. My English is not very good."

"Like high," as soon as he had mouthed the words, he knew that he was sounding like a fool.

"Hi? I still don't understand," her countenance put on a quizzical expression with a furrowed brow.

How was Mr. Dipstick going to undo his verbal clumsiness? He forced himself to think.

"*Perdóneme. Estoy agitado porque comí mucho postre y tomé mucho café,*" he reasoned that if she didn't understand his English, he might as well try to use his Spanish. [Sorry I'm jittery because I ate too much dessert and drank too much coffee.]

"Ah, I understand now," her frown had disappeared from her face, "The sugar and the coffee have affected you. I need to practice my English more."

"Your English is better than my Spanish." They both beamed.

She took out a thick bound book from her brown suede bag. She showed it to him. She was reading "*The Complete Works of Jack London.*"

"Have you checked out '*Call of the Wild*' yet?" he asked.

"Yes. It was very good," her sparkling emerald eyes glistened as she twisted her head slightly. "But I wouldn't want to be in the Yukon. It sounds too much like Patagonia. Do you know Punta Arenas?"

He pulled up his seatbelt and shifted in his seat so he could see her better. She had an infectious smile.

"No, sorry. I didn't get to travel much in Chile," he said as he adjusted the seat upright. "I'm a student too. I go to the University of San Francisco. That's in San Francisco." *Duh, that's so lame. Why I am such a dork today? I feel like I'm on a bad acid trip.* "I was doing my junior year abroad at the University of Valparaiso. I'm just now coming home."

"Oh, I love Valparaiso. It is so enchanting," she was so full of energy, so vivacious. "Those funiculars are so much fun. And such brilliant colors! The city is like a *caleidoscopio.*"

"I was stoked on La Sebastiana. One of Pablo Neruda's houses."

"I love his poetry."

"Me too. In fact, he is going to be one of the Latin American authors that I am going to do my senior thesis on."

"He loved life to the fullest."

"Yes."

"And his women also," she grinned.

Her joie de vivre was contagious. She and Andrés continued to converse incessantly.

He showed her the book that he was currently reading.

It was a dog-eared paperback copy of Mario Vargas Llosa's "*Conversation in the Cathedral.*"

"You are from Peru?" she asked. "Your parents are from Peru?"

"No, I'm from the States," Andrés said. "My dad and mom passed away when I was very young."

"I'm sorry about your parents."

"No problem. I was raised by my uncle and aunt," Andrés said matter of factly. "My parents' families were from Mexico."

"But you are reading in Spanish." she observed. "Very good."

"My Spanish is okay, but not great. That is one of the reasons that I went down to Valparaiso."

She handed back his book.

The airline hostess came back and offered them milk and warm chocolate chip cookies. Astrid and her father declined. Andrés "forced" himself to indulge.

There was an announcement over the speaker system advising the passengers that they were 150 miles from their final destination and that the weather in San Francisco was 74 degrees Fahrenheit.

"It doesn't seem to be that warm here," Astrid remarked.

He didn't reply. He started to slip out of this surrealistic experience. Now he was beginning to draw a mental list of what he had to do when he got home.

A tall lanky man wearing a San Francisco Giants baseball cap bumped into Andrés' shoulder rushing forward to the restrooms before the final descent.

Moments later there were reminders over the loudspeakers to put away the tray tables, to set the seats upright, and to pass all trash, newspapers, and glasses to the center aisle while the flight attendants came by.

The jet pitched slightly as it approached the airport with the San Francisco Bay on the starboard side. After a smooth descent, the plane bounced onto the runway. The wheels screeched for what seemed an eternity.

Astrid made the sign of the cross upon the safe arrival.

The doors opened and the passengers started to disembark in a semi-orderly fashion. A tired looking young woman was lugging two toddlers and a big diaper bag was shoving her way past behind them. There were several short, broad-shouldered, older women who seemed to be toting their weight in shopping bags and packages. Andrés waited patiently in his seat as the passengers exited. He guessed that Astrid would have a difficult time both escorting her father and hauling their boxes. At last, everyone had left and one male flight host was helping Mr. Schmidt amble with his cane up to the front exit door.

A wheel chair was waiting for Mr. Schmidt, with an airline porter assisting him into it. Astrid was right behind, followed by Andrés burdened down with their packages. The drop dead gorgeous airline hostess threw out a throaty "thank you, sir" whisper as he exited past her. He could taste her perfume. His hormones kicked into high gear.

While Schmidt was having an amiable chat with the Filipino porter and Astrid was at her father's side, Andrés performed all the burdens of a pack animal. After the ten-minute jaunt that seemed like ten hours to him, they arrived at the immigration inspection area. People were milling around like ants. Andrés was prepared to separate from the Schmidts and go through the "U.S. Citizens Only" line when the porter told them to follow him. He led them through a special "handicapped" queue and they expeditiously went through without a hitch. In customs, Astrid summoned a skycap to help them with their luggage.

Finally, they all exited the terminal. A chauffeur, who looked like the alter ego of The Incredible Hulk, greeted the Schmidts. This sculpted android wore livery that would have looked more appropriate on Frankenstein, but he easily piled their half dozen pieces of luggage on to a baggage cart.

Andrés felt wimpy compared to this Goliath. The chauffeur took the boxes from him without saying a word. He saw Astrid talking to her father in an animated manner. Finally, Schmidt nodded his head.

Astrid ran over to Andrés. "Where do you live?"

"My pad is over by USF. The University of San Francisco," he replied in bewilderment.

"Great! We are going to give you a ride home," she eagerly grinned. "You have been such a *caballero*."

"It is not necessary."

"We insist," she said as she grabbed his arm.

"Okay, no problema," he demurred. "No sweat."

CHAPTER 3

GERM KNÖDEL

Friday, November 25, 1921, Vienna

"How far up is it?" Mayr was debating the climb, up the stairwell in the dark.

"Just 27 steps to heaven's gate," Micaela lured him. "It's the first door on the right."

cx

Earlier in the evening, Mayr had wanted his customary dessert with his coffee. Thimig had lit up a cigarillo and informed his dining companion that he had an engagement that evening.

"In this weather?" blustered the professor as the buxom bar maiden cleared the dishes from the table.

Thimig fidgeted a little too long. He thumped his free hand on the table nervously. "I need to interview a young lady this evening." He did not look his companion in the eye. "For my latest play."

The professor was well aware that Thimig was married. Mayr was now being exploited by his dwarfish associate as a convenient alibi. The professor hated to be disrespected and vowed to get even with Thimig.

"Let me pay the check," Thimig said, trying to mollify his host for the evening.

The big man did not respond, but Mayr's face vividly portrayed that he was not happy.

"Order your coffee and dessert," the little man struck at Professor Mayr's weak point, his stomach for sweets.

"Okay. Okay," barked Mayr, waving him away with the flick of his wrist.

Thimig extinguished his cigarillo in a saucer. He slid on his overcoat and rushed over to the bar wench who was carrying six steins of beer to a faraway table. She yelled at him to be patient, but he insisted he had to leave. He finally put a handful of bills into the pocket of her dirty apron and ran out the door.

Mayr frequented this tavern because it had an old Tyrolean cook who made the most delectable dessert in the city. He always asked for the Germ Knödel that was a dumpling bursting with plum jam and topped with poppy seeds. Tonight he ordered this and a mélange.

Singing began from the tables next to the fireplace. Goblets were held high and clanked together. Bawdy toasts were shouted. "Prost du Sack, auf die Weiber, zack, zack, zack!" [Cheers, you prick, onto the girls quick, quick, quick!]

Mayr belched before he was half way done and licked the frothy milk from his moustache. His kidneys were betraying him and before he finished, he arose from the table to go the WC. The urinal with its discolored tiled wall reeked with an unbearable stench. He tried to hold his breath against the vile odors while tending to his bladder. Eventually he escaped. Gasping for fresher air, he made his way back to his table.

"I'm sorry. Were you sitting here, kind sir?" inquired a pallid girl with brunette ringlets falling from her head and lots of makeup, snuggly wrapped in a dark tawny-colored shawl.

Mayr's mouth was agape. He stared deeply into her dark pooled eyes. Then he noticed a trace of plum jam resting on the corner of her mouth.

"Do you mind if I sit here for a few minutes?" she wiped her face with the back of her lacey glove that she then immediately took off.

He smiled at her. It was a devilish grin. It had taken him a moment to realize that she was a girl working the streets.

She smiled back at him coyly.

"Would you like a drink, miss?" he examined her. He knew the ritual.

"Sure," she shrugged her shoulders. "White wine."

The wine came. The demimondaine pulled out a little blue vial from her black booty bag. When the wine arrived, she poured out some drops from the vial into her glass. She tipped her head back and drained the liquid elixir.

"Sorry, miss, but I have to go," he started to put on his jacket. He lived in Graben that was really not that far away.

"Please, don't leave," she pleaded plaintively. "They will make me go back into the cold."

"How about if I buy you another drink?" he suggested as he pulled out his wallet.

"I know a better way to spend your money," she urged him coquettishly.

The persuasion won out. He paid for the glass of wine and the two bundled up.

She grabbed his arm and they slowly navigated their way to a narrow, ochre-colored multi-story building.

The young girl talked to the oldish matron who answered the door. Mayr handed the madam a wad of banknotes. The girl instructed Mayr to go up the three flights of stairs and enter the first door on the right.

As he labored up the unlit and serpentine incline, he asked himself if he was selling his soul to the devil. At the end of the 27-step climb, he groped around in the darkness and found a loose door handle. He carefully jiggled it and entered the dimly lit, dank, and moldy smelling room. There was a basin and a little water ewer on a small wooden table.

Moments later she crossed the little threshold toward him. She began disrobing in front of him as he rested on a rickety lounge chair. She began with removing her red ribbon with a cheap cameo that she had tied around her neck. Then she took off her glove, slowly and sensually with her tiny teeth.

The candle flickered as she continued through her wanton performance that was well rehearsed. The shadows danced across the wall.

CHAPTER 4

JET LAG

Sunday, June 9, 1974, San Francisco

Andres arrived home late that Saturday night, jet-lagged and very tired. He dropped his one suitcase onto the floor and headed straight for his futon bed. It was too late to unpack. He would do that tomorrow. Andrés' head rested on a pocked foam pillow without a case. The air was stagnant in his room. The rented basement apartment had been empty for a least a month since his roommate had graduated and gone back to Boston. Andrés owed him a half-month's rent in arrears because he wanted to keep the place for his last year at USF. It was very close to campus and the landlords were a couple of carefree guys who were alumni of the school.

His eyes closed and he thought of the foxy stewardess. She was hot. He couldn't quite get to sleep. He went over to one of the basement windows and opened it. The openings were protected by wrought iron gratings. The cool air crept in. It was so refreshing. He needed to air out his apartment anyway.

Andrés' mind was racing. He thought about the ride home in the Schmidts' big green Mercedes limousine. Very cool!

cx

Sunday morning came and his clock radio kept blinking twelve o'clock. He really didn't know the correct time. He actually didn't even care.

He jumped into the shower that was part of the bathtub, where he found the water freezing cold. No hot water! He quickly washed his shoulder length black hair. His body was a garden of goose bumps. He dried himself off swiftly and started to get dressed. He pulled his hair into a ponytail that he secured with a rubber band.

The mirror was cloudy. He wiped it with his wet towel. He looked at his reflection. "Dear Lord, do I really look that gross?" He shaved diligently around his thin moustache, trimmed his long sideburns and tried to remove some of the scruffy hair from under his neck.

He went to a little cloth bag and pulled out a small gold cross earring with atom size turquoise stones. This he inserted into his left ear lobe. A semi-clean white tee shirt, a pair of jeans, and an old camouflage jacket and he was ready to go.

Andrés loaded two old yellowish pillowcases with his dirty clothes and went to the neighborhood coin-operated laundromat. There was a young African-American mother holding a swaddled infant on her lap, rocking back and forth. It looked like she was using half a dozen machines. A little girl ran up to her to show the mother what she had found on the linoleum floor.

He started two loads and walked next door to the Café Don to have a caffè latte accompanied by a croissant with butter and jam. It reminded him nostalgically of his recent days in Valparaiso when he was laughing and yelling with his Chilean schoolmates. They teased him about his Spanish. He reciprocated by reminding them that Chile always lost to the Argentinean national soccer team.

Andrés came back into the laundromat to transfer his wet clothes from the washers into the dryers. The little girl who must have been about four years old, observed what he was doing.

"My mother does that," she told him in a soft whisper.

"Do you help your mother?" he played along.

The little girl nodded yes. The mother tilted her head back and rolled her eyes.

Andrés then gave the munchkin a stern look, "Why aren't you in school?"

The child ran over to her mother and gave her a plaintive look.

"Tell him that today is Sunday," the mother told her. "There is no school on Sundays."

The little girl came back to Andrés and smartly said, "No school on Sundays."

"Oh, okay," Andrés tried to suppress a smile and looked at the mother. "May I give her a piece of g-u-m?" He was spelling it out carefully so the little girl would not be disappointed if the answer was no.

The mom shook her head affirmatively. Andrés pulled out two sticks of spearmint gum for the youngster and for himself.

ك

About two hours later, Andrés was back in his apartment, folding his clothes. He was packing them away in an old, dilapidated pressboard chest of drawers, when there was a knock at the door.

The sour odor in the room seemed to have finally dissipated by keeping the windows open and was replaced by the smell of clean laundry. Andrés turned down the pop music on the clock radio.

"Welcome back, Andrés," said a tall, slender man with black short hair. "We're glad you're back."

"Come on in, Maurice" Andrés beckoned. "I'm trying to straighten up the place. I got in late last night."

Maurice was the landlord. He took a seat on one of the green vinyl beanbag chairs. The two exchanged light conversation for a while.

"John made you these biscotti," Maurice smiled. "He knows they're your favorites."

Maurice's attire was very preppy with a white v-neck tennis sweater. He was well groomed and looked youthful, even though some people thought John was his son rather than his partner.

"There should be two packages and some magazines on the table over there. I didn't know if they were important," he pointed to a voluminous stack. "Also, there is a box of stuff that your roommate left behind."

The name of the roommate was not mentioned because he was not on good terms with the landlords.

"Do with them as you wish," Maurice was secretly hoping that Andrés would dump the whole thing into the trash.

Andrés asked Maurice if he wanted something to drink, even though he had only water.

The landlord declined. He got up to leave. "John is coming home soon." Andrés stopped him with a motion of his hand and went over to a paper bag still in his suitcase. He pulled out two souvenir leather bookmarks from Valparaiso and gave them both to Maurice.

"Oh, thank you. You shouldn't have."

Andrés shrugged his shoulders and smiled.

"Have to go. John will be waiting."

As Maurice got up and started to make his way to the door, he turned and remarked, "Don't fret about the rent this month. Pay us when you can."

ॐ

The grocery store was a cool place to hang out. People did their shopping on Sunday night for the rest of the week. Andrés went down his list and ticked off the items as he placed them into his cart. Bread. Peanut butter. Strawberry jam. Cheese slices. Lunchmeat.

On the way home he stopped at a public telephone booth. The service for his home phone had been disconnected during his absence. He called his aunt and uncle in San Antonio letting them know that he was fine and had had a good time in Santiago. The operator interrupted every few minutes and told him to deposit more quarters. He promised his aunt that he would come to visit them after his graduation in May. He didn't have any plans after that.

Andrés was really tired when he returned home. He made himself some grilled cheese and ham sandwiches and was in bed by nine o'clock.

CHAPTER 5

MICAELA

Wednesday, April 19, 1922, Vienna

The young woman was shaking in the makeshift bed. There was the patter of light rain outside the old building on Seilerstrasse. Two other companions stood around her, one wiped the forehead of the feverish patient while the other cooed over her with soothing words.

"Micaela, do you want us to call the doctor?" the redhead with pensive hazel eyes asked.

The bedridden girl was in a sweat, shook her head no, and weakly blurted out, "I could use a few drops of my medicine though."

"You know you can't," softly reprimanded the other woman attending her. "It would be bad for the baby."

"Just a few drops to let me sleep," she pleaded. "It couldn't do much harm."

The two friends both shook their heads.

The sixteen-year old Micaela was so pallid with dark circles around her reddened eyes. Her skinny frame of a body looked like a serpent that had devoured a pig. She was almost five months pregnant and clearly showing.

Meanwhile, they all could hear screams and the creaking of some furniture coming from upstairs.

"Laurette has taken the patrolman into house arrest again," the two giggled.

Micaela coughed. A little spittle of blood emerged.

An odor of urine permeated the room. The poor girl had wet herself again. One of the women went to grab a clean, wet cloth.

Micaela closed her eyes.

Suddenly, without warning, the door swung open.

"You have to leave by Friday," ranted the dwarfish madam who barged into the room abruptly.

The two younger women were visibly frightened by the sudden intrusion.

"Jesus, Mary, and Joseph! Micaela, what in heaven's name is wrong with you?" continued to bellow the little lady in a fashionable crimson satin dress with her silver grey mane gathered into a bun. "This place stinks and you look hideous!"

The redhead and the other woman pulled back as the madam approached the bed, holding a white silk handkerchief over her nose.

"I'm going to send you over to Doctor Lohnes," Madam Regina asserted. "He'll take care of the problem."

The fragile figure opened her eyes. Tears ran down her cheek. She painfully nodded no.

"All right! All right! You young people! You think you know everything," the older woman lamented throwing up her hands. "Wait and see. You and your child will both starve when you are out on the street.

"I can't support you. You are costing me money when you don't work. You already owe me hundreds! I don't care if you don't know who the father is. You can persuade one or two of your gentlemen friends that the child is theirs. They will pay. I know, they will pay," the venom gushed from her mouth. "I want the money or you are out of here by Friday. You better make it right."

The two other women dared not say anything.
Micaela began sobbing as her little torso convulsed.

CHAPTER 6

SENIOR THESIS

Monday-Tuesday, June 10-11, 1974, San Francisco

After he had his telephone service turned back on, Andrés wandered over to the University of San Francisco college campus. The sky was overcast. He could barely see the St. Ignatius Church in the distance. Some co-eds were shooting hoops at the basketball court.

He couldn't believe that the telephone company wanted ten dollars to turn the service back on. Fortunately, he talked them out of another deposit because there was still money in the account that his roommate had left uncollected.

In order to take his senior thesis seminar this summer, Andrés would have to register for that class now. Hopefully, there would be room and he wouldn't have to be wait-listed. He crossed the mottled lawn and headed for the Admissions Building. There was the smell of fresh cut grass.

In addition to the registration forms, he had to fill out some financial aid papers. He also had to provide the school with personal history and health information. Andrés was attending USF on a partial scholarship, but he had also accumulated several student loans over the last three years. He hoped that there were no longer any debtors' prisons.

Andrés Miramón had been born in San Antonio in 1953. His father had been killed when a train ran into a municipal bus when Andrés was only one year old. His mother moved in with her brother, René, and sister-in-law, Dora. His uncle was Andrés' mentor and best friend.

Studying was never Andrés' forte. He did just enough to pass. When his mother moved away and got remarried, he remained with his uncle. She had passed away when Andrés was only eight.

He never got into serious trouble. He occupied his time by reading any book he could get his hands on . . . the Hardy Boys series, "*The Count of Monte Cristo*," and stories by Rafael Sabatini and Emilio Salgari. The local library staff knew him by his first name. They would always forgive his fines for overdue books.

Uncle René had raised himself up by the bootstraps. He finessed his teenage blacksmith skills into becoming a decent linotype operator at the local newspaper.

He tried to share with his nephew some avuncular wisdom about pursuing one's dream, but always having a Plan B that could enable one to make a decent living. Andrés would just nod his head and pretend to go along with the program.

Aunt Dora was sad when Andrés moved away to San Francisco. She wanted him to settle down in San Antonio where people were friendly and decent. None of that crazy hippy stuff and Free Love that California was famous for. Maybe marry a local Chicanita and give them a "grandkid."

A few years later, when Andrés declared his major in Comparative Literature, he knew that he had disappointed his guardians. He also thought that he probably would never come back to Texas to live. Damn that Jack Kerouac!

It took Andrés most of the day to complete the cumbersome paperwork that he finally turned in at the school clerk's office.

Afterwards, he left the campus and walked a block to the bank to check on his account balance. He had very little money. He had to decide between going to school or eating for a month. It would be July before he would receive a financial aid check.

Another block over was the post office. It was closed when he swung by late in that afternoon. He would have to come back another day.

og

The next day, Tuesday, was a little chilly and Andrés grabbed his jacket and multicolored scarf. At least this morning there had been hot water for his shower. He skipped shaving per his loose routine. He left the house and waved good morning to the elderly man next door who was watering his chrysanthemums and other colorful plants. The old man gave him a smile with a scarcity of teeth.

He crossed a busy street where buses and trams were hurrying hundreds of people to work. Finally, he arrived at the post office. There were at least twenty people ahead of him. An Asian lady held a big cardboard box. Some scruffy-looking students sported USF green and gold sweatshirts. A middle-aged brunette wearing her nurse's garb snapped her gum.

When he finally reached the window, he showed his California driver's license as identification for the retrieval of his mail. It showed 40 Tamalpais Terrace as his address. He really didn't drive, but he needed something besides his student ID: 5'8", 155 lbs., black hair, brown eyes. He was given a large white plastic box that contained letters, bills, flyers, and more junk mail. Initially, it seemed to weigh about five pounds. By the time he returned home sweating, it was weighing closer to fifty.

It was late in the afternoon when Andrés started to sort his mail. The evil smells of his abode were finally gone. His clock radio was tuned to an "oldies but goodies" station. Andrés threw wadded-up junk mail into a small trashcan to the left of his feet. He scored one point for each basket. To the right went the bills. Magazines and letters he placed next to him.

The chamomile tea that he had prepared warmed him up a bit. He had covered his legs with a blue and red afghan that an old girl friend had crocheted for him.

There were applications for Visa credit cards, ads for Medicare supplemental insurance, a dozen wrong addresses, and seven old Christmas cards.

He took a sip of his hot beverage. So far the tally was sixty-one points. In front of him sat an oversized, fancy pink envelope. He tried to open it too quickly and was rewarded with a painful paper cut on his thumb. He ran to the bathroom to get some toilet paper to stop the bleeding.

With a bit of struggling, he managed to extract a pink cardstock invitation. He was stunned to see who the sender was.

The printed invitation said that Mr. Schmidt was having a birthday celebration for his daughter Astrid on Saturday, June 15 at 3 o'clock. There was a telephone number to RSVP and the home address.

At the bottom of the invite, there was a friendly note written with a fountain pen:

A mi amigo Andrés,
Gracias por todo. Ojalá que usted pueda asistir a la fiesta.
¡Cumplo dieciocho años!
    Su amiga,
    Astrid

His mouth formed a smile. He would have to attend the party. Awesome! What about a present?

CHAPTER 7

USCHI

1929, Vienna

Her pain was over. Micaela lay on a bed with her glassy eyes staring upwards at the paint that was peeling from the grayish green ceiling. The doctor had pronounced her death. He wiped the blood from his hands onto the butcher apron. One of the young women came in with a basin of water and some old rags to clean up the gruesome scene.

Micaela had endured until she was 24 years old, trying to survive and raise Augustin. After Madam Regina had expelled her from the brothel, she came to live in an apartment flat owned by the demimondaine, Ursula "Uschi" Sokol, a well-kept woman.

"Uschi" had a big heart, but an even bigger entrepreneurial sense. She had been raised in Frieberg with a father who worked in the neighboring mines and who habitually beat Uschi's mother. Her father had even tried on several occasions to sexually abuse her, his own daughter. When a young local militia corporal had paid attention to Uschi and promised her the sun and moon, she readily ran off with him. She was only sixteen, but she knew that she was destined to a miserable life if she remained at home. The abduction and the seduction eventually became a nightmare for the soldier. He really didn't have any paying employment; he relied on monthly stipends from his uncle who was a former admiral in the Austrian navy.

They ran away to Großschirma where they found lodging at a local gasthof. He would force his little beauty to parade among the customers in the inn while he collected coins until he passed out or the tavern closed. On occasion he would get agitated and jealous and accuse the patrons of trying to take liberties with Uschi. Finally, one night this segued into the young corporal killing another soldier in a barroom brawl.

Uschi and her lover fled to Vienna where they took refuge in a cheap pension. He had evolved to accusing Uschi of encouraging other men. He continued to drink excessively until one night at a restaurant, he struck Uschi with the back of his hand. She flew across the table knocking over plates and drinks.

A well-dressed older man of Arabian descent and swarthy features put his hand on the soldier's shoulder. He tried to calm the young man down.

The young corporal called the interloper out.

"Let go of me, towel head!" his speech slurred. "Mind your own business!"

"Please, my friend, calm down."

"Stay out of my way or I will demand satisfaction!"

The situation escalated until finally the pair went outside into the murky alley.

"I challenge you a duel, you blackheart," the young man pulled out his ceremonial sword and brandished it toward the gentleman.

"As you wish," the older man pulled out a pistol and shot his opponent in the heart.

The police arrived within the hour and at least six witnesses swore that the fatality was prompted by an attempted robbery.

The robber had disappeared into the darkness.

Meanwhile, Victor Mansour escorted the poor girl to his palatial living quarters. He was a gold and precious metal trader from Greater Lebanon. In the beginning, he just bought Uschi flattering clothes, lavished her with jewelry, and wined and dined her at the finest restaurants. She became his renowned paramour and was the talk of the town, especially among the diplomatic corp. Her classic beauty and innate intelligence made her a very exclusive commodity.

Unfortunately, Mansour was forced to return to Beirut under the latest French mandate or face confiscation of his business and properties. He knew that Uschi could not survive a life in Lebanon, so he passed on to her a small leather bag of precious stones when he departed.

Now she did not have to work the streets in the cold. But before Uschi operated on her own, she worked briefly for Madam Regina. She wanted to learn the business aspect of her profession. It was there that she met Micaela for the first time.

Finally, when Uschi was established, she rose to the elite class of her profession. Uschi could pick and choose. She wore the finest clothes and dined at the best restaurants. Because she felt so advantaged, she took pity on young girls who had suffered unfortunate experiences. There was sweet Marie who had a child fathered by the local priest of her town, the toothless Henrietta who had been gang raped and beaten by soldiers, and Patrizia who was a schizophrenic. They all were supposed to pay their benefactress back for their food and lodging, but most of the time Uschi lost money.

When Micaela was thrown out of Madam Regina's, Uschi invited the expectant mother to her residence. Room and board was charged, but rarely was it collected. In fact, when

Micaela had a difficult time trying to suckle little Augustin, Uschi hired a French wet nurse. This woman was a former prostitute who had had her face slashed by her maquereau for allegedly holding out on him.

After Augustin was born, Micaela went back on the streets, again working for Madam Regina. She also had to kick back a percentage of her earnings to Uschi for rent. Her precocious son spent his evenings being raised in Uschi's brothel. There he was always pulling pranks with the ladies' under garments, and thereby was given the nickname *"Teufl"* or "Little Devil."

As Augustin got older he would converse with customers on all subjects and in all languages. For these parlor tricks, he was rewarded with chocolates and small coins.

His mother became increasingly ill and demented until she died of consumption. She had been addicted to laudanum for years in her quest to cope with her miserable life, and toward the end she could no longer even recognize her own son. He was almost seven years old when his mother passed. He had never known his biological father.

Uschi loved looking into Augustin's blue eyes. After Micaela died, Uschi assumed custody of the child and brought him back into her home to be raised as her own.

The following year Uschi and her new patron, Dieter, picked up and moved to Munich. They brought Augustin with them. Dieter Müeller had been a German military attaché to the Austrian Nazi Party. For Dieter, Uschi represented everything that exemplified the best of the Aryan race. Dieter was kind and generous to her.

Although Uschi and Dieter never married, together they raised Augustin as their own. Micaela had never known who her son's biological father was. There had been hundreds of candidates among her Viennese clientele, but that was the risk that her profession ran if one got pregnant. The boy was known now as Augustin Teufl. He was sent to an exclusive scholastic academy where he excelled beyond all expectations. His teachers raved about Augustin's genius.

"This prodigy will set the world on fire," bragged Dieter to his military cohorts.

CHAPTER 8

THE BIRTHDAY

Saturday, June 15, 1974, San Francisco

He dug his hand into his pocket to look for change while he walked down Turk Street to Masonic to catch the northbound bus. Andrés would have tried to walk it, but he was running late. It took forever for the hot water in the shower to come on, and he couldn't find his Brut cologne.

Luckily, he had clean clothes. He had quickly hitched on his brown corduroy jeans. At first he was going to wear a yellow turtleneck, but it didn't seem to match. He opted for a blue and white tablecloth patterned Levi shirt, a navy blue parka, and his scarf. Awkwardly bending over, he put on his Macalister suede shoes and rushed out the door.

It took him less than five minutes to navigate his way to the bus stop, stepping around an Irish setter being walked by a young African-American couple, an older Russian lady pushing a shopping cart loaded up with groceries and a bottle of jug wine, and a tired looking Hindi mother with her three kids.

The air was chilly, but the overcast from the morning had almost burned off. The exhaust fumes of the cars and buses fouled the air. How this contrasted to the fresh air in Valparaiso, situated on the coast with its wonderful ocean breezes, he reminisced.

The bus driver gave him a dirty look. "You still owe five cents."

Andrés had not paid attention to the fact that bus fares had been raised while he was away.

"Sorry," he said remitting the extra nickel.

The bus was only half full and he sat behind two young girls chatting away in Cantonese. He looked out of the window as they passed by storefront shops and pastel-colored houses. By the time the bus entered one of the Presidio gates, he was the only passenger left.

He asked the bus driver where he should get off, but she didn't know. Andrés was subsequently dropped off in the middle of a cypress and pine forest. The smells were great, but he was now lost. There was no one around.

Andrés walked in a westerly direction until he saw a mail truck. Quickly, he ran to it and inquired of the mail carrier where 531 Gibbon Court was located. The postman pointed his index finger in a southerly direction.

He looked toward the curvy road that sloped upward. There were no cars coming or going. He started to walk. There was no sidewalk on either side of the road. Near the top of the grade, he observed the beginning of a hiking trail splicing off to the right. The path was covered with wood chips and looked rather desolate.

Andrés was totally disoriented. He decided to continue straight ahead and avoid the hiking trail. The air was moist and there were fresh pine scents engulfing the wooded area.

A few minutes later he heard voices down the incline. He stopped and listened. The sounds grew louder. He heard laughter. In front of him, Andrés spied four hikers walking uphill towards him. He stopped and waited.

A tall, light brown haired young man around Andrés' age

approached him and asked, "We are looking for a trailhead somewhere around here. You haven't seen it, eh?" Moments later his other male colleagues also carrying backpacks caught up.

Andrés informed them that he had passed such a spot and pointed up the hill. He spied the Canadian maple leaf decal on the first hiker's hooded sweatshirt.

One of the other guys pulled out a map. The Canadians were trying to decide where they were and how to get to the desired hiking path.

Andrés joined them and saw that they had a diagram of the Presidio grounds with its trails and roads. He asked to see it and eventually found the vicinity where the Schmidts resided.

The five walked up the slope to the wood chip covered path. At that point they all said their good byes. Andrés hurried along the road where he had previously traveled. He had been going the wrong way for over half an hour. Now he was worried about being late to the party.

A squirrel ran by and stopped in the middle of the road, knowing no fear. Andrés was sweating. He took off his parka and wrapped it around his waist.

⊰

The large oaken door opened up to the elegant interior of the three-story, Spanish-styled barracks with a red tiled roof.

"Welcome, Mr. Miramón," greeted the middle aged, grey haired maid. "I'm Nan Hill. We have been expecting you."

Andrés uttered something unintelligible in return as she took his parka, scarf, and a newspaper-wrapped package. The foyer had a large marble statute in the middle. He thought he was in the Versailles Palace.

A fleeting figure raced down the staircase.

"Oh, I'm so glad you came," Astrid grabbed his arm and hung onto it. She had her auburn hair in big curls that complemented her green eyes and emerald silk dress.

"I'm sorry that I'm late," he mumbled feeling like a fool. "I got lost."

"Don't worry," she was still fastened to his arm. "I'm still getting used to this place, too."

She escorted him into a huge drawing room with three crystal chandeliers hanging from the ornate ceiling. The walls were covered with tapestries. There were lace-covered tables with platters of cold and hot food. A white frosted double-tiered birthday cake stood in the corner. Soft classical music was playing from speakers implanted into the walls.

"May I bring you a beverage, sir?" the shaved-headed valet inquired.

"A screwdriver, please."

"Very good, sir," he replied. "And you, miss, are you still good with the sparkling water?"

"Yes, thank you, Bert," Astrid bowed. "This is my friend Andrés."

They walked over to a table that had charcuterie, cheeses, olives, and a thousand other little appetizers. Andrés tried to be circumspect as he filled his little white china plate with the goodies. It took him a minute to realize that no one else had touched the food.

Having grown up in San Antonio, his background was very simple. His mother had struggled to raise him. They had been poor, but Andrés was always clean and well groomed. After his mother died, his aunt Dora and Uncle René made sure that Andrés had his daily allotment of rice, beans, and tortillas. Andrés didn't have his first hamburger until he was eleven. His first pizza came during high school when he was on the baseball team. Right now he couldn't have ever dreamed about eating this type of cuisine.

Astrid gave him a small fork and a white cotton napkin. They started to stroll over to the gold-colored sofa.

Suddenly, there was a strange stillness in the room. A short, full-bodied woman was making her entry. She was dressed in a long black gown suitable for the Spanish Inquisition and walked slowly across the room toward the pair. Her black hair was pulled back and braided into a coiled bun. She wore no makeup. Her hands were clenched and she stared directly into Andrés' eyes. She had the same solemn comportment as his third grade teacher, Sister Mary Attalia (affectionately, nicknamed Sister Mary Attila the Hun by the students).

"*Tía, quiero presentarle . . .*" Astrid tried to interject. [Auntie, I want you to meet . . .]

The aunt put up her index finger as a caution, "Remember, my dear, we will only speak English, especially with guests."

"Yes, auntie," the girl bowed her head.

"Welcome, Mr. Miramón," the older woman said in a subtle tone as she extended her hand. "I have heard a great many things about you. I am Matilda Grossman."

Andrés shook the hand lightly, "Pleasure to meet you, Mrs. Grossman."

The woman smiled back at him weakly, "I am not Mrs. Grossman. I am Astrid's aunt and guardian. You may call me Doña Grossman."

"When is Father coming down?" inquired the niece.

"I don't know. I will have Bert locate him. He needs to receive his guest." Doña Grossman walked off and the environment came back to life.

Andrés lost his appetite. He felt that some portentous

incarnate had entered his soul.

"Come on," said the girl with a smiling face. "Let's sit back down."

They did, but Andrés kept one eye peeled toward the salon entrance.

In her bubbly fashion, Astrid shared that she was enchanted with her new living quarters in San Francisco. It was quite different from their situation in Santiago where her family had more household staff.

Andrés picked at his food. Astrid took a grape from his plate and plopped it casually into her mouth with a little giggle.

Finally, Bert, the butler, entered the room accompanying an older man walking slowly with a cane. Before her father had entered, Astrid had whispered to Andrés that Schmidt had suffered a debilitating stroke in 1966 that had left him partially paralyzed. With physical therapy and an iron will he was almost ambulatory. Unfortunately, the side effects of the pain medication had caused premature aging. His hair had turned gray and thereafter, he became bald. His face radiated a million wrinkles. Schmidt was not one for self-pity and tried his best to be independent although everyone fawned all over him.

"Welcome, Andrés," greeted Mr. Schmidt heartily, extending his hand. "Thank you for coming, my boy."

"Thank you, sir, for inviting me."

"You should feel very special. You are our first official guest," Schmidt said in an amusing fashion.

Bert pulled up a chair for his master and then retreated to the back of the salon. The father, daughter, and visitor engaged in light social conversation.

Andrés again related in more detail that he was entering

his senior year at USF. He was majoring in Comparative Literature. He told his hosts that for the summer he would be taking a seminar that was designed to prepare him to write his senior thesis. He stated that he would compare and contrast the writings of Pablo Neruda with the writings of Jorge Borges and Mario Vargas Llosa.

"Very interesting," proffered Mr. Schmidt pensively. "Just their works? Or their philosophies, values, and personalities also?"

Andrés was about to quickly retort that this was to be a paper on literary styles, but held himself in reserve for a second.

"Does a writer jot down simply words?" further inquired the elder. "Or does he also share his political views? His religion? His soul?"

In less than a minute, Mr. Schmidt had turned Andrés' worldview upside down.

"I really don't know," feeling dumbfounded, Andrés tried to rebound. "I should ask my professor. He has to approve my topic anyway." He really didn't want to feel stupid in front of Astrid.

Mr. Schmidt barely moved his hand and suddenly, Nan was there by his side.

"Yes, sir," the short lady in the maid's uniform responded with a slight French accent.

"When Matilda returns, please serve us the hot dishes," he directed.

"The table in the dining room is set, sir. Whenever you are ready," Nan responded. "Would you like me to call on her, sir?"

He made an invisible motion toward her.

"What are you thinking about becoming after you

graduate?" Schmidt turned his attention back to Andrés.

"I really hadn't given it much thought," he answered. The truth was that he hadn't given it any thought. He probably didn't have enough money to enroll in graduate school where he would have to do attend if he wanted to teach at the collegial level. Maybe he could try to teach high school.

"Did my daughter tell you that she will begin classes at Mills College in September?"

Andrés was surprised. He realized that he knew very little about the Schmidts. He had done most of the talking during their conversations.

"Oh, awesome," he blurted. He looked away from Mr. Schmidt and turned toward Astrid. "Do you know what you want to major in?"

"I am thinking Art or Art History."

There was a pause and everyone looked around.

"Pardon me for being late," the woman in black said. She turned her head, "Nan, we will be proceeding to the dining room."

Obediently, the three people arose and walked toward the open salon door.

The large black oak table was set for four persons. There were several pieces of silver flatware and crystal vessels for each setting. Andrés felt awkward that there were no other guests for Astrid's birthday party. *Oh, well, she has only been here a week*, he thought, *not much of an opportunity to meet many people.*

Andrés looked at the spoons, then the forks. He frowned. He was not familiar with dining etiquette or place setting protocols.

"Do you know many people in the Bay Area?" he tried to ask diplomatically.

"Not yet. But I know you," she teased. "I still need to go over to Mills to get my orientation package and finalize my housing arrangement."

"Are you going to live on campus?" he had hated living on the campus at USF during his freshman year. There was too much juvenile behavior and partying and smoking marijuana.

"Aunt Matilda has been making all the arrangements," Astrid asserted. "I will be in the International Students Dormitory."

"That's awesome."

The first course was brought in by Bert. It was a clear chicken broth with chicken chunks and julienned vegetables. Andrés was trying to observe which piece of silver he was supposed to use.

Matilda, who was sitting to his right, grabbed his hand. He was momentarily startled.

"Let us pray," the matron began. "Oh, Lord, bless our family and our guest for the food we are about to receive . . ."

Astrid held his other hand. It was warm. Her head was bowed and her eyes were closed as she prayed along with her aunt.

After the "amen" everybody selected the big spoon furthest to their right. Mr. Schmidt had a little difficulty doing so. It appeared that he was left-handed.

Bert came in and poured a little sauvignon blanc for everyone, except Matilda. A toast to Astrid's birthday was given.

The soup dishes were cleared away.

The salad was the next course. The romaine lettuce was dressed simply with oil, vinegar, salt, and pepper. Andrés was generously spreading butter on the dark bread roll.

The conversation centered around Mr. Schmidt asking Andrés for suggestions about things to do in the Bay Area.

"There is lame, touristy stuff. Like going to Fisherman's Wharf or Alcatraz," his eyes drifting upwards as he tried to think. "But there are some very cool museums inside Golden Gate Park."

"Wonderful," the old man seemed to have winked at Andrés.

Nan removed the dirty dishes and soiled flatware from the table. Andrés carefully wiped the corners of his mouth with the white linen napkin.

Bert carried in the main course that was a pork tenderloin dish with roasted apples and an exquisite Calvados sauce that Nan assisted in serving. There were scalloped potatoes, carrots, and peas on the side.

Andrés was already getting sated before he could start the tantalizing dish. Meanwhile, Bert poured him some Riesling in another wine glass and refilled his water glass. Astrid was constantly staring at Andrés and smiling pleasantly at him.

Andrés slowly resumed eating. He had hated eating peas growing up. They had tasted like tin. However, these petit pois were divine.

Matilda was deathly quiet during the meal. She deferred to Mr. Schmidt during the dialogues. She did not eat much. Her eyes seemed to steal toward Andrés often.

Andrés was only able to finish half of his plate. He felt guilty because he had been raised to eat everything on his plate and not waste food. He was always the starving student and couldn't afford to eat well. Now he was eating Michelin star quality goodies and squandering the experience. His stomach was so full.

Mr. Schmidt "suggested" that they take their coffee in

the study that had a giant picture window overlooking San Francisco Bay and Alcatraz. The Golden Gate Bridge was not quite visible. There were dozens of sailboats skating atop the white caps. There was a hint of a fog coming from the west. Schmidt ambled slowly into the room with a cane in his left hand and his daughter supporting him.

To the right of the room, the birthday cake glowed. The top layer had eighteen candles burning brightly. The bottom layer had *"Feliz Cumpleaños"* written in chocolate icing around it.

Astrid jumped for joy. They all sang the Chilean version of "Happy Birthday":

> *Cumpleaños feliz*
> *Te deseamos a ti*
> *Feliz cumpleaños Astrid*
> *Que los cumplas feliz.*

Everybody clapped. Astrid was about to blow out the candles when her father put out his arm.

"Let's sing the English version," he laughed. " *Happy Birthday to you . . ."*

The group was now rambunctious and everyone was laughing except Matilda. Nan the maid and Bert the butler had joined in the festivities.

After taking a deep breath, Astrid blew out the eighteen candles. Nan extracted them from the cake. Wax had dripped on the yellow cake with vanilla frosting. Fortunately, Andrés always had room for dessert.

Bert poured coffee for everyone, except Matilda who took a chamomile tea. Andrés took his beverage with plenty of cream and sugar.

Now it was time to open presents. Astrid received presents from the Schmidt household staff in Santiago that Matilda had transported a month earlier when she had come to set up the new household.

❀

Matilda Grossman was the sister of Astrid's mother, Carmen. Their father was German and the mother was Chilean. Their mother tongues were German and Spanish. Carmen was always in high spirits growing up while Matilda was always stern and judgmental. Carmen excelled in school and was very popular. Matilda had different aspirations and was reclusive. She entered the Order of the Immaculate Heart of Mary. It was at the Colegio Villa Maria in Santiago that Matilda became fluent in English. Eventually, she was sent on a mission to Peru to work in a Quechua village. Unfortunately, in 1956, her sister Carmen died in childbirth. She felt guilty for being so estranged from her sister. She had cared for children that she had very little familial connection with, except for their almighty souls. After going into a retreat for a week, she met with her Mother Superior. Sister Mary Matilda, as she was known, was granted dispensation from the bishop to leave the nunnery and rescind her vows. Six months later, she took charge of raising Astrid at Schmidts' mansion in Santiago.

In 1966, Matilda became head of the household. It was not known if it was because Schmidt had suffered major health issues or if her management style commanded it.

Under Matilda's tutelage, Astrid's education was first class. Astrid was proficient not only in Spanish and German, but could hold her own in English and French. Matilda was a hard taskmistress and read her Bible while Astrid practiced the piano on a daily basis.

When Johann Schmidt decided to move to San Francisco, he sent Matilda ahead in early May to set up the household at the Presidio residence. The Schmidts would still maintain their Chilean home with a skeleton staff after the transition was implemented.

Matilda had met with the Presidio administrator who gave her leads on staff employment, residence requirements and restrictions, and other useful information. The maid and the butler came highly recommended by the Human Resources Director of the Presidio. The young Mexican cook, Maria, came from one of the best Italian restaurants in the city. The chauffeur, Erik, was furnished by the consulting firm with which Schmidt was working.

❧

Someone had given Astrid a beautiful white wool sweater. Nan folded the wrapping paper as soon as the birthday girl unraveled each package. There were brown calfskin gloves, a Waterman fountain pen, and a diamond tennis bracelet. Astrid was so excited. She uttered dozens of thank yous.

Toward the bottom of the pile, there was a package wrapped in old newspaper . . . the Sunday Herald-Examiner comic section, to be exact. Astrid read the card and grinned at Andrés.

❧

Andrés had gone to his first summer school class the day before. It was a seminar on how to write a senior thesis. He wanted to make sure that whatever topic he selected, his professor would approve it. He had seen too many seniors procrastinate and end up bombing on their projects.

Professor Jameson had a ruddy face and a stringy goatee. He called all the students "boys" or something similarly indifferent. He gave them a short overview of the course that included timelines for senior thesis proposals, executive summaries, outlines, etc. Andrés barely took notes. He was adrift trying to think of a fitting gift for Astrid, a girl he barely knew. Immediately after class, he rushed to the college bookstore and bought a birthday card with the picture of the Golden Gate Bridge on it. Mentally he thought that he should buy her a USF sweatshirt. Unfortunately, he didn't have the money and he didn't know her size.

⚙

Astrid now exuberantly unwrapped Andrés' gift, throwing the newspaper behind her. She let out a shriek of joy. The present turned out to be used hardback copies of John Steinbeck's "*Of Mice and Men*," Helen Hunt Jackson's "*Ramona*," and Carlos Fuente's "*Aura*," the last book being in Spanish. These came from Andrés' treasure trove of old books that he had collected over the years and were his only signs of wealth. Nan wadded up the old newspaper into a ball that she would discard later.

Astrid got up from the sofa and came over to give him a kiss on the cheek. For this he felt embarrassed because his gifts paled to what Astrid had amassed this evening.

It was getting to be close to eight o'clock. Matilda gave Astrid the suggestion that the party should start winding down because everyone was getting tired.

Astrid transformed herself into the dutiful niece. Moments later she once again thanked Andrés and bid him good night.

Andrés was all ready to leave when Schmidt summoned him with his left forefinger.

"Andrés, thank you for coming over this evening. I know that you must have a lot of studying to do. Astrid has really enjoyed your company."

Andrés at first was speechless, but finally he recovered, "Thank you, Mr. Schmidt for the invitation. You have a beautiful home. I had such an awesome time."

"Sit down, my boy, for a minute," he gently grabbed the young man's arm. "I was wondering if you could do me a big favor."

"Sure. What is it?'

"As you know, my daughter has just arrived into a different environment. It is going to be difficult for a while for her to adjust and get acclimated." Andrés was nodding his head as Schmidt went on. "Her first priority is to master the English language. This is the only way that I see that she can excel in college.

"My initial instinct was that we should hire a woman to tutor her, to orient her around the city, and to help her grow into a fine, young lady," he paused and looked deeply into Andrés eyes. "But Providence has brought you to us. Andrés, you are a noble young man. If you could be her mentor this summer, I would be in your debt.

♋

"*¡Madre de Dios!* Johann, you can't be serious," Matilda remarked to her brother-in-law as they sat in his private office earlier that afternoon. "He's too young."

"Well, I got a good feeling about him while conversing with him when Astrid and I flew here to join you."

"But we don't know anything about him."

"He's a nice boy. He seems trustworthy," he looked her in the eye. "And he is very respectful."

"Is he religious?" Matilda persisted. "He can't be one of us. We don't need any radical students around. You know what they are doing back in Chile."

"Why, Matilda , I am surprised at you," Schmidt smiled at her. "I had almost forgotten that you had taken a vow of charity."

Her face reddened.

"And besides, he is an orphan," he added empathetically.

Matilda knew that her arguments were futile. She knew her brother-in-law all too well. He had already made up his mind and he rarely changed it once he decided on something.

"I just want Astrid safe and sound," she made a last ditch effort.

"Me, too," he replied softly. "But, Matilda , we are not going to be able to protect her forever. She will have to fend for herself. You know that we have to expose her to a little reality."

Matilda didn't respond. She bobbed her head ever so slightly. She had yielded to Johann mentally.

"Besides, my dear sister-in-law," he tried to allay her concerns. "It's only for the summer. What could go possibly wrong in a few months?"

慘

"If you accept, Andrés, it would require you to assist her twice a week. You would help her become proficient in English, knowledgeable in U.S. customs and culture, and more importantly, protect her. I know that you are a gentleman. You have already demonstrated that to me. I could offer you $50 a week plus expenses."

Andrés was stunned. He would be a babysitter for the summer. Heavens knew that he desperately needed the money and Astrid was a nice girl. "Right on, Mr. Schmidt," he reached out to shake the older man's hand. "Thank you very much, sir."

"Two things, Andrés. The first one is man-to-man. Astrid is very innocent. I know that you will not take advantage of her or expose her to any type of depravity."

Andrés didn't know if that was a question or a parental

directive. "Yes, sir, I understand."

"The second thing is that you must not tell her of our business arrangement. Agreed?"

Andrés nodded his head.

"Wonderful. Thank you, my young man," the elderly man clapped his hands softly. He turned around and directed an order to the butler, "Bert, please have Dieter take Andrés home."

The butler acknowledged the request and bowed.

It took Andrés five more minutes to say his thank yous and give his good byes. He put on his parka and scarf.

Outside in the driveway the back door opened to the large green Mercedes and he climbed in.

"I live at . . ."

He was abruptly interrupted by the chauffeur, "I know where you live. I drove you home last week."

Andrés had forgotten that. He was exhausted from the day's experience. He belched. He would have a good night's sleep on a full stomach.

He looked down at his lap. Nan had given him a care package, including a piece of cake. *I'm totally stoked!*

CHAPTER 9

TEUFL

Summer of 1936, Frankfurt/Vienna/Berlin

Uschi and Dieter remained together without the benefit of marriage. They thought the informal arrangement kept their relationship fresh and interesting. Dieter Müeller had been a German military attaché to the Austrian National Socialist German Workers' Party. He had been specifically assigned to Vienna. Although he had recently moved back to Frankfurt with Uschi and Teufl, Dieter still had to make his monthly trips back to Vienna.

Dieter spent much time with Teufl during the child's formative years. The guardian realized how bright the boy was. He knew that his charge absorbed everything that he observed. Uschi sent Teufl for his formal education to an exclusive private academy, the Schule Deutsche. On Sundays, Dieter and he would go fishing and hunting. Dieter would never miss an opportunity to preach Aryan superiority to the youngster. Soon thereafter, Dieter enrolled the youth into the local German Youth club when the boy turned ten. Eventually, Teufl dropped out because of the rigid physical regimen and military orientation.

When a swarthy classmate once tried to befriend Teufl, Dieter's fiery temper and threats to the school had forced the expulsion of the "foreigner." While Uschi didn't agree with the indoctrination, she did not refute anything her "husband" said. She loved the fact that Dieter was taking responsibility for helping to raise the child.

In the summer of 1936, Dieter procured two tickets to the Summer Olympics in Berlin. He and Teufl took the train to the site and spent two weeks of quality time together. There they saw the Führer address thousands of German citizens. Hitler promised them that all nations would be humbled by the Fatherland's exceptional athletes.

Days later Dieter was drinking heavily. He was so infuriated that a black U.S. athlete had won four gold medals. He was yelling out racial epithets in the tavern. He was finally asked to leave by the bartender. Dieter then threatened to close the place down because he was a member of the SS. Teufl never demonstrated any emotion when his guardian engaged in his racial superiority proselytism.

That same year, Dieter decided to take Teufl to his favorite brothel on the Kurfürstendamm in Berlin. He told Teufl that he was giving him a coming of age gift now that Augustin was turning fourteen. Dieter told the madam that they didn't want any dark ones. He paid for both of them and they entered the salon.

Teufl was initially unmoved by the scene. He had been raised in a brothel and naked women did not arouse him.

☙

Years before in Vienna, his mother Micaela was with her john in one of the brothel bedrooms while Augustin was roaming the halls of Madam Regina's establishment. The boy was only wearing underpants. Normally, the other prostitutes paid no attention to this four-year old child. He was innocent enough. However, that night he had an erection.

"Who are you doing, little man?" chided one of the working girls in the passageway. Her other two companions giggled.

The second one blinked her eyes and said, "Looks like he is ready." The ladies snickered even harder now.

Augustin's knew they were talking about him, even though he didn't understand exactly what they were saying, His face reddened. He felt so ashamed. He was afraid that his mother, Micaela, was going to punish him. He didn't know what he did wrong. His little eyes started to tear up.

"Leave him alone, you whores," screamed Uschi who had rushed to the poor child's rescue. She had come to visit Madam Regina and happened upon the teasing incident.

"I could give him a freebie," smirked one of the prostitutes disregarding the reproach. "The little bastard needs a little break in his life."

"Unknown father. Loser mother. He's screwed for the rest of his life," smirked another.

"Get out of my sight, you bitches!" Uschi cried as she picked up a ceramic pitcher. The three girls made haste and left. Uschi picked up Augustin and took him away.

From that day forward, Augustin would undermine his three tormentors. From an early age, he had observed the practices and routines of the ladies of the evening. He was bright enough to know how to extract revenge. He would poke holes in their condoms or pour rubbing alcohol into their douche bags or wet their makeup powders. If he got caught, they laughed it off thinking that he was only trying to be cute. However, for Augustin, these were acts of vengeance. He was Teufl.

☙

During those hot and humid August days in 1936, Teufl was mesmerized by how much pain an athlete could endure for the competition. Dehydration. Cramps. Collapsing.

Delirium. However, it had been the sight of the Italian-American, Louis Zamperini from the United States, zipping through his last lap in 56 seconds that made Teufl realize that he wanted to work in the medical research field and learn about the human body.

Dieter was happy with Teufl's career decision and procured a position for him in the apothecary at the University Hospital Frankfurt a.M. Teufl was a quick study. By age 15, he knew more than some doctors and nurses.

CHAPTER 10

GHIRARDELLI CHOCOLATE

Tuesday, June 18, 1974, San Francisco

"I love this!" Astrid plunked her spoon back into the chocolate syrup covered chocolate sundae. Her emerald eyes sparkled as she beamed toward Andrés. Her modest figure was being assaulted by the ingestion of hundreds of sinful calories. Her reddish hair was neatly tucked into a smart, black knitted hat. She was rambling about this and that. Her eating utensil was conducting a concert. She seemed to be a kid at heart.

Andrés, by nature, was a carefree person. While he was responsible most of the time, he lacked initiative. He went with the flow of life. Now he was in the position of being a mentor to this young girl. Andrés didn't know exactly what he was supposed to do. He felt like a babysitter to this young lady. Well, it was easy money. Or was it?

೮೩

Andrés had phoned the Schmidt house on the previous day and talked to Doña Grossman. He asked her when he should come over to meet with Astrid.

"Be here promptly at ten o'clock," directed Astrid's guardian.

This morning he had gotten up extra early and showered. He hated his alarm clock. Andrés looked at the mirror over the sink. His light brown skin had faded during his stay in

Valparaiso. He took his razor and trimmed his thin black moustache and long sideburns. He brushed his hair back and put it into a ponytail that he secured with a rubber band.

In his left earlobe, he carefully inserted the gold earring. His black turtleneck shirt was fairly clean, so he put it on. He finished his wardrobe off with a pair of faded blue jeans and a multicolored woven belt he had purchased in Chile.

This time he knew the correct bus stop and when to jump off at the Presidio. He rushed over to the Schmidts' house and actually arrived five minutes early. He was greeted by Nan in a very friendly manner. He was escorted to the study. Moments later Matilda Grossman entered.

"Good morning, Doña Grossman," he almost bowed.

"Good morning, Andrés," the woman in black said in a tone that could almost be taken as friendly. "How are you this morning?"

"Fine," he fixed his eyes on her. She seemed inattentive to his response.

"This is from Mr. Schmidt," she efficiently shoved a white envelope with an embossed family logo into his hand.

Andrés was perplexed for a moment. He decided that he should fold it in half and open it later.

"Do you know where you are going today?" she started to interrogate him.

"I thought we would start off with some touristy things, like Fisherman's Wharf," he tried to read her face without any success. "Places that I usually take my friends when they come to visit from L.A."

"L.A.?"

"Los Angeles."

"I think it would be prudent if you didn't teach Astrid any slang, don't you."

"Of course, Doña Grossman," his face reddened. He knew that he needed to be super-conscientious. His financial situation depended on it.

Astrid poked her head into the doorway.

"Good morning, everyone," she gleefully greeted the two. "I'm ready."

She sauntered in with a long umber plaid wool skirt over some russet leather boots and a cinnamon sweater.

"Remember, my dear, that your main objective is to practice your English."

"Yes, tía. I mean auntie," she laughed. "Ready, Andrés?"

"Erik is going to drive you to your destination, dear," the older woman held her niece's attention. "Go with God."

Andrés said goodbye and the two left the room. As they were leaving, they heard the guardian shout, "Make sure you are home by five."

Moments earlier, Andrés had convinced Doña Grossman that a return ride was unnecessary. Astrid had to learn the public transportation systems in San Francisco. Reluctantly, the guardian had assented.

Astrid escorted him down some stairs to the lower level at the back of the house. From outside of the garage there was a panoramic view of San Francisco.

The forest green Mercedes limousine was humming. The chauffeur was standing next to the car. This chiseled muscular Goliath seemed rather young to be a driver. He was at least 6'2" with a blond flat top and icy blue eyes.

"Good morning, Miss Grossman," Erik said subtly as he opened the back door of the car and let her in. She slid across the tan leather seats.

"Oh, good morning, Erik," she greeted him back.

Andrés followed Astrid into the huge back seat of the car.

"Where are we going today?" asked Erik.

Astrid looked at Andrés who replied in an overly loud voice, "Fisherman's Wharf."

"Very well, sir."

Within twenty minutes, Erik had dropped them off. Despite it being a weekday, the area was crowded with sea gulls and foreign tourists, both making lots of commotion. Several languages could be heard as scores of people mingled into the souvenir shops. T-shirts. Coffee cups. Key chains.

Astrid wanted to wander into every little store. She picked up and scrutinized every little stuffed animal, comical greeting card, and ashtray.

At first Andrés was bored, but surprisingly, he took advantage of the situation.

"Every time you pick up something, you have to tell me its name in English, okay?" He thought that she would either be motivated to learn English more rapidly or would quit shopping. In either event, he thought it was a win-win situation.

Unfortunately, she was willing to play the game. If she didn't know a word or mispronounced it, Andrés made her repeat it three times.

The smell of the marine air blended with the food odors in the restaurant areas. There were small samples of clam chowder being passed out by the various seafood stands in front of the well-established restaurants.

Andrés had surreptitiously opened the envelope from Mr. Schmidt while Astrid was trying on a sweatshirt. Inside he found ten ten-dollar bills with a note that said, "$50 in advance and $50 for expenses." He was shocked. He hadn't had a hundred dollars in his hand for quite a while. He carefully transferred the money into his wallet that now became difficult to fold and put it into his back pocket.

They stopped at the food stall in front of the Alioto's Restaurant and ordered two clam chowders that were served in their own sourdough bread bowls. The air was a bit nippy and the hot liquid went down really well. Andrés ate his with vigor. She more or less played with her food. In the end she only ate half of hers. From the remaining bread, they tore off little chunks from the "bowl" and threw them on the sidewalk. Dozens of seagulls came squawking down, fighting amongst themselves for the morsels.

They walked westward and visited the red-bricked Cannery buildings. There was more shopping. Astrid finally bought herself a pink sweatshirt that said, "Yo Amo SF." Andrés explored a bookstore that played piped in classical music.

From there, the pair strolled along the Aquatic Park. There was an African-American man with a straw hat and big smile, playing guitar and singing fun ditties. There were hippie types sitting on old Army blankets on the grass and selling tie dyed clothing, beaded jewelry, and sweet scented incense (which seemed to disguise the pervasive smell of marijuana). Older men were walking their little yelping dogs.

Andrés and Astrid took a break and sat down on an old wood and concrete bench. They stared out at Alcatraz. The waves lapped up. Seabirds soared overhead. A sea lion could be heard calling to his mate. She took some photos with her camera. She made Andrés pose in a few of them.

Astrid looked at a map and suddenly laughed. "Are you ready for a Spanish lesson?"

"What?" his brow furrowed with bewilderment.

"Once upon a time, before the prison was built, this island had either calla lilies on it or pelicans on it," she had assumed the role of the instructor. "That is what the word Alcatraz means in Spanish."

Andrés pondered that explanation. So much of California had Spanish names. He could improve his Spanish by going through the geographic names in the local atlas. Atascadero. Manteca. Salinas. Los Gatos.

They got up from the bench. The fog was rolling in and started to veil the Golden Gate Bridge. The dozens of sailboats in the bay bounced on the crests of the water, homeward bound. A scruffy looking man holding out a Dixie cup came up to them and asked for a quarter. Astrid opened up her little leather handbag and pulled out a dollar.

They walked to Ghirardelli Square that was just up the hill. Minutes later they were eating chocolate sundaes.

∽

It was getting late. They had just left Ghirardelli. It was past three when they climbed upon the cable car. They were both tired, but now were on a sugar high. She laughed as the trolley clanked.

"We're back in Valparaiso!" she blurted as the wind blew into her face.

Andrés was finally loosening up. He smiled back at her.

She took more photos. Andrés was afraid that she was going to drop or lose her camera.

Finally, they arrived at the end of the line at Market Street. Astrid wanted to walk back to Union Street.

"Another day," he begged off. "I have to get you home by five."

She had wanted to argue or persuade him otherwise, but she didn't.

There were more street people. Business suits. Bag ladies. An Andean band with their pan flutes.

Andrés and Astrid hopped onto a tram and then transferred to a bus.

There were dropped off by the Presidio at the corner of Lombard and Lyon. Andrés was going to lead them through the Lombard Gate that probably would have made them late. Fortunately, Astrid knew a shortcut. There was a staircase that went directly from the street up to her house.

They ran up to the front door. They were sweaty and winded. Astrid pulled her house key out of her handbag. She climbed the first step.

"I had a great time, Andrés."

"Yeah, me, too."

She leaned over and kissed him on the cheek.

CHAPTER 11

THE PRODIGY

December, 1940, Frankfurt

In 1938, Dieter Müeller spent the whole year in Vienna during the Anschluss, when Nazi Germany was taking control of Austria. At the same time, Teufl was becoming a medical prodigy. He was promoted to lab assistant under Dr. Ottmar Freiherr at the University Clinic Frankfurt a. M., where he worked with vaccinations and other experimentations. Additionally, two days a week, Teufl worked in the Public Health Office of the hospital where marriage fitness certificates were processed. He shuttled the kilometer distance between the hospital and clinic all week long. Teufl rarely went home. He slept in an empty ward in the basement of the hospital. The young man rarely trimmed his wispy handlebar moustache or hair. His clothes were normally unkempt.

Dr. Freiherr permitted Teufl to attend medical classes and observe surgeries. At times, Teufl was allowed to be present during certain procedures and was even allowed to assist the nurses. Teufl did not pass out at the sight of blood or cringe at touching organs. The miasma of dead bodies had no effect on him whatsoever.

Teufl was focused on one thing only: the human body. He rarely communicated with Uschi who was heartbroken by his absence. Uschi was at a loss without the company of her two men.

On those occasions when Dieter returned home to see Uschi, he also visited Augustin. He bragged about Teufl to anyone who would listen.

When Teufl was not working, he studied his medical books. In German, French, or Italian. He had a lust for knowledge. He walked around the hospital officiously in his lab coat, toting a clipboard. His social life was nil. Teufl had no close friends. He only communicated with the doctors and his superiors. By 1940, he had achieved a stellar reputation at the hospital.

"Teufl will make a fine doctor," one would say.

Another would remark, "Teufl will make a great surgeon."

And a third would opine, "Teufl will transform the medical field."

೮੪

It was getting close to the Christmas season. The snow began to fall and the patients arrived wearing their long coats. The doors let in blasts of cold air. The hospital floors were getting icy wet and slippery.

Teufl's watch showed that it was past seven o'clock. His normal routine for meals was to eat at the hospital cafeteria. The food was hot and the prices were cheap. He really didn't care about the taste of the meals, although he was partial to meat.

This evening he walked up the one flight of stairs to the cafeteria. He wasn't wearing a sweater. He felt the chill inside the building. While in line, he stopped and pointed at some cabbage soup. The chunky lady with a dirty handkerchief tied around her head ladled him a bowl. It had healthy chunks of pork and potatoes swimming in it. He carefully put it down on his tray making sure that he did not burn himself or spill it. He grabbed some thick slices of brown bread and a cup of steaming coffee.

After paying, he went to look for a place to sit. Normally, he sat in the corner or at a table that faced the inner courtyard of the hospital. But tonight, all the tables were occupied with trays of dirty dishes, medical books, or people playing cards.

There was a nurse sitting by herself. She was in the middle of her meal. She was wearing a white uniform which accented her olive colored skin. Teufl knew that Dieter would have reproached him for even looking at such a woman. He asked politely in a weak voice if he could sit at the table.

She shrugged her shoulders and her right hand said to go ahead. She scooped up a spoonful of carrots and peas.

He tried not to stare at her, but her auburn hair and green eyes captivated him. It took him a minute to begin eating his soup.

She finished her meal and quickly wiped her mouth with a napkin. She had not made eye contact with him at any time during his presence. She picked up her tray and left without a word. She went to the back of the dining area and bussed her dishes.

Teufl was fixated on her. Her name badge had read "K. Urmuz." Maybe he would run into her again.

CHAPTER 12

PET CEMETERY

Saturday, June 22, 1974, San Francisco

There was an early morning drizzle as Andrés walked toward the Schmidts' home. A green army camouflage jacket, his colored scarf, and an Oakland Raiders cap protected him against the elements. Birds watched him from their telephone line perches.

♋

The week had gone by quickly for Andrés. He had stopped by a Mexican taqueria on the way home Tuesday evening after his day with Astrid and ordered a giant bean and cheese burrito.

When he finally fell upon his bed at home, he opened his wallet and counted out the money he had left. The newfound wealth was burning a hole in his pocket, but he had expenses he had to pay.

On Wednesday morning, he walked upstairs from his basement lodging and clanged the lion's head knocker. John opened the door.

"Hey, baby boy," John gave him a big hug. "We've missed you."

"Did you get the postcards?"

Although it was chilly, John wore tight jeans and a purple tank top that highlighted his tattoos.

"Yes. Thank you," John motioned him into the house.

"Do you want some coffee? I just made these outrageous cinnamon scones."

"Bummer! I would love to, but I have a bogus homework assignment that is due Friday," Andrés sighed. He had a sweet tooth and was obsessed with John's baked goods. "I need to go buy a new ribbon for my typewriter. Have to turn in an outline for my senior thesis by Friday. Kinda sucks."

John frowned with his youngish baby blues.

"Just came by to drop this off," Andrés gave him an old envelope with $25 enclosed for back rent.

John thanked him. "I'll make sure to give it to Maurice. He needs to give you a receipt. You know he won't let me do it."

Andrés gave him a kind smile, "No problem. I'm not splitting out of here any time soon."

"Just a sec," John disappeared. A minute later, he came back with a scone wrapped in a fuchsia-patterned napkin. "One for road."

"Thanks, man," Andrés took his leave.

He ran around the neighborhood doing his errands for the remainder of the morning.

The next two days he worked on his thesis topic, trying to make it focused. He had liked Mr. Schmidt's ideas about researching the philosophies, values, and personalities of Neruda, Vargas Llosa, and Borges and incorporating them into his paper. By late Thursday night, he had finished typing it up.

Andrés went to his one-hour class on Friday and turned in his proposal. Several students had dropped out of the class, but there were still a dozen or so left. He knew two of the guys in the room and briefly talked to them.

Anthony, who was a pre-law major, was going to do his

thesis on the John F. Kennedy assassination. Simon, who belonged to a progressive political group on campus, wanted to discuss the United States' invasions around the world, from Mexico to Southeast Asia.

The professor gave his lecture with his face always glued to his notes. He never made eye contact with any of the students. It seemed that he was oblivious as to whether the students were there or not. It was the professor's summer job and he was getting paid, so why should he care? Andrés wondered if the professor would simply rubber-stamp the thesis proposals or would he actually read them and make comments. Andrés did not want to take any chances. He did not want to spend the whole year writing and rewriting the thesis.

∞

It was Saturday and he had taken the shortcut to the Schmidts' home that Astrid had shown him. He was supposed to be there by ten.

Nan met him at the door.

"Good morning, Miss Hill," he nodded.

"Good morning, Andrés. Please call me Nan. Everything is less formal here," the maid winked with a broad grin. "Besides, Doña Grossman wants Astrid to learn colloquial English and customs."

He smiled back.

Astrid soon joined them and he was invited into the study where Mr. Schmidt was sitting in a wheelchair.

"How are you, my young friend?" the patron stuck out his hand. "Sometimes I need a little assistance getting around," he said in a light manner pointing beneath him.

"Fine, sir."

"Would you like a cup of coffee?"

"No, thank you, sir," replied Andrés. He didn't know whether to thank Mr. Schmidt for the money or not.

"So tell me how the other day went," Mr. Schmidt inquired. "Astrid said she learned a lot."

"She is very bright," Andrés was trying to be diplomatic. "Her English is very good. I wish my Spanish was half as good."

This brought a sign of satisfaction to the older man's face.

"We're going to work on her accent a little bit," Andrés added. "And maybe, make her speak a little slower."

They conversed for a while. Doña Grossman entered the room and saluted everyone.

"Where are you youngsters off to today?" she had taken charge.

"I actually thought we would walk down to the Palace of Fine Arts. It's one of my favorite places."

"Excellent," remarked Mr. Schmidt slapping his legs with both hands.

"Then walk along to Chrissy Field and Fort Point," Andrés then started to smile, "and then to a surprise place."

"Just make sure you are home by five," commanded the matron.

"Would you like to join us for dinner tonight, Andrés?" offered Mr. Schmidt.

Andrés replied affirmatively.

"Do you like football?" asked the older man. "I guess here they call it soccer. Erik and I have a bet on the World Cup games. I already owe him. Germany, that is West Germany, beat Chile. I don't really follow sports that much any more."

Andrés had played baseball in high school. He really didn't know much about soccer until he went to Chile. Everyone over there was a total fanatic. Cars driving up and down the streets, horns tooting. People hanging out of windows as they waved their banners. People of all ages wearing red with white trim national team shirts. Students carrying and flashing posters supporting Universidad Católica, Universidad de Chile, or Colo Colo.

⊳

Astrid and Andrés took the flight of stairs down to Lyon Street. She thanked him a thousand times for the wonderful time she had the previous Tuesday.

As they walked down the hill, he made her identify various things. Ferns. Traffic light. Hair salon. At times he made her give him a brief description of a thing or event.

"What is that lady wearing?"

Finally, they arrived at the Palace of Fine Arts. She took several photos of the magnificent structure. She even persuaded an eager Japanese tourist to take their picture together.

Andrés gave her the twenty-five cent tour of the 1915 Panama-Pacific Exposition rotunda as they strolled around the lagoon, and past the eucalyptus trees. They stopped and looked at the white swans and listened to the mallards honking. She took more photos. She was forced to recite more words and descriptions for her mentor.

They spent almost an hour at the Exploratorium, interacting with several exhibits and bumping into dozens of energetic children who were running from one thingamajig to another with no parents in sight.

It was past noon when they crossed Mason Street and started on the Bay Trail toward Chrissy Field. They followed the path that bicyclists, joggers, and dog walkers shared with them. The cool ocean breeze tickled their nostrils. They could smell the salt in the air.

"Are you getting hungry, Astrid?"

"Yes. And how about you?"

"I was born hungry," he smiled.

They grabbed a couple of hot dogs, potato chips, and soft drinks from a food cart near the marine sanctuary.

"How do you say *mostaza*?" she asked.

"Mustard," he answered and pointed to the other condiments. "Mayonnaise, catsup, relish."

"And what are these?"

"Barbequed potato chips. My favs."

They sat on a cement bench.

"Astrid, why did your family move up here?" he was trying to be sociable. "It sounds like you had an awesome life in Santiago."

"Oh, we did," she replied, a little more reserved than she had previously been with him. "It was for my father's work."

"What kind of job does he have?"

"He works for a pharmaceutical company. The company has offices all over the world," she took a large swig of her soda. "He is working with the U.S. government at Letterman Hospital. I think it is some sort of research. I really don't know. He really hasn't told me."

"That sounds awesome," remarked Andrés, "getting to travel all over the world for your job."

"Where are we going now, Andrés?"

"To Fort Point."

"Oh!"

"Are you getting tired?"

"No, but I need to use the bathroom."

Within a few minutes, they found the public restrooms.

"Point Fort. What a strange name for a place," she said. "I don't understand."

"Fort Point," he corrected her. "I don't either."

The seagulls were soaring over their heads. The Golden Gate stood majestically in front of them. She took more photos.

The air was getting cooler. Astrid grabbed Andrés' arm for warmth.

He felt that she was getting fatigued. He was sweating even though he was cold.

They finally reached Fort Point and grabbed some pamphlets at the site. They sat down on a small wall. He made her read the entire brochure out loud.

"Just relax. You are doing fine."

"I don't know some of these words."

"Just try."

They explored the stronghold, going up and down the stairs that hugged the fortress walls. Now they were both exhausted. They exited the historical site and stopped at the main entrance.

"Can we rest for a few more minutes, Andrés?" she pleaded.

"Sure," poor planning on my part, he thought.

He stared at the gravel in front of him. His feet ached. He would be feeling miserable by dinnertime, if he at all survived.

"Hey, you guys want a ride?" solicited a muscular, bald headed guy wearing a navy blue warm up suit. He was straddling a bicycle taxi.

"Can you fit us both in?" Andrés asked excitedly.

"For five bucks, I could fit ten more."

The cold whipped through their faces as the driver peddled furiously down the trail. They bounced on the irregular clay surface and skidded in the muddy sections.

Faster and faster they went. Astrid held on tight to Andrés, constantly squeezing him.

The jock dropped them off near the buildings back at Chrissy Field. Andrés took six dollars out of his wallet and handed them to the bicyclist.

"Thanks, man. You saved my life."

The Superman bicycle taxi flew off. They were left standing by a public restroom.

A group of skateboarders zoomed by them.

"Let's take a break," he said. She did not argue with him. "Do want something to drink?"

"Yes, please," she looked a bit raggedy.

He walked over to a beverage cart that was tattooed with stickers and bought two cans of Pepsi.

"Are you too tired?" he looked at her. "Or can you walk another five or ten minutes? Remember, I promised you a surprise."

"No, I'm fine," she perked up like she just had a shot of adrenaline. "I'm ready when you're ready."

They walked slowly up the incline into a graveyard surrounded by pine trees that exuded forest smells. There were hundreds of small white wooden markers scattered throughout this shabbily kept cemetery underneath the Highway 101 culvert.

"Is this a cemetery?" she asked puzzled by why he would bring her here as a surprise. Macabre?

"Yes," he stood in front of a sign that said, "Pet Cemetery." He smiled at her.

They walked up the path that was encroached upon by overgrown grass.

"Okay," he pointed to a little headstone. "Please read what it says."

She had no problem reciting some of the epitaphs to the dogs and cats that had been the loyal pets of military families from all parts of the world. She took a photo of Andrés standing in front of several gravesites.

Walking around, Andrés and she giggled about attributions to rats, goldfish, and canaries. She took more photos.

"You better be careful," she teased. "Or some mouses will rise from the dead."

"Mice."

"Okay, mice."

They traipsed back up the hill toward her home, fading with each step. Astrid would stop every once in a while and pick a little white flower or a blue one.

They arrived back at the house ten minutes before five.

Bert escorted them into the study where Mr. Schmidt was reading the San Francisco Examiner.

He asked them the usual pleasantries and could see they were exhausted.

"Andrés, would you like a little sherry before dinner?"

"No, thank you, sir," Andrés said in a weak voice. "But could I please trouble you for some coffee."

"Why, of course, my young friend. Anything for you, my dear?"

She shook her head. Bert immediately left the room.

"So tell me what you two did all day," Schmidt said sipping his amontillado sherry.

Astrid went through their itinerary, elaborating on how beautiful this was or how interesting that was.

"And we ended up at the Castillo de San Joaquin . . ."

"Where?" Andrés interrupted, almost spilling his coffee. He was caught off guard by her rendition of the day.

"You know, Fort Point," she smiled mischievously. "Remember you made me read the history of the fortress out loud."

Andrés' face turned crimson.

After she had finished with the summary of the day's events, she excused herself and left the room to get ready for dinner.

Mr. Schmidt started to roar with laughter.

"Behind that angelic smile, stands a very bright young lady," he gave Andrés a conceited grin. "Don't underestimate her."

☙

"Okay, Boehner," said the demanding voice on the other side of the line. "Did you find the information yet?"

Erik had driven the Mercedes to a public phone booth about a mile away from the Schmidt house.

"Negative," the Schmidt chauffeur replied. "I have searched his study, his bedroom, and the other places in the house. Negative so far."

"For the money we are paying you," said the interrogator, "we should have the damn report by now. Shit!"

"Did you find anything at his office or lab?" Erik countered.

"Hey, listen, asshole, I'm the one who is asking the questions. Do you understand, jerk off?"

"Yes, sir."

CHAPTER 13

THE MEETING

January, 1941, Frankfurt

Teufl tossed and turned in his makeshift bed. He had had trouble sleeping. Although the little room was cold, his body was sweating. Teufl kept thinking about her, that young nurse in the cafeteria. He had really never had a love relationship in his eighteen years. Dieter had taught him that prostitutes were the best way to release tension. These women who worked the streets only wanted money anyway. They would do anything or everything for it, any time or any place.

Maybe tomorrow night after his work at the clinic he would drop by the Venus brothel. He always avoided the dark girls and the Slavs.

Teufl reminisced over the scent of the mystery girl's skin. Her essence had overwhelmed his senses. Everything was wrong about her. He knew that. Dieter would have severely reproached him for his total disregard of the Cause. In his mind, he knew that the woman was an outrage against Aryan purity.

Cʒ

A few nights later Teufl went back to the cafeteria at the same time as before. The tables were again all occupied. The visitors and the medical staff were conversing amiably. Where was she? He scanned the room. Finally, he spied her in the corner with several other people. Upon further observations, he realized that she was associating with fellow nurses.

He threw his food into the trash receptacle and went back to his lab. That night he had more bad dreams. He was angry with himself for falling prey to a lesser being. She was an evil temptress. Dieter had told him that Eve was the cause of disharmony in the universe. She had seduced Adam. Now, the forbidden fruit was the scourge of the world for all men. The Garden of Eden had been lost because of a woman.

Saturday came and he told himself that he was not going to the cafeteria. Well, maybe just for a cup of coffee. He bought his coffee and walked around the cafeteria. He did not see her. He was relieved. Yet, he stayed at a table by himself waiting for her to appear. It was almost nine o'clock when he finally left the eating area.

Maybe it was her day off? He thought. He himself rarely took time off. Maybe she was sick. She probably worked with a lot of sick patients who had infected her. Or maybe she was terminated. Why would she be fired?

Teufl had to find a way to discover in which section of the hospital she worked. She seemed too young to work in surgery or in the emergency room. He seemed to recall that her surname was Urmuz. *What kind of name was that?*

His body was getting tenser every day. He couldn't concentrate on his work. He was arriving late at the lab and missing classes.

Finally, he spied her one afternoon when he was taking his lunch in the cafeteria. She was sitting at a table talking to a young man fashionably dressed in a suit and tie. The man was very animated conversing with her, gesticulating with his hands. She seemed to beam every once in a while. She kept eating while her tablemate talked.

Teufl watched the scene coldly. *Why was she encouraging*

this fop? Teufl questioned why he should care about this young woman whom he really didn't know. *She's probably just like the other whores on the street.* He tried to feign indifference in his mind, but his blood was boiling as it ran through his veins. *Who was this interloper?* Teufl wondered. It was obvious that this male was trying to pursue her. He shouldn't care. She didn't even appear to be Aryan. His was an illicit desire. Teufl clutched his pencil in his left hand until it snapped in two.

The clock struck two and several people got up from their tables to return to work. The girl got up to leave. The young man reached for her hand and asked a question. Teufl didn't know what was said.

An orderly carrying a tray full of dirty dishes passed in front of him. He could not see what happened. When he finally was able to see the table again, she was gone. The young fellow was wiping his mouth with a napkin and got up to leave.

Teufl was late for class, but he decided to follow the fellow. They walked down the hallway.

The young man went into the WC. Teufl waited outside. He pretended to be reading the employee bulletin board.

Five minutes later the interloper exited, wiping his hands dry with his handkerchief. The man walked down the long corridor. He passed an old man in grey overalls mopping the floor. He continued toward the stairwell and began to descend.

A few moments later, there was a shriek from the bottom of the stairs and a loud thud.

"Someone get a doctor!" a woman screamed. "A man has been hurt."

Teufl looked down from the top of the stairs and sneered with satisfaction.

ca

A week had passed since the incident in which a young resident doctor had been critically injured after slipping and falling down twenty-seven stairs at the hospital.

"May I join you?" Teufl seated himself across from her without waiting for a reply. He took the bowl of lentil soup and bread roll off his tray and placed the items in front of him. She was reading a tattered and dog-eared copy of Time Magazine. Someone had inked a swastika over Hitler's face that adorned the front cover.

Her green eyes looked up at him, but she said nothing.

"Haven't I seen you in the Gastroenterology Department?"

Suddenly, she looked up, "That's where I work."

"Hi, my name is Augustin," he extended his hand. "Augustin Teufl."

She shook his hand. Her warm touch burned a hole into his soul. The room became silent to him. The lights seemed to dim. He was finally with her. He had met his destiny.

"Keichelle," she slowly pronounced with a little bit of a strange accent. "Keichelle Urmuz."

"How long have you been a nurse here?" he combed back his hair with his hand.

"Three and a half months. But I am not a nurse. I am an assistant," she hesitated in explaining what she did. But Teufl had already investigated her working situation.

They remained in silence.

"I have to go," she started to get up.

"It was a pleasure meeting you, Keichelle," he arose from his chair.

She left. Teufl's heart was pounding. He went back to his office. The lab was empty. Everybody had already gone home from work.

He tried to work but could not concentrate. At about a quarter to eleven he exchanged his lab coat for his black overcoat.

There were only a few night nurses on duty at the hospital. He walked up to the main level. The floors were being mopped by scrubwomen on their hands and knees and disheveled janitors were carrying trash sacks away.

He waited by the employees' entrance. The swing shift was finally leaving. Dozens of workers were putting on their heavy coats and hats to brave the snow outside.

At first he did not recognize her. She was only wearing a crocheted dark grey scarf knotted under her neck and a flimsy jacket as she departed from the hospital. Her shoes were not suitable for the inclement weather.

As she walked down Theodor-Stein-Kai Street in the cold and dreary night, Teufl slowly tailed her, making sure he was not spotted. Taxis would flash their lights as they drove by. A drunk was urinating on a wall. Teufl walked past a tavern where the smell of beer and cigarettes even polluted the sidewalks.

Keichelle stopped at the corner and crossed the street. She looked behind her. Teufl quickly slid into a doorway. A black cat jumped out, giving him a fright.

She made her way across the dimly lit Friedensbrücke that crossed the Main River. Teufl maintained his distance. After crossing the bridge, she turned left onto Speicherstrasse and proceeded for two more blocks.

She passed an old man walking his short-legged dog. The dachshund left a souvenir on the freshly fallen snow. Keichelle turned right on Wertstrasse and eventually turned left at the next block that was Rottweilerstrasse. At a large brick building, she paused and then proceeded to carefully climb the front stairs. She almost slipped. At the top, she fumbled with a key, unlocked the weather beaten front door, and finally entered into the unlit apartments.

Teufl crossed the street until he was opposite the building. He slid into the shadows and waited. Finally, there was a light that illuminated the window shade on the third floor.

Specks of snow clung to his face. He stood there watching the little glow upstairs. He felt the palpitations of his heart as he sighed.

The illumination finally went out, but he could still picture her shadow.

CHAPTER 14

LEGION OF HONOR

Wednesday, June 26, 1974, San Francisco

"Do you like my new earrings?" Astrid pranced into the room pinching her earlobes showing off the gold studs. She was wearing long navy blue slacks and a white Mills College sweatshirt.

"Sure," he didn't know what to say. "They're awesome."

He arrived a few minutes early that Wednesday morning and had been escorted into the Schmidts' study. Doña Matilda handed him an envelope. Andrés, in turn, handed her an envelope, the one he had been given the week before.

"What is this?" asked Matilda.

"Oh! I just included receipts for expenses," he meekly told her. "If I didn't have a receipt, I wrote the amount on a piece of paper. I still have $11.42 left."

"Very good," she seemed pleasantly surprised.

ო

Andrés was slowly being seduced by the prospect of a weekly paycheck. He could start paying off his back rent and other bills. He would still have to get a roommate for the fall semester. However, more food in his refrigerator was also good.

The times between visits to the Schmidts had been hectic. He had been exhausted by his time with Astrid that prior Saturday. This was Andrés' rationale for sleeping in on

Sunday. He decided not to work on his thesis. He did his weekly laundry and went to the grocery store. He bought a five-pound bag of rice and some carrots and celery.

The next day, Monday, he went to the university library and starting writing down the bibliography for his senior paper.

"Excuse me," he approached the librarian in her horn-rimmed glasses wearing a kelly green sweater. "Where is the Latin American section?"

"Anthropology, history, or literature?"

"Literature . . . Pablo Neruda."

She told him that it was upstairs in the stacks to the back. "You may also want to check out the poetry section."

Andrés spent the whole day there.

As he was unlocking the front door of his lodging, he heard the phone ring. He fumbled with his keys and finally answered the phone on the fifth ring.

"Hello, Andrés," a soft voice said on the line. "This is Astrid."

"Hey, what's up?" he knew that he was supposed to go over to her home the following day.

"Am I interrupting you?" she hemmed. "Are you busy?"

"No, I just got home," he was throwing his notebook onto the little table he used for a desk.

"You can't come over tomorrow. I'm sorry. I have an appointment at Mills College for my orientation. Father and Aunt Matilda are taking me over there."

Andrés was taken aback. Had he done something wrong? Was he out of favor? He needed the money!

He wanted to say something, but his mouth wouldn't open.

"Are you still there, Andrés?" there was a pause at the

other end.

"Yeah, I'm here."

"Can you come on Wednesday instead?"

"Sure!" he said relieved. The goose that laid the golden egg was back.

"Father said we would make it up to you. For your inconvenience."

"No problem."

"Great. I would like to go to the Legion of Honor. Is that all right?"

"Sure."

CB

Wednesday finally arrived.

"Erik is waiting for you outside," advised Matilda. "See you back here by five o'clock."

Astrid led Andrés down the back stairwell to the garage level of the house. The green limousine was idling.

"I got you a little souvenir," she said coyly. She handed him a wrapped package.

"Thanks."

"Well, open it."

He tore it open without much finesse. It was a grey Mills College cross-country tee shirt.

"I hope it fits," she said, "I got you a large." She had purchased it as a compensatory gift for changing the appointment date from Tuesday to Wednesday. Astrid wanted to buy Andrés more presentable clothes.

I hope it's not a woman's shirt, he mentally grimaced. "Thanks. You shouldn't have." He tried to smile. *I'm going to lose this in my closet*, he decided.

Erik dropped them off in front of the Legion of Honor in Lincoln Park. There were yellow school buses parked in front. Teachers and parent volunteers were escorting gaggles of young children into the museum. Astrid took a photo of Rodin's "*The Thinker*" in front of the neoclassical building.

"I have a list of a dozen museums that I have to see."

They spent the next two hours absorbing European art from the seventeenth, eighteenth, and nineteenth centuries. She was disappointed that she was not allowed to take photos. Every once in a while they would eavesdrop on a museum docent explaining a painting.

"Another example of Impressionism is Edouard Manet's *'At the Milliner's*,'" the guide expounded. "Note the bold brushwork."

Senior citizens in the guided tour kibitzed about the colors of the painting and the type of hat that was portrayed. Astrid and Andrés finally broke away.

They progressed into the Spanish art gallery. Astrid suddenly scurried over and stood in front of a large painting. She rolled up her museum brochure and spoke into one end like a megaphone.

"Another example of Spanish Renaissance is El Greco's *'St. John the Baptist.'* El Greco who was born under the name of Domenikos Theotokopoulos . . ." she was giggling as she spoke.

Andrés could not refrain from laughing with her.

"You're too much," he said nodding his head in disbelief as he took her elbow and led her away.

They ambled over to the bookstore. She perused all the art books and finally bought one on Impressionism. Andrés saw that it cost $30. That was way beyond his financial means. He bought a lonely postcard of Monet's "*The Grand Canal*" as a memento for himself.

"It's about twelve thirty," she said looking at her leather

banded Bulova watch. "Are you hungry?"

"Sure," he grinned. "You know I'm always hungry." They both snickered.

She grabbed his arm and they worked their way outside. She dragged him along. They stopped in front of a yellow taxicab. Andrés was bewildered.

"Where do you want to go?" he inquired, feeling a pain at the back of his head.

"You'll see."

"We can eat at the cafeteria here."

"Come on."

The cab driver, whose taxi license showed him to be Wayne Dong, drove them to the Sutro Cliffs in less than ten minutes.

They got out and she paid the fare.

"Hey, I'm supposed to pay," he insisted.

"Don't worry about it " she put a reassuring hand on his shoulder.

"Please don't tell your father," he hemmed. "I made him a promise." Andrés was embarrassed. He had made an agreement with Mister Schmidt. On the one hand he couldn't tell Astrid that he was being paid by her father to be her mentor and babysitter. On the other hand, he should have asserted himself and paid for the cab. He did not want to lose control of the situation.

"I know that already," she smiled cagily. "It was my idea in the first place."

Andrés did not know whether he felt betrayed or relieved. He tried to recover his composure.

She grabbed his arm and they walked into the restaurant.

"Schmidt. Party of two," she asserted to the host.

"Just one minute, please," advised a tall young man with

long black sideburns who was wearing a rainbow colored tie. "We are getting your table ready."

Andrés led her outside to a waiting area overlooking the beach. They had a view of the former Sutro baths and the beautiful seascape from the railing outside the foyer. The ocean breeze slapped their faces. They could smell the saline air. Seagulls flew above them, hoping for someone to drop a morsel of food their way.

"Right this way," the host came outdoors and politely escorted them back downstairs. The table was set against the window and gave them an excellent view of the waves breaking on the shore. The foam bubbled up to the restaurant's supporting pillars.

"What's this all about, Astrid?" he said to her in all seriousness. He was outside his element.

"I just wanted to make up for yesterday."

"This isn't necessary," he tried to play down the situation. "I'm cool."

"It's just that I see us as friends. Not boy friend and girl friend," she looked deliberately into his eyes. "I just don't want you to feel like one of our staff."

He tried to read her green eyes. He saw that she was trying to be serious.

"That's cool. I have no problem with that."

An older pixie blonde waitress approached them.

"How are you two doing today?" she took out her pad and without waiting for an answer asked, "Can I bring you something to drink?"

The two ordered iced teas.

"The special of the day is a pan fried calamari steak," she said. "I'll be right back to take your order."

Andrés made Astrid go through every menu item. If she

didn't know what it was, he explained it to her.

"I liked the clam chowder we had the other day. That's what I'm getting," she told him in a lighter tone.

"Sounds good. Me, too."

The waitress came back and they told her what they wanted. The busboy brought them water and some sourdough bread and butter.

"*Gracias, amigo,*" stated Andrés instinctively.

"*De nada, señor,*" was the reply.

Astrid looked stunned at the exchange. Andrés read her mind. "Latinos work in all the restaurants in the City. Even in the Chinese ones."

"Really?" She looked at him incredulously. She couldn't believe what he was saying.

"Sure thing!" he answered as he offered her a slice of the sourdough bread. "Some of the best chefs in the Italian restaurants are Mexicans."

She declined the bread. "You'll have to point that out to me."

"Do you want to see North Beach and Chinatown this Saturday?"

She gleefully said yes.

The chowders came. "Anything else I can bring for you?"

"Tabasco, please," he said.

She ate slowly. He tried not to gulp his food, but he did. She was only half done, when he finished.

"That was most excellent."

He noticed that she ate her soup with her spoon going away from her, rather than towards her. *What's with that?* He pondered. *Oh, well.*

"So, Astrid, what was your favorite painting today?" he switched into his tutorial mode.

"That is an excellent question," she seemed to become serious. "I don't have favorites. I think each painting has its own worth and meaning."

"What do you mean?"

The waitress came by and offered them coffee and dessert. He was tempted, but he declined, as did she.

"For example, I think that Rembrandt's works portray a stark reality while Reubens' reflect a lighter nature and a sensual passion," her knowledge of art went far beyond her years. "These contrast with El Greco who is consumed by suffering."

"Whoa!" he put up his hand. "I think that you are going to be the most awesome art history student at Mills."

She laughed and then went on to describe her visit to Mills College the prior day and what classes she would eventually take. She paused and then said, "My father wants me to start an art gallery business."

Andrés had no idea what that would entail.

"Do you know any artists?"

"Father has friends and associates all over the world who have precious art collections," she was envisioning her destiny. "In fact, when I graduate from college, he is going to take me to Europe. I am dying to visit El Prado, the Hermitage, and the Louvre." Andrés could barely afford to go to the local museums and movie theatres.

As if on cue, the waitress appeared and placed the check in front of Andrés who gulped when he saw the total. He reached for the envelope that Doña Matilda had given him earlier that day. So this was the difference between being a tutor and a friend. He knew that in the Latino culture, the male always got the bill, even if he was dirt poor. Ah, chivalry.

Before he could continue, Astrid grabbed the check

folder and inserted a credit card.

"Astrid, it's my responsibility," he protested.

"No, it's father's treat," she replied, and then added with a mock frown. "Are you sure that you don't want dessert?"

CHAPTER 15

IN THE EARLY MORNING RAIN

February 1941, Frankfurt

Over the next few weeks, Teufl would try to time his walk from the clinic to the hospital to correspond with Keichelle's commute to work. He would wait inside a little café at the corner of Speicherstrasse just before the Friedensbrücke. He knew that she had to check into work by 11 a.m. He calculated that she would have to pass by sometime after ten-thirty. Teufl was now also trying to comb his hair and wear a clean shirt every so often in anticipation of seeing her.

It was at his third surveillance attempt that he saw her approach. He threw some coins down on the table and ran out the door.

She was wearing the same flimsy coat that she wore on the night that he had followed her. The temperature was around zero degrees Celsius, but the sky was blue and clear. Birds circled silently overhead by the Main River.

"Good morning," he called out, the words steaming out of his mouth, as he tried to catch up with her.

She didn't even stop.

"Keichelle!" he gasped as he was running out of breath.

She paused and looked around.

"Oh, it's you," she said somberly, steam exiting her mouth. He finally caught up to her. He was not in good physical condition and his heavy overcoat weighed him down. She continued her walking.

"Are you going to work?" he tried to be cheerful.

"Yes," she started to speed up, her shoes sloshing in the wet snow. "I'm late."

He didn't know whether to believe her or not. It seemed that she had plenty of time, but maybe she had to change clothes or do some other preparation.

The temperature had seemed to warm up a bit. There was a wind blowing from the west. A young mother was pushing her child in a baby carriage toward them over the bridge.

"Do you mind if I accompany you?"

"No, as long as you can keep up," she said in a scowling tone.

Fifteen minutes later they arrived at the employees' entrance of the hospital.

They had not uttered a word to each other during the entire jaunt.

He opened the heavy door for her and let her pass. She continued onward.

"See you later," he mumbled.

03

He hurried back to the lab. He was totally exhausted when he arrived at his office. There was a handwritten note on his deck. It was from Dr. Freiherr. It was on official letterhead.

"I am still waiting for the clinical results on the African subjects. See me immediately."

Teufl had been remiss in his responsibilities as of late. Teufl rifled through his papers. He had been preoccupied with Keichelle. The she-devil. He grabbed a thick file.

He changed into his lab coat and went into the laboratory. He opened one of the three refrigerated units where hundreds of vials had been cataloged and stored. He took the first tray to the sample table and started the clinical protocols, writing down the results. He kept repeating the routines for the remaining vials.

A wizened janitor came in around midnight and startled him. Teufl had been working non-stop for almost twelve hours without a break. He was frantically trying to catch up on his work. He gave the janitor a dirty look. Augustin did not want to be bothered. He had too much to do. The old man vanished in a hurry.

The clock said 5:20 when Teufl left the report on Dr. Freiherr's desk with a cover note early that morning.

"Here are the results you requested."

He had lost respect for the pedantic doctor who no longer did his own lab work. Teufl even had to sign all the official forms and documentation because Freiherr was too busy to be bothered by administrative red tape. Teufl thought that the aged man did not have to make excuses or even follow the rules. The lab could not run without young Teufl. *Old Freiherr should retire to some Bavarian retirement spa,* he thought.

Teufl had been wound up throughout the night. His mind had not even wandered once to thinking about Keichelle. He had felt her slight.

His stomach growled, but he felt sleepy. He couldn't decide if he should take a nap back at the hospital or get something to eat.

The doctors and clinical assistants started to arrive. He put on his overcoat and left the building. It was pouring rain.

ଔ

Uschi's apartment in the ritzy part of Frankfurt occupied two stories. She did a lot of entertaining with politicians and high-ranking military personnel. Dieter often had private meetings with Nazi party leaders in his office at her place, where Uschi played the charming hostess.

Teufl entered Uschi's place and went immediately into the kitchen and looked inside the icebox. He pulled out some cheeses, ham, and butter that he soon inhaled with some bread. He washed all it down with milk that he drank straight from the bottle.

Although he still had a house key and his own bedroom, he rarely visited his former guardians.

"Anyone home?" he yelled. There was no answer.

He went upstairs to his bedroom and grabbed a medium size valise. There were photos of him with Uschi and Dieter on the dresser. He had never had any toys. Dieter had thought that it was too degrading for young boys to have any plaything while growing up, except a toy gun. How else could they learn to grow up to be real men?

Augustin grabbed a few shirts and underwear and stuffed them into the bag. He had shelves of books in German, French, Italian, and Russian. He packed a few into his suitcase and started down the hall. He suddenly stopped and put down the valise.

He walked back until he came to Uschi's bedroom. The door was open. He observed that no one was there.

"Uschi, Dieter, are you here?" he wanted to make certain that he was alone. There was no response.

Covertly he went into the boudoir and entered the closet. It was scented with a mélange of honeysuckle and mothballs. This small but separated space functioned as two walk-in closets. In the first section, he saw evening gowns, furs, and dozens and dozens of shoes. He started browsing through the clothes until he found a medium weight, dark brown wool coat. He grabbed it and shoved it under his arm.

He wandered into the next section that housed accessories, hats, and more shoes. He found a tan wool cap that he stuffed into his pants' pocket. Finally, he opened one of the carved wooden jewelry boxes that played "*Für Elise*." He pilfered two silver barrettes.

Suddenly, Augustin heard a door slam downstairs. Teufl ran out of the room and grabbed his suitcase. The coat did not fit into the valise. He went back into his bedroom and hurriedly unpacked the books and half of the clothes. After much effort he succeeded in fitting the coat into the bag. Beads of sweat gathered on his forehead. He could hear his heart beat throbbing through his head.

He ran down the stairs. The door to the kitchen opened in front of him. A female figure approached him.

"Oh, Master Teufl," the maid said. "It is so good to see you."

He bowed.

"Mistress Sokol is attending a luncheon and Master Müeller is out of town. Shall I tell them that you called upon them?"

"Please do," he said anxiously and swiftly exited the premises.

CHAPTER 16

THE FORTUNE COOKIE

Saturday, June 29, 1974, San Francisco

Erik maneuvered the Mercedes expertly among the buses, taxis, hotel vans, and cars heading toward Union Square. He stopped at a passenger unloading zone in front of the St. Francis Hotel and dropped off Astrid and Andrés.

The cable car clanged as it raced past them. Andrés grabbed Astrid's hand and started to run across Powell Street. A horn sounded and something was yelled out the window of a passing car.

"Welcome to San Francisco," Andrés said sarcastically as they made it to the Union Square side.

They walked toward the center of the plaza.

"Stand over there, Andrés, please," she took her camera out of her tan leather purse.

He complied and she took several shots, each time reminding him to smile.

"What's that statute called?"

"I think '*Victory*,'" he responded, "I don't usually do too many touristy things."

"You've done an excellent job so far," she smiled.

They proceeded across the square. She paused and looked all around her. People of all ethnic and racial backgrounds walked by them. Different languages were being spoken. A panhandler came up to her and jingled his plastic cup in front of her. Andrés shooed him away.

"Hey, I want to go there," she pointed her finger.

Andrés looked over. It was Macy's. "What's happening over there?'

"Shopping," she looked at him as if he had asked the dumbest question in the whole world.

"No way," he put his hands on his hips. "We are supposed to be working on your English and doing cultural things."

"We could practice terms for clothing," she proffered with an innocent look.

"You should go with your aunt or a girl friend," he said dispassionately. As soon as he had uttered the words, he knew he had acted rashly.

She did not argue with him. She became sullen.

Two guys dressed in jeans and Levi's shirts were eating hot dogs. As they passed by, Andrés smelled the tantalizing grease and started to get hunger pangs.

"Okay, let's go," he grabbed her elbow and led her up Stockton Street. She didn't resist.

The incline was steep, but she was wearing black leather flats and had no problem with the climb. Andrés' black Converse tennis shoes were splitting apart at the soles and he was having difficulty trying to negotiate the slope.

They eventually arrived at the Dragon Gate at the entrance to Chinatown. On Grant Street they passed an antique shop that had jade paintings, cloisonné vases, and a smiling fat wooden Buddha statue. The narrow street was crowded with Chinese people. A grandmother with a shopping cart was leading her little granddaughter down the sidewalk. They passed an herb shop and a place that sold live chickens. Some of the buildings had pagoda styled roofs.

"You must think that I am a spoiled brat," her green eyes

looked over to him, as they stopped at a signal that none of the other twenty or so pedestrians obeyed.

"You got that right," he said severely, and then started to smile. She punched him in the shoulder.

They walked into the Hong Kong Restaurant where dozens of tables were filled with people speaking Cantonese and selecting various dishes from carts pushed by plainly dressed girls. An officious waiter seated the pair and asked them if they needed menus. Around the room there were embroidered silk paintings depicting the mountains of Guilin or women in traditional garments.

"Is this *comida chifa*?" she inquired. "When I went to the private girls' school, we would sneak out to eat Chinese food. It's so good."

A young girl pulled her cart in front of them. She offered them chicken feet or broccoli. They politely declined.

"This is dim sum," he tried to explain. "You order from the food carts."

"How do you know what's on the cart?"

"You don't," he snickered. "That's part of the treat."

The aromas of garlic, ginger, soy sauce, and scallions permeated the room. Hot jasmine tea was brought to their table.

Andrés made the selections on behalf of both of them. Wonton soup. Char siu bao, har gau, and cheong fan (steamed barbeque pork-stuffed buns, steamed shrimp dumplings, and rolled rice noodles). Astrid, with her camera in hand, took photos of the dishes and of the interior of the restaurant.

Watching Astrid trying to use chopsticks was comical. She ended up skewering her pork bun with them. Slightly embarrassed, Andrés asked the waiter for a fork. Mechanically, he placed a fork by her plate and filled their glasses with more ice water.

"Well, I guess you are not going to learn much English here," he remarked.

"I learned the word 'chopstick'," she said in a girlish tone.

They passed on the egg custard desserts. They were sated.

The check came and with it, fortune cookies. Astrid looked at the little treat with amazement.

"There's a paper inside," she said bewildered. "How strange."

"With your fortune on it."

"You are teasing me."

"No, really, just check it out," Andrés broke up his cookie and pulled the little paper message out of it. He read it to her:

"Your dearest wish will come true."

He popped the cookie into his mouth to seal the deal.

"Oh, this is great!" she voiced in a fun loving voice. "What's your wish?"

"I don't have one."

"Sure, you do. What is it?"

He really didn't have a wish. He lived day by day. He was just along for the ride in life.

"Don't know yet," he sidestepped the issue. "It's your turn. Open it."

Astrid carefully broke the cookie in half. She took the fortune out and left the broken cookie parts on top of her plate. She read hers to him:

"Friendship is an ocean of which you can not see bottom."

"That's pretty awesome."

ઝ

It took them almost 45 minutes to walk over to Telegraph Hill. They passed men in the park, smoking foul smelling cigarettes and spitting and playing cards.

Andrés' shoelace broke when he had to tighten his right shoe. He had to knot it and relace it. This delayed them. The jaunt had caused them to get sweaty. They had their sweaters swung over their shoulders.

"We sure have been walking a lot lately, don't you think?" she remarked.

"We're just cruising so far. You haven't seen anything yet."

They climbed up the innumerable wooden stairs that led from Kearny Street up to the Coit Tower, stopping several times to catch their breath. Tourists with backpacks raced down. There were tons of plants all along the way up.

Finally, they reached the summit, hot and exhausted. In front of them was a giant structure with a statue of Columbus in the foreground.

"This is Coit Tower," he gasped as he pointed.

Astrid was looking the other way. "*¡Que maravilloso!* I love this view!" She pulled out her camera and took panoramic shots until she ran out of film. She reloaded her camera.

She asked a tall Swedish tourist to take their photo. He took at least five from different angles.

Eventually, they entered Coit Tower. They viewed the murals throughout the structure. Astrid was overwhelmed.

"Are you dragging?" Andrés asked after they had finished their tour.

"No," she replied. Andrés knew that she would never admit to it.

"Unfortunately, we have to walk back down," he said. They started to cross the parking lot when a taxi pulled up and dropped off three passengers.

"Come on," he grabbed her. "We just got lucky."

They rode back down to North Beach and got off in front of Saints Peter and Paul Church facing Jackson Square.

Minutes later they were sitting at an old wooden table in the Caffe Trieste in North Beach inhaling the wonderful coffee aromas. The patrons were smoking and gesticulating while speaking Italian. The waiter brought over two gigantic cappuccini, an almond biscotti, and an anise biscotti.

Andrés dipped his cookie into his coffee drink.

"Did you have a cool time today?"

She nodded affirmatively, "But I think you tried to kill me. My feet hurt."

"Bummer! You should get yourself some jogging shoes."

"But I don't jog."

"It's what people wear when they walk."

"I don't understand."

It was late, so they walked to a nearby bus stop where they waited next to a young Latina mother with two children. The wind had started to pick up and clouds were forming over the bay.

"Andrés, I had a great time today," she said, smiling at him.

"Yeah. Me, too."

"You know that you are my only friend," her tone changed and sounded slightly morose as she turned and stared down at the sidewalk.

He put his arm around her. "Hey, you just got here. At Mills, you'll be one of the most awesome dudes."

"Duds?" she looked puzzled.

"No, dudes," he was grasping for a description. He didn't want to say "chick" or "babe." "You know like girl . . .young woman . . . *mujercita*."

They both laughed. She reached over and kissed him on the cheek. Andrés was paralyzed.

❧

Meanwhile, back at the house, Erik was busy rifling through Schmidt's desk. Earlier he had dropped the old man off at his office near the Letterman Hospital in the Presidio.

Erik had entered the locked office downstairs using one of the spare keys he had of the entire domicile. He had relocked the door after him. Most of the drawers contained papers and billing receipts related to Schmidt's association with Sellarebu Pharmaceuticals [SPL].

The bottom right drawer was locked. He tried his burglar tools, but was trying to be very careful not to scratch the lock.

Suddenly, he heard a noise outside the room. He stopped and became perfectly still. The sounds were getter louder. He recognized that someone was vacuuming the hallway. It was probably the cleaning girl. She might come in to dust the office and empty out the trashcan, he thought. His cover would be that Schmidt had asked him to pick up some papers that he had forgotten in the office. The cleaning girl really only spoke Spanish and he was sure that she would not question him.

Finally, after five minutes, the noise ceased. Boehner thought he heard footsteps leaving. He put away the burglar tools and took out a set of fingernail clippers with a small hooked file attachment at the end. In less than three seconds he had jimmied opened the locked drawer. He carefully rummaged through the documents. They were piles of legal documents. None seemed to be the information that he was supposed to be looking for.

When he finished his search, he relocked the door as he exited the office. He walked out the exit that led to the downstairs garage.

From the partially opened hall closet, a pair of eyes had secretively observed Erik's escape.

CHAPTER 17

THE UMBRELLA

April 1941, Frankfurt

Teufl had changed his walking route from the clinic to the hospital so that he could pass close to Keichelle's residence and attempt to intercept her. He watched for her patiently from the nearby café.

Finally, on an inclement day with rain pouring down in buckets, he observed her getting drenched as she scurried by. He escaped out the café door and tried to pursue her.

"Keichelle!" he cried out in the storm.

The wind of the storm was howling and she could not hear him. He shouted out again as loud as he could.

She hesitated and turned around. He opened up his umbrella and placed it over her. She didn't say anything. They began to walk shoulder-to-shoulder into the black sheets of rain, getting drenched. She was only wearing her flimsy coat, which by this time was completely soaked.

The cars sped by and splashed water on them.

"I hope you have dry shoes back at the hospital," he yelled above the din of the downpour.

"I'll find something," he thought he heard her say in a resigned voice.

Newspapers flew by, as did a broken charcoal grey umbrella. The pair had to negotiate puddles and overflowing drains. More than once they sank into shallow pools of muddy water.

At last, after what seemed an eternity, they reached the hospital.

"Thank you," she said hoarsely in a serious manner.

"Do you have another coat?"

She nodded her head no.

"Keichelle, meet me at the cafeteria at seven tonight," he called out.

Her hair looked like an old mop. She was shivering. She did not respond, but rushed off, sopping wet.

附

His body also quivered. Teufl had gotten drenched on his trek back to the clinic. He tried to work in his office but his mind was distracted. Or was it his heart? He went to the hospital cafeteria at 6:45 that evening and found an empty table. He did not get anything to eat. He was waiting for Keichelle.

At the top of the hour, people started to come into the dining area. Keichelle was not among them. A group of four next to him were laughing and discussing a patient who had defecated in the middle of a waiting room. He was repulsed by such insensitivity. He had witnessed hundreds of cases of human suffering.

"Thank you for rescuing me this morning," a grateful voice came up behind him. He turned around and saw that she was in a white nurse's uniform. A pair of powder blue cloth slippers, however, covered her feet. These were the kind that patients wore.

"You're welcome," he smiled at her as she sat down with her bowl of vegetable and bean soup and piece of dark bread.

"I probably should have bought you dinner for that nice act," she had definitely changed her tone from the prior encounter, he thought.

She then noticed that he had no plate in front of him. "Aren't you eating?" she asked incredulously.

"Oh, I am not hungry," he didn't want to leave her alone in order to get something to eat. "By the way, I am Augustin Teufl."

"You told me that the last time we met. I didn't forget. You have a reputation around here for being some sort of medical wunderkind."

A crimson tide overcame his face. Was she mocking him? He wondered. The remark seemed a bit impertinent.

"I asked around about you. I don't generally talk to strangers," her green eyes looked softly at him. "I'm sorry if I appear rude or ill-mannered. I'm probably both."

On the outside she was tough and a survivor, but internally, she seemed to have a good heart, he observed.

They chatted briefly. She opened up to him and revealed that she was twenty years old, but felt that she had endured a dozen life times. Keichelle spoke matter of factly. She and her sister had been raised in an orphanage in Constanţa. They had been victims of child abuse, but were rescued by Doctor Weinglas and his sister who later adopted the two girls.

Now Keichelle was a nurse's assistant in the Gastroenterology Department.

She was late coming to dinner tonight because she had to clean up after a very ill patient.

Teufl had already known about the type of menial work that she performed at the hospital. Now he glanced over to the table that had been making inappropriate remarks about a sick person. He made a mental note of each of their faces.

"I have to go," she said.

"But you just arrived," he started to panic. Was she just

going to eat and run?

"The head nurse in our department hates me," she said nonchalantly.

"Oh, really," his brows furrowed. "Who is that?"

"Old Fraulein Rossum," she heaved a sigh. "She's short, stout, and old. She should have been put out to pasture decades ago."

"Sounds like a lovely person," he coyly grinned.

"She is the one who made me clean up the mess in the waiting room even though she knew I was on my way to eat. I can't be late or I'll be cleaning every WC on my floor." She arose to leave. Teufl got up from his chair also.

"Keichelle, I saw that your coat was soaking wet," he started to stammer. He pulled out a large article of clothing from a chair next to him. "Here is a coat. It's an extra one from my stepmother. It's probably too big for you, but no one is going to notice in the rain."

There was a moment of silence as she looked down at the woolen coat. At least she would be warm.

"Thank you," she said dismally. She was embarrassed and started to leave the table.

"Do you want me to escort you home tonight?" he called after her.

She spun and nodded affirmatively. She mouthed out the word "eleven." He gave her a thumbs-up sign with a little stifled smile.

"There's a hat in the pocket," he called out not knowing if she had heard him.

CHAPTER 18

HAIGHT

Tuesday, July 2, 1974, San Francisco

The Schmidts' house actually consisted of two three-story residences melded together. It had been part of the officers' residences when the Presidio was a military base. The bedrooms of the Schmidts were on the top floor of the first residence. They were joined to the servants' quarters at the same level of the second residence by a double door that was always locked. Only Nan and Bert were permitted to use that secured passage.

The study, library, drawing room, dining room, kitchen, and other main rooms stretched across both floors of the two residences. There were two garages on the bottom floor with driveways facing eastward. One garage housed the green Mercedes limousine. Erik had his living quarters next to this garage. The other garage had been partially converted into Mr. Schmidt's private office.

Early Tuesday morning, after dropping Mr. Schmidt off at his place of employment, Erik rushed back to the house and started to berate Nan.

He face was beet red and he was seething. "Those people should not be working here," he yelled, pointing to his collar. "She ruined my shirts. They're not white anymore. I don't know what the hell she used to wash them."

"You should probably bring this up with Doña

Grossman," Nan replied imperturbably. "The cook was hired by her."

"I don't know why they hire these people from Guatemala or Nicaragua or wherever the hell she is from. They don't even speak English."

He rubbed the top of his short flat top and shook his head in disgust.

Bert had heard the shouting and summoned Doña Matilda, who came downstairs to meet with the chauffeur.

"Good morning, Erik," the matron greeted him. "Is there a problem?" she asked in a neutral tone.

He described the problems that he was having with Maria the cook.

Matilda then asked him if he was paying Maria extra for the washing and ironing.

"Of course not!" he declared forcefully.

"Now, Erik, you know she shouldn't be doing your laundry anyway," she said in a conciliatory manner. "She's being employed as the cook. She had great references from the Mark Hopkins Hotel."

"Okay, then Nan should do my clothes."

Matilda remarked with a demeaning glare, "That's never going to happen. If you are not satisfied with the situation here, you are free to eat off site and have your laundry done elsewhere." She didn't wait for a response and walked away.

CB

Andrés had called his uncle on Sunday and everything seemed to be fine back in San Antonio. The weather back there was humid and in the high 90s. After hanging up, he left the house for the laundromat. Sadly, he took inventory of his clothes. His shoes were falling apart, his jeans had holes in them, and the collars on his shirts were worn. He planned to wear only white tee shirts for the school year.

Astrid had invited him to a Fourth of July celebration at the Golden Gate Club at the Presidio. It was being sponsored by Mr. Schmidt's consulting firm, Sellarebu Pharmaceutical Laboratories (SPL). Andrés thought that he needed to buy some new clothes with his next paycheck.

On Monday, he had gone to campus and picked up his completed assignment that had been reviewed by the professor. His senior thesis topic was approved, but the instructor had made a few suggestions about needing to be more focused and analytical. Overall, Andrés was pleased. He now had to start hitting the libraries at least twice a week.

೦ಽ

Both Andrés and Astrid sensed something was amiss with Erik as he drove them through Golden Gate Park that morning. If Andrés had heard correctly, the chauffeur had muttered some kind of remark under his breath about babysitting a spoiled brat and her hippie boyfriend. But Andrés was too busy calling out points of interest to Astrid to really pay close attention, and quickly forgot about Erik's asides.

They drove casually past the windmills at the west end of the park and did the serpentine drive throughout Golden Gate Park. Andrés pointed out Kezar Stadium where professional football had once been played.

"Andrés, why do people in the States call it football. Everybody in the world knows that soccer is the real football."

"Who told you that?"

"My father. He told me that U.S. football is more about passing and running."

"You have to be kidding!" he felt that she was attacking a core cultural value. He gave a little laugh, "That's America's number one sport."

"That's not really true. Soccer is the number one sport," she contradicted him. "The United States is part of North America. And, of course, you do remember that Chile is in South America."

He didn't know how to respond. Maybe being so ethnocentric was an intrinsic cultural value. God bless America!

Erik grimaced as he stopped the limousine in front of the Japanese Tea Garden. Dozens of tourists with cameras dangling from their necks were coming in and out. A woman with a pink umbrella held high over her head was leading the group. The sky was overcast, but it was warm. Astrid decided to leave her black leather jacket in the limousine. She thought that she would be comfortable enough in her tan cashmere sweater and black wool pants.

After they were dropped off, Andrés and Astrid walked into the Spanish-style De Young Museum and waited in a long line to purchase tickets. In front of them, there were a half-dozen African-American youngsters who were being led by an Angela Davis look-alike. When she told them to do something, they obeyed instantaneously.

Astrid wanted to explore the pre-Hispanic sections first. They passed through various salons, starting with the pre-Columbian displays. She knew a lot about the Incas and could spout off their various historical periods, but she really got enthused about the Aztecs and Mayans. She was amazed. Sadly, no photography was allowed.

They continued into the Spanish colonial sections.

"I can't believe that the Europeans ripped off the natives' gold in the name of Christianity," he remarked facetiously. "How many indigenous people died or suffered in order to adorn European churches?"

"Andrés, please don't say things like that in front of my aunt," she beseeched him. "She is very religious. She used to be a nun."

"Just messing with you," he smirked. He couldn't afford to antagonize Doña Matilda and thereby lose his paycheck. He hoped that the Inquisition was over.

The contemporary textiles and costumes exhibits were also interesting. She stared at some of the full-length theatrical gowns.

"We should go shopping," she teased.

A baby was crying. The mother picked the young child up and started to rock him, but he kept up the blubbering.

"It's time to jam," Andrés' eyes rolled.

"Jam?" she looked at him.

He made a hitchhiking type motion with his right hand toward one of the exits. She understood that he wanted to leave the wailing walls.

They left the museum after making a book purchase. People were eating their picnic lunches on blankets that sprinkled the surrounding lawns.

"Are you getting hungry?" he asked her as they walked eastward on the gravel path.

"No," she tugged on his arm and exclaimed, "Hey, you promised to take me to Haight-Ashbury!"

"No way," he grimaced, looking straight ahead.

"You should take me there anyway."

"I don't believe you. Why would you want to go there?"

"Lunch?" she gave him puppy dog eyes. She paused for a moment. "No, really, my friends back home said it was the one place I had to visit and get them souvenirs. Come on, Andrés"

"Your aunt is going to flip out."

"No, she won't," she started to skip. "Andrés, I love the smells of these flowers and plants."

They walked through the Panhandle section of Golden Gate Park, hopping over dog droppings. Andrés remained silent. There was garbage strewn throughout the grassy areas. The smell of marijuana permeated the air around them. Skinny, skanky, longhaired stone heads were beating on trashcans and screeching out acid rock songs. Astrid's eyes ogled a heavily bearded old man who was naked save for a tie-dyed tee shirt and was squatting in the middle of the dirt path.

The Haight welcomed them with its psychedelic head shops, second hand clothing stores, and rancid smelling bars. Eventually, they stopped at the TGD Café and grabbed a quick croissant sandwich.

A barista with nose and ear piercings recommended the Acapulco Gold shop as the place to buy souvenirs. It was only a block away and they found it easily.

Jasmine incense hit them as they entered the charming shop with its colorful caftans, Dungeons and Dragons figurines, and all sorts of crystals. Astrid was like a kid in a candy store. She literally touched every item in the store.

"What kind of stone is this?" she asked.

"Amethyst," hissed the longhaired brunette with a blond streak, sitting behind the counter reading the Detroit Free Press.

Astrid could not understand what was said. She finally ended up buying some rainbow-colored beaded bracelets for her friends back in Chile and a sweatshirt that said "I Love the Haight."

"Where to now?" she asked.

His feet ached. His head hurt. Andrés was already spent for the day. Matilda had given him another envelope when he had arrived that morning. He was supposed to pay his rent by today. He wanted to go home.

"Hey, do want to check out where I go to school?" he probed. "I have to run a quick errand at my pad. It's real close to the school."

"Sure, I would love to see it!" she jumped with excitement.

He carried her purchases and they arrived at his dwelling about fifteen minutes later. He was exhausted.

Andrés gingerly went up the steps and rang his landlords' doorbell. John appeared wearing a Cordon Bleu cooking school apron over his pink tank top and tight jeans.

"Hey, you!" John emoted. "Great to see you." His eyes wandered over to Astrid who was waiting on the sidewalk.

Andrés reached into his pocket and drew out the envelope that had two twenty-dollar bills to pay toward his back rent and for the current month.

"Both of you, come on in," John motioned to them. "Who is your cute little friend, Andrés?"

"This is Astrid. She's from Chile. She's going to Mills in the fall."

Astrid climbed the stairs and extended her hand, "Pleasure to meet you."

"I'm John," he took her hand and led her through the door in a debonair fashion. "I just finished making some brownies."

Andrés really didn't want to tarry there and handed John the rent money. On the other hand, John's pastries were to die for. Maybe one brownie wouldn't hurt.

The living room was impeccably decorated in bright yellows and whites. Andrés and Astrid collapsed onto a white leather sofa that was situated in front of a dark mahogany coffee table. The three started to converse about this and that. Astrid inquired about the erotic artwork and photos mounted about the room. John's eyes lit up when he found out that Astrid was art major.

"My partner just picked up this black and white print from a photographer named Mapplethorpe," John pointed to the photo over by the baby grand piano. "He's supposed to be hot."

While the other two were deep in conversation. Andrés inhaled two brownies filled with toasted almonds and chocolate chips and a glass of milk.

"Thanks, John, we really need to get over to school."

"Here, take these," there were four more brownies wrapped up.

"Are you ready?" Andrés seemed to be asking her, but was actually hinting that they were leaving. "We need to go my apartment for a few minutes. Is that all right?"

"Why, of course," she said a little too eagerly.

On second thought, he remembered his commitment to Mr. Schmidt. It wouldn't seem proper for her to come over alone to his apartment. He would be unable to lie. Appearances would trump reality.

"Astrid, I'm only going to be a minute," he retreated. "Why don't you stay here with John and I'll be right back."

Astrid seemed stunned at what he proposed. She just stood there.

"Is everything all right?" Andrés was puzzled.

"Andrés, in my country, a young woman can not enter or stay in a man's house unaccompanied," she looked embarrassed as she explained the predicament to the two men. "My aunt would crucify me."

John seemed to have read Andrés mind. "Don't worry, you two. We can all go down stairs. I'll be your chaperone," he laughed and led them to Andrés' basement apartment.

Andrés' place was a mess with his dirty clothes strewn all over the floor. It was dimly lit and cold. In one corner was an area that served as a tiny kitchen. There was no television. His school papers were scattered happenstance all over the table that served as his desk. He was searching for the forms that he had completed for fall registration and his student health application.

"This is alternative art," John whispered to Astrid, pointing to the Los Lobos and the Grateful Dead posters tacked into the wall. A macramé plant hanger dangled from the ceiling. The flora was more dead than alive.

"Okay, I got the stuff," Andrés made his way to his front door.

As they parted, Andrés added, "Hey, John, can I borrow an iron? I have to press a shirt. I'm going to this fancy party with Astrid on the Fourth."

"Sure. Do you want to come up this evening or do you want me to leave it in your place?"

"My place, please. You know where the extra key is hidden. Thanks."

The pair escaped to USF and the main administration office where Andrés turned in the necessary forms. He gave her a cursory tour of the campus and led her to the building where he took most of his Arts and Sciences courses for his Comparative Literature and Culture major. They huffed and puffed as they negotiated the several flights of stairs. Today there were only secretaries present. The two stopped to recuperate and read the bulletin boards. There were rooms for rent, odd jobs, and available free pets. The baby turtles made the two laugh.

Fifteen minutes later at the University Center, Astrid sifted through the sweaters, caps, and other articles of clothing. She bought still another sweatshirt.

"Yo, Andrés," a familiar voice called out. "When did you get back?"

A girl with long brown hair hanging down to her waist and dressed in a rose halter-top and skinny jeans was staring at them.

"Hey, what's up, Judy?" Andrés responded coolly. She was a junior with whom Andrés had had an on-again, off-again relationship. They would date, go to her place, make love, and then break up. The spats would be over trivial matters. She preferred Proust and James Joyce; he detested them and liked Dumas and Verne. She favored Joni Mitchell; he favored Joan Baez.

"Who's your friend?" Judy inquired, envy seeping from her pores.

"Oh, this is Astrid. She's from Chile. I'm her tutor this summer."

Astrid extended her hand and gave a curt smile.

"Tutoring in what?" Judy's words were laced with jealousy.

Astrid felt belittled. She had been insulted by the girl and trivialized by Andrés.

"English."

"Gotta go. Give me a ring if you want to have some fun," the girl disappeared.

Astrid and Andrés started walking home.

"Your girl friend?" she asked meekly.

"Ex."

That night when Andrés returned home, he found the iron on his table. Next to it, there was also a beautiful blue and burgundy striped tie from Magnin's, the high-end department store in San Francisco. There was a hand-scribbled note under it:

"A gift from Maurice. She's a keeper. Have fun on Thursday."

CHAPTER 19

THE BARRETTE

May, 1941, Frankfurt

They had met twice for dinner at the hospital cafeteria before she agreed to have coffee outside of the work environment with him. They met at the Baseler Platz Kaffee Haus from where Teufl had originally covertly observed her. She thanked him for the coat and the hat on each occasion. Even though the coat was too large for her, she wore it with grace when she met him at the Kaffee Haus.

Keichelle took her coffee with milk and sugar. She declined anything to eat. She now gave him a pleasant smile while they chatted.

She deflected most of the personal questions that Teufl asked. By now he had found out most everything about her from her personnel files. She worked from 11 a.m. to 11 p.m. everyday for seven straight days. She got every eighth day off.

Keichelle did not dress stylishly, but her green eyes and auburn hair hypnotized Teufl. He had a subliminal longing to touch her olive skin, but something held him back.

Teufl asked her about her favorite books. She told him that she didn't read much, but her sister did. He had tried to find out about Keichelle's likes and dislikes, but met with little success. Keichelle said that she had very little opportunity to divert herself. In addition to working, she had to take care of her adoptive mother who was now blind. She had to cook for her, clean up after her, and when not too tired, socialize with her.

Teufl had hit a nerve with her. Now Keichelle started to ramble involuntarily. She stared dreamily out the window, no longer looking at Augustin. She spoke of her adoptive father, Dr. Ludwig Weinglas, who had taken a position in Pediatrics at the Frankfurt hospital when she was six years old. The doctor's spinster sister, Elise, was a social worker who had raised her and her sister.

Dr. Weinglas had died in 1933 when Keichelle was twelve years old. Her "mother" (Ludwig's sibling), her sister, and Keichelle lived off the family savings, but their funds became depleted when Elise became blind. Keichelle was forced to start working at a tender age in order to help support the family. She initially had to take on menial jobs until she procured employment at the hospital through a family friend of her father.

Her eyes started to well up with tears. Teufl sighed. His heart ached.

"Keichelle," he looked directed into her floating pupils. "If you could go anywhere in the world, where would it be?"

"Italy."

ⳇ

On her next day off, they rendezvoused at the coffee house and spent the day walking around the Palmengarten. They visited the different pavilions and greenhouses. They laughed when they saw cacti trying to survive in the cold weather.

"It must be from southern Germany," they joked.

They took an afternoon break to have ham and cheese sandwiches on buttered buns in a small outside picnic area.

She asked him questions about his work. He was vague

in his answers and only shared that it was clinical lab work.

Keichelle was in an elated mood. When the check came, she reached for it first.

"Keichelle," he uttered, "I'll pay." He was shocked by her attempt.

"No. It's my treat," she beamed. "I finally got a promotion!"

"What!" he seemed surprised.

"Yes, old Fraulein Rossum just retired," she underscored. "I'm the new head of nursing in my department! I don't know how I got it."

"Congratulations!" he beamed at her. "We need to celebrate."

✓

All week he thought only about his date with Keichelle. Now that she had a better position in the hospital, he thought that she should start cultivating herself with literature, music, and the arts. He himself needed someone to share his acumen. He had finally found a woman who did not trade her body for money or power.

He planned for them to go the Goethehaus. Teufl wanted to do something that would impress her. He decided that he would buy her some works by Goethe. He would even inscribe a dedication to her.

It was around nine o'clock one morning and he was walking around Frankfurt trying to locate a bookstore close to the main train terminal. The streets were crowded with commuters going to work from the suburbs. The consumptive derelicts had their tin cups out for stray pfennigs. There was a slight mist of steam arising from the sewers after the early morning rain.

He crossed the boulevard and almost stopped in

midstream. Exiting from a small bakery was Keichelle. A middle-aged man helped her put on a black cloak. He was of small stature with black hair and a black frizzy beard. He wore little spectacles on his bulbous nose.

Teufl walked right up to them. The man smiled at him, but the woman did not.

"Good morning," Teufl said calculatingly.

With a big smile, the man returned the greeting. The woman barely nodded, her green eyes were stolid.

The surface of Teufl's body seemed poised, but his blood was boiling. So this was the reason Keichelle was indifferent to him. For an older man! Financial security! What else could it be? All women wanted money. They really didn't believe in true love. He couldn't think straight. He wouldn't tolerate this. He had pulled strings to get her a promotion. The ingrate!

Teufl turned around and walked to the clinic. He threw himself into his work. He was behind in all of his projects. The clock on his desk said that it was a quarter to eleven. Teufl threw on his coat and raced down to the café by Keichelle's house.

He didn't go in, but waited in the shadows. He would confront her on her way to work for trying to take him for a fool.

Within ten minutes, a slender figure swimming in a dark brown woolen coat was walking forward. Something didn't seem right to him. He wanted to jump out and ask her why she had denied him that morning. Something inside his psyche stopped him. He let her pass by, she being oblivious to her near peril.

A few days later they met at the café before going to the Goethehaus. Teufl had toiled day and night in order to bring his clinical projects up to date. He still had outstanding paperwork to complete at the hospital.

The weather was moderate and the sun was out. Keichelle was wearing a black sweater over a long grey woolen skirt. She was in a pleasant mood.

He would be systematic in approaching her for the rebuff she had given. He would make sure that she would feel that she should never have been born, after he was done with her.

"Hey, Keichelle, how come you didn't say good morning to me the other day when I saw you at the bakery?" he said in a seemingly teasing tone.

"What are you talking about?" she said defensively.

"When you left the bakery," he said in an irreproachable manner, "with that old man."

"What bakery?"

"You know the one by the train station."

"That wasn't me."

"It looked just like you."

"Was the man about this tall?" she lifted her left hand and held it a few inches above her head.

"Yes," she was going to confess, he thought.

"That was probably Zharko."

"Who's Zharko?"

"It's my sister's boyfriend."

"What does your sister look like?" he asked incredulously.

"Why just like me, of course. We're identical twins."

For the rest of the day, he treated Keichelle like a goddess. He was her slave. He had behaved like a jealous fool.

At the Goethehaus, they walked up and down the stairs. The descriptions for the exhibits in each of the fourteen rooms were extensive. The legends gave the historical perspective of the city of Frankfurt, the biography of Goethe, and a synopsis of German Romanticism. In the museum section, he bought her a copy of *Faust* and inscribed it:

Liebe Keichelle,

Wir werden für immer zusammen sein.

Augustin

[To Keichelle, we will always be together, Augustin.]

Keichelle's face turned crimson when she saw the inscription. It looked like she wanted to protest, but she didn't.

❧

On occasion she would let him hold her hand. He spent every conscious moment thinking about her, wanting to possess her. Her next day off was on a Sunday. They went to the Cathedral of St. Bartholome and observed the mass.

"You make me very happy," he boldly pronounced after several glasses of wine later at the gasthof.

She smiled.

He reached into his jacket pocket and pulled out a paper wrapped package and handed it to her across the table.

Her face twisted in puzzlement. She opened it. Inside there were two silver barrettes. She picked them up and turned them in her hand as if she were examining unidentified foreign objects.

"I can't, Augustin," she attempted to hand them back.

"You must," he insisted. "I can't wear them."

She gave out a nervous laugh. She withdrew her hand.

Later that evening she gave him a kiss good night.

CHAPTER 20

FIREWORKS

Thursday, July 4, 1974, San Francisco

Night had fallen when the Mercedes pulled into the Golden Gate Club. A young man wearing a light grey security windbreaker directed the vehicle to the passenger-unloading zone. Erik opened the door first for Astrid and Andrés, and then carefully assisted Mr. Schmidt out of the vehicle. Although Matilda had specifically instructed Erik to make sure that her brother-in-law utilized a wheelchair, the older man adamantly refused.

"I'm no damn cripple!" he growled as he grabbed his silver knobbed cane. "I can manage." He took hold of Astrid's arm with his right hand.

While Erik left to park the limousine, the threesome proceeded and entered the red brick building. They were checked in at the reception area and were given red, white, and blue lanyards with their names and affiliations printed on them. Cigarette smoke escaped from small reception rooms as they passed by. The foul odor made Andrés nauseous, but he felt that he could not complain since he was merely a guest.

Heads turned as Astrid entered the gigantic room wearing a navy blue dress and adorned with white gloves, a white belt, and a white pearl necklace. The ruby red shoes finished the costume. Most of the bald gentlemen and overly made up ladies were at least three times her age.

"Isn't this beautiful, father," she pointed toward the floor-to-ceiling picture windows and the hanging chandeliers. They went over to the large pane and observed the sailboats riding on white caps toward Golden Gate Bridge.

"Wonderful, my dear, simply wonderful," he put his arm around her. He turned to Andrés, "Thank you for joining us, my boy."

Andrés nodded politely. He observed the other participants around them in their tailored suits, elegant dresses, and statuesque military uniforms. He had dug out his navy blue corduroy pants and grey tweed sport coat. He also wore the beautiful tie that John and Maurice had given him. He had even taken the bus to the Schmidts' home so he wouldn't arrive sweaty or late.

In the large formal room, encircled by wooden panels, historical landscape paintings, and flags positioned in the corner, ruddy-cheeked men drank their cocktails while they conversed and smoked. Their wives hung on to each word and laughed accordingly. Andrés observed that a few of the spouses were barely older than he was. The military men wore enough medals, ribbon bars, and braiding to supply a carnival. Trophies were the name of the game.

The threesome slowly strolled around. Astrid's father introduced his daughter and her escort to everyone he knew. Schmidt declined the hors d'oeuvres offered by young men in classy waiter garb. Andrés was not bashful and took more than a few canapés. Astrid only poked at her appetizers.

"Why, there you are, Johann," proclaimed a rosy-faced large framed man with nicotine stained teeth. "And who are these fine looking youngsters?"

"This is my daughter, Astrid, with her escort, Andrés

Miramón," he pointed out. "This is Arnold Neumann, my associate at the lab."

They all exchanged greetings. Neumann took Schmidt's elbow with both hands and started to lead the older gentleman away.

"We'll be back in a little bit," Schmidt proffered as he twisted his head back. "We have a few things to discuss." The two older men left the two youths.

Andrés pointed to the other side of the large room and Astrid followed close to his side. As they strolled, neatly attired waiters offered them flutes of champagne, but they declined.

"Do you want to look for some punch?"

"Yes, please," she replied.

But before they had taken any more steps, Erik rushed toward them and blocked their path.

"Where's your father?" he demanded. The two youngsters pointed over to the far corner where they had last seen Schmidt in an animated conversation with Neumann, two other middle aged executives, and a three star general in dress blues.

Erik abruptly hurried over to the small gathering, shook hands with Neumann, and led Schmidt away. He found a couch for his charge. Schmidt was grumbling at the interruption.

Meanwhile, Andrés was sampling several more hors d'oeuvres as the servers came around. Astrid gave him a sweet smile as he snacked. They walked over to the punchbowl, avoiding the corporate VIPs and their entourages.

Andrés was beginning to pour Astrid and himself some reddish punch.

"Hi, y'all," they were confronted by a buxom woman

with a brunette beehive hairdo. "I'm Trudy Maddox."

Andrés and Astrid smiled politely and lifted their cups toward her.

"We just moved out West from Georgia," she volunteered with her thick as molasses Southern accent. "I just love Frisco!"

Astrid twisted her head and furtively whispered into Andrés ear, "*¿Qué dijo?*" *What did she say?*

He tried to repress a smile. "We're college students." And then turned to Astrid and softly muttered, "*Ella es de sudamérica.*" *She is from South America.*

Astrid silently mouthed, "*¿De verdad?*" *Really?*

"Well I declare, there must be a thousand colleges in this state, you know," she pertly said. "My husband, C.K., just started working over at the Stanford Bioengineering Department down in Palo Alto . . ." While she was speaking, Andrés smiled politely along with Astrid. "I'm trying to get a teaching position. In Atlanta I used to instruct . . ."

Mrs. Maddox gave her captive audience her entire life history while imbibing on the free flowing alcoholic drinks that came by with Swiss watch punctuality.

Astrid kept poking Andrés and grimacing. She kept whispering that she was having a difficult time understanding the woman. *What kind of a foreign dialect of English did the lady speak?*

"I still am learning about The Next Generation . . ." She fanned herself with a program brochure. "What brings y'all to this little ole soirée?"

Andrés was about to respond on Astrid's behalf, but uncharacteristically restrained himself.

"My father was working for The Sellarebu Pharmaceutical Laboratories in Santiago, Chile. He was working for them for a long time," Astrid was speaking slowly and enunciating. "He is now working for them here in San Francisco with The Next Generation Project at Letterman Hospital."

Andrés nodded approvingly. He was proud of the way Astrid had responded. He squeezed her hand and gave her an appreciative wink.

Mrs. Maddox's monologue was dragging on until suddenly Andrés was jostled from behind. He felt two hands lightly grabbing his shoulders accompanied by the stench of cigarette smoke.

"Sorry to intrude," Neumann said in an exasperated tone looking directly toward Astrid. "Do you know where your father is?"

The interloper's expression had alarmed her. "No," she replied.

"Well, if you see him, please tell him that I am looking for him," he gave a scowl. "Thank you." He released his grip on Andrés and scurried away.

They apologized to Mrs. Maddox and explained that they needed to find Astrid's father and that it was a pleasure meeting her. It took a few minutes to extricate themselves from her. She was still talking when they escaped.

Andrés took Astrid by the hand and led her through the multitudes. He wanted to grab a few more appetizers but he exercised some self-control.

They trolled their way through the large room looking for her father. The throngs had multiplied with commensurate noise, cackling, and laughter.

"He should be with Erik," her face displaying displeasure. "Erik is supposed to take care of him."

A tray of hot dogs, cut into thirds, passed in front of them. Andrés inhaled the biting smell of mustard. His mouth salivated. He quickly snatched one.

They exited through the double oak doors into the main passageway, bumping into new arrivals. They proceeded to the left where there were two small salons that were hosting private receptions. The National Science Foundation was sponsoring the closer reception room. No one challenged the pair as they entered. The participants here seemed to have whiter beards and thicker glasses. The two walked toward the middle of the room and found a large round table strewn with shrimp, smoked salmon, and an assortment of cheeses and breads. Andrés and Astrid both grabbed little white plates and took some samples.

Astrid grabbed several red, white, and blue napkins for them. They enjoyed their little respite. Their reconnaissance was unsuccessful and they left without incident.

The second small reception room was filled with more military types. Judging by the drinks in their hands it seemed that it was hosted by Johnny Walker or Jack Daniels. A solidly built gentleman greeted them at the entryway.

"Hello, can I help you?" his body blocked the doorway like an offensive tackle.

"Yes, please," Astrid smiled innocently. "We are looking for my father. Doctor Schmidt."

"Yes, miss," he bowed. "He is over against the back wall," he pointed. "Welcome to Evergreen Air. Please enjoy." He nimbly withdrew himself.

The military personnel were quaffing their drinks like soda pop and smoking gigantic cigars. The air was almost unbearable to breathe.

As Andrés and Astrid approached, they could hear the animated conversation between her father and Neumann. Erik was standing close at hand.

"It is really important, Johann!" the associate's voice implored. "We need to share the Seele Project report with them. They're up my ass!"

"They can wait," was the calm reply.

"We have to keep them happy!" Neumann pleaded angrily. "The administration is breathing down their throats!"

"We will. We will."

Astrid stepped forth, "Father, is everything all right?" Her voice filled with concern.

"Why yes, my dear," he gently clasped her hand. "Arnold here is just working too hard. Time is money. Isn't that right, my friend?"

Neumann gave a faint smile that exposed his yellow teeth.

"You two run along. Erik is taking good care of me," Schmidt looked down at his watch. "When do the fireworks begin?'

Someone answered, "9:30."

The young pair took their leave.

"Let's get out of here," Andrés began to rush out the door. "This place is too wasted."

They moved on to the other salon and made a beeline to the table with the seafood. Most of it was now depleted, so they nibbled on the smoked Gouda cheese and the baguette slices.

As the hour grew late, people gradually started to pull away and make their way outdoors through a side door. By this time, Andrés and Astrid had joined the exodus. They took their place behind a cement balustrade in anticipation of the spectacle.

The air was chilly and a light mist nibbled on the observers. Fortunately, the sky above was still clear and a few stars shone. Astrid was now shivering. She pressed her body against Andres. He gently put his arm around her. She leaned her head into him and snaked her arm around his waist underneath his jacket.

The Golden Gate was lit up. There were boats in the bay that were also illuminated.

A military band began by playing a march. There were oohs and aahs when the fireworks shot up and exploded in front of them in kaleidoscopes of color. A second or two later there were the delayed bangs and whistles.

Her body jolted with each new burst in the air.

"I love it! I love it!" she squeezed him. "This is fantastic!"

In the distance, dogs were howling. The smell of burning sulfur slowly crept toward them. People clapped and yelped all around them.

The twenty-five minutes of pyrotechnics reached its finale with the "War of 1812 Overture" playing in the background as red, white, and blue sparks flared through the sky.

Astrid pressed herself closer to Andrés. He noticed that she was still shivering in the chilly outdoors. She slowly grabbed the front of his shirt causing his head to tilt forward. She drew her other arm around his neck and embraced him. She kissed him on one side of his lips, and then on the other side. Andrés wanted to pull back. Her back slowly arched as his lips touched hers. He pulled his head back. He remembered his promise to Schmidt. But she was determined and started to kiss him on the neck. He couldn't resist her passion. The heavens exploded.

CHAPTER 21

THE LOCK

May, 1941, Frankfurt

Eight days after Augustin had given her the barrettes, he and Keichelle went to see *Don Giovanni* at the Opera House. They were among the hundreds of patrons mingling in their stylish finery. Elegant vehicles dropped off their charges. The night was still and the partial moon illuminated the skies. Cigar smoke permeated the air. Women wearing flowing gowns and chandeliers of jewelry laughed at whatever their escorts said.

Keichelle had never been to a musical performance before. This was one of the most thrilling moments in her life. Her auburn hair was in a bun pinned by the silver barrettes that Augustin had given her. Her dress was plain and she didn't wear any earrings or bracelets.

Augustin and Keichelle were seated in the side orchestra section of the theatre. They could see the beautiful sheen of the costumes. The voice of the lead baritone in the aria "*Il Mio Tesoro*" brought two ovations from the audience.

During the intermission, Keichelle peppered Teufl with dozens of questions about every aspect of the opera. He loved being her mentor. He shared his soul with her. Since he was proficient in Italian, he gave her his insights into the plot. She did not understand why there were demons in the last act and why Don Giovanni did not repent.

Teufl then said to her, "*Questo è il fin di chi fa mal, e de' perfidi la morte alla vita è sempre ugual.*" [Such is the end of the evildoer, the death of a sinner always reflects his life.]

At supper they continued to discuss the music, the plot, and the characters.

"Do you really think that there was such a man as Don Giovanni," she asked naively.

Teufl laughed like a man who knew all things about life, "Of course, my dear, there are thousands of such men around."

They each imbibed in a glass of sparkling wine. She was feeling tipsy.

"Augustin, I need to ask you a big favor."

"What is it?" he seemed surprised. "Ask and it is done."

"You know about the marriage fitness certificates, don't you?"

"Yes, I handle them for the hospital."

"Well, my sister Sandrine and Zharko want to get married," she paused and looked into his eyes. "And they need to have the marriage fitness certification approved."

"It shouldn't be a problem. Have them come to my office at the hospital on Tuesday. At 10 o'clock. They need to bring birth certificates, passports, and any other sort of identification cards. Has either one been married or divorced before?" he slipped into his administrative persona.

"No. I should say no for my sister. I don't know for sure about Zharko."

"When do they want to get married?"

"Next month."

"Am I invited to the wedding?" he taunted.

౭

On Tuesday morning, Teufl could not believe his eyes.

Sandrine was the spitting image of her twin sister. The same auburn hair flowed over her shoulders. The identical green eyes and olive skin faced him.

He gave Sandrine and her future husband Zharko the three page form to fill out.

Teufl then went through a list of questions with each one to determine their racial purity. Sandrine could not answer several questions about her birth or her birth parents. All she knew was that the Weinglases siblings adopted her in 1923. She showed Teufl adoption papers from the Constanța orphanage averring that she was born in 1921 under the name of Sandrine Urmuz. She showed him birth declarations for herself and her twin sister, Keichelle Urmuz.

Sandrine and Keichelle currently lived in Frankfurt with their adoptive mother, Elise Weinglas. Sandrine confirmed that there was no blood relationship between her and the Weinglas's. She had not been brought up religiously and she was not Jewish.

Teufl was ticking off each box on the form as he went down the list of questions. If the answer was nebulous, he wrote down a favorable notation. He still couldn't believe how much Sandrine resembled Keichelle.

Zharko smiled through the whole process, but he fidgeted nervously in his seat. More than one time he stepped outside the office to smoke.

When it was his turn to answer questions, he was more succinct in his answers. His name was Zharko Delčevç and he was born in Macedonia in 1912. He had no prior marriages or issue (to his knowledge). He tried to make a joke.

He had gone to the university in Frankfurt and earned his letters. He had opened up a bookstore. It became successful and he moved to a larger place in an area that had more pedestrian traffic. In 1937 he had hired Sandrine at his store and after a few years they became engaged. He also showed documentation and receipts to Teufl.

Initially, Teufl had despised Zharko because he had thought that the latter was his rival with Keichelle. Now he felt an unexplained kinship with him. They were mutually obsessed with the identical twin sisters.

The interview had taken over an hour. Zharko had unexpectedly invited Teufl to lunch. He wanted to show his appreciation.

Later in the day, Teufl brought all the documentation over to Dr. Magnussen and requested that the application be expedited. He was envious of Zharko's simple life and his love of books. Teufl, on the other hand, was born with a supreme intellect and brilliant mind. His brain was always racing, trying to solve the next problem or invent the subsequent permutation. His colleague informed him that there would not be any problems. The routine background check would simply be pro forma.

Teufl was too excited to work. He waited for Keichelle in the hospital cafeteria. Now that she was the head of nursing for her department, she had more flexibility in her meal times. When Teufl asked to meet at an earlier time than usual, she assented.

"I don't think that we'll have any problems," he boasted to her. "They will just do a routine background check."

"Augustin," she grabbed his hand with both of hers. "Thank you for all of your help."

"No problem. We should get the certificate in a few days."

She smiled. Her face glowed. Her skin radiated.

His heart was full. He was so happy. He had found his destiny.

"Well, what are you going to do when Sandrine gets married?" he inquired innocently.

"We're all taking my mother to New York to live," she said matter of factly.

"Are you going too?" he asked, immediately disheartened.

"Yes," she answered sullenly. "Zharko has relatives there. He can get a good job there."

She had stabbed him in the heart. His spirit was broken. This was how she repaid him. She was ungrateful. His faith in her was destroyed.

Teufl's mind raced. *Why don't I ask her to stay and marry me?* He struggled within himself. He had had a lifetime of indoctrination about the appropriate "look" of the Aryan race and Keichelle did not fit. He couldn't do it. Instead he chose to blame her for leaving him.

Teufl's mouth formed a smile and patted her hand. He wished her the best.

His mind was filled with Dieter's admonishments about the duplicity of women. They were all consumed with financial arrangements and money.

Tears welled up in his eyes. He was distraught and angry at the same time. He turned his head away so that she could not observe him.

"I don't know how to repay you," she reached over and squeezed his forearm.

He paused and thought for a second. "I would like a lock of your hair."

PART II - CAFFÈ MOCHA

CHAPTER 22

THE WORLD CUP

Sunday, July 7, 1974, San Francisco

"¡GOOOOOOOOOL!" bellowed the Spanish-speaking television announcer.

"*Scheiße!*" screamed one of three shaved-headed guys that were sitting at a communal table with Erik.

"That is total b.s.!" yelled his comrade. "That f__king English ref! He has his head up his ass!"

There was loud cussing and screaming when the Netherlands' team was awarded a penalty kick within the first two minutes in the World Cup against West Germany.

Erik had been invited to watch the world soccer final with Schmidt, but Erik had told him that he would be watching the game with friends. He really didn't like being a caregiver to the old man.

Erik had been a U.S. Air Force brat and as a teenager had lived at various airbases throughout West Germany. After doing a stint in Air Force Special Operations, Erik did security work for Lockheed Aircraft. He eventually quit because it became a desk job and he liked action. Teal Associates had picked him up to provide international protective services for their clandestine military operations. Presently, he had been recently hired by Neumann of Sellarebu Pharmaceutical

Laboratories to be Schmidt's chauffeur and security person.

He patiently sipped his Löwenbräu at the Sudwerk Haus among the angry crowd.

"Why don't you quit your whining, you cry babies," came a voice from another table. There were five brawny guys wearing red, white, and blue garb.

"F__k you, you f__king assholes," the first skinhead jumped up and started waving his fist.

"Let's step outside," intimidated the second bald companion.

"They should have gotten rid of your kind, like they did the Jews!" berated the last of the trio.

"F__k you!" the Dutch fan table returned fire. "Let's do it." The Dutch guys started to stand up, beer bottlenecks in hand.

Suddenly, there was an earsplitting noise from behind the bar. "Everybody remain calm or I'm calling the police." The bartender with the handlebar moustache was waving a portable air horn. "Go ahead! Sit down, I said!"

There was a lot of grousing and cussing.

"Wait until after the game, asshole," one of the skinheads yelled over to the other table.

"I said stop it!" the bartender shouted apoplectically. "They still have 87 more minutes to play!" He shook his head in disbelief.

Erik eyed his tablemates. He grudgingly appreciated the solo run down the field by the Dutch forward, Cruijff. Hoeneß had made an unwise foul in the penalty area. West Germany had struggled against East Germany two weeks before, but still looked like the team to beat. He had won almost every bet that he had made with poor old Schmidt.

People were singing soccer fight songs. The noise level was

at a fever pitch. The game was being televised on a Spanish language station, because the bar proprietor disliked the U.S. sports station that used British announcers that no one could understand and who made cavalier comments about the play on the pitch. Erik had learned Spanish when he was in Texas. When his parents divorced, he had moved to New Braunfels with his father who was a retired colonel.

The Heidi look-alike bar waitress came around with her tray. He ordered another beer and some bratwursts. The announcer in his excitable delivery made the game interesting, even though West Germany's game was lethargic. Hölzenbein made a brilliant run, but was fouled in the Dutch penalty area. The English referee awarded West Germany a penalty kick with which they scored. The majority of spectators in the bar jumped up and clapped. The game was now tied. Someone slapped Erik on the back.

"F__king ref!" came from the Dutch.

"Now we're even," rejoined the skinheads who were now laughing and giving the finger to their rivals.

The aficionados sat back down on the benches. The tone of the crowd had now simmered down. Erik patiently waited for his bratwursts.

He reacted to the passion that the Spanish announcer delivered with each touch of the ball. Then suddenly, right before the end of the half, Müller scored a goal for West Germany. The fans went wild, jumping up and down, twirling each other. The score was now 2-1 in favor of West Germany.

The half ended and finally the brats were set in front of Erik. He dipped them into some hot mustard. The French fries were salty and soggy, but he was hungry. He wiped his face with the paper napkin. He needed at least two more sausages, but he did not see speedy service coming. He went to the small restroom that reeked of urine and cigarette butts. There were no paper towels left, but at least he washed his hands and dried them on his pants.

He slowly snaked his way back to his table through the multitudes. His beer was still where he had left it.

The second half was more exciting. Both teams had nearly scored goals. The fans went ballistic when Müller scored, but the goal was disallowed because he had been offside.

"That f__king ref! Go back to England! How much are you being paid?" the crowd jeered at the television.

People were getting buzzed and their words were slurred. They kept standing up and bumping into each other. Erik had been jostled several times. He controlled himself.

One of the skinheads yelled out disparagingly, pointing to an empty table. "Hey, guys, the fokkers left. Ha-ha-ha." He gave the finger toward the ceiling.

At the 85th minute, Hölzenbein was fouled again. Everybody vaulted to his feet. Erik felt a little pinch on his neck, but didn't think anything of it.

The patrons booed when the referee did not award a penalty kick.

"That f__king ref!"

CHAPTER 23

THE DOCTORS' TRIAL

December 9, 1946, Nuremberg, Germany

Sandrine's hands felt clammy as she listened attentively to the presiding judge of the tribunal.

"Count One. Between September 1939 and April 1945, all of the defendants herein, acting pursuant to a common design, unlawfully, willfully, and knowingly did conspire and agree together and with each other and with diverse other persons, to commit war crimes and crimes against humanity, as defined in Control Council Law No. 10, Article II, . . ."

Sandrine stared at the three United States judges sitting on the bench. They were elderly grey-haired men wearing judicial robes. There were the flags of the Soviet Union, Great Britain, the United States, and France behind them. She wrung her hands fretfully.

"Count Two . . . involving medical experiments without the subjects' consent, upon civilians . . . of which defendants committed murders, brutalities, cruelties, tortures, atrocities, and other inhuman acts. Such experiments included . . ."

Sandrine did not understand the English being spoken. She, like the hundreds of persons now in room 600 of the Palace of Justice, wore headphones that provided simultaneous translations from English into Russian, French, and German. The tonal quality of the apparatus was filled with static and she strained to hear. Turning up the volume only exacerbated the problem.

"High-Altitude Experiments. Freezing Experiments. Malaria Experiments. Lost (Mustard) Gas Experiments . . ."

She observed the 23 defendants whom she understood to be mostly doctors. They had their German defense attorneys with them along with dozens of assistants scattered among the tables facing the judicial bench. Scores of army personnel were in attendance, either as participants or as security guards.

"Bacterial Infection Experiments. Bone, Muscle, and Nerve Transplant Experiments. Sea-Water Experiments . . ."

Stacks and stacks of papers were piled in front of the judges, the prosecutors, and the defense attorneys. Assistants were shuffling the various files. The 325 foreign press correspondents had a special seating section for them. The 400 members of the public sat in the back of the hall in wooden chairs.

"Epidemic Jaundice Experiments. Spotted Fever Experiments. Poison Experiments. Phosphorus Burn Experiments. Sterilization Experiments . . ."

Sandrine burst into tears. Her head was bobbing back and forth. Her nose was running. Her sobbing was uncontrollable. The man next to her put his arm around her and gave her his handkerchief. He knew what she was feeling. These beasts had infected his Polish parents with tuberculosis.

Jerzy "George" Kulongoski was part of the War Crimes prosecutorial team. He was assisting the U.S. Nuremberg Military Tribunal in the case against the defendant, Dr. Rudolf Brandt.

"Count Three . . . involving the execution of the so-called 'euthanasia' program of the German Reich, in the course of which the defendants murdered hundreds of thousands of human beings . . ." This "euthanasia program" was the systematic execution of elderly, insane, incurably ill, deformed children, patients in nursing homes, asylums, and hospitals. They were termed the "useless eaters."

This time it was Kulongoski who gritted his teeth and cringed. He squeezed Sandrine's hand. He had escaped to England before the Nazi Germany invasion of Poland. Most of his family had perished during the incessant Nazi bombings on Warsaw. He had been a law student and now had dual English and Polish citizenships. Jerzy had spent the prior 18 months working on the Nuremberg trial cases for Great Britain and the United States. Most of his responsibilities involved preparing prosecutorial witnesses for direct testimony and cross-examination. His main responsibility today was Sandrine Urmuz.

"Count Four. All named defendants are guilty of membership in the Schutzstaffeln Der Nationalsozialistischen Deutschen Arbeiterpartie, commonly known as the 'SS' . . ."

 Cß

"Please state your full name for the record," directed the special prosecutor to Sandrine in English.

Finally, twenty days into the trial, she would be able to tell her story. Kulongoski had coached her the last few days. She was wearing a grey twill jacket over a black sweater and skirt. The interpreter placed a bible in front of her and she swore in German to tell the truth. Everything she said was being simultaneously translated.

"Sandrine Urmuz," she replied. Kulongoski had advised her to take a deep breath before each answer, to speak slowly, and to enunciate. She dug her fingernail into the palm of her hand in order to avoid the jitters.

The middle-aged prosecutor with a very distinguished beard asked basic background questions in English, which the interpreter then asked Sandrine in German. Her eyes were solely concentrated on these two men. She did not want to look at anyone else.

She recounted about how she and her sister had been raised in an orphanage in Constanţa, Romania, until Dr. Weinglas and his sister adopted them. The initial questions were simple.

"Miss Urmuz, what happened to you in May of 1941?"

"There was a loud beating on our door very early one morning," she took a deep breath. "Some soldiers dressed in long black coats rushed in and arrested my sister and me."

"For what reason?"

"I don't know. We were so scared," tears started to well up in her eyes. "We just screamed that there had to be some mistake. They told us to be silent. They grabbed us and forced us into a wagon."

"How old were you?"

"Twenty," she rubbed the back of her neck. She was feeling the stress rising.

"What was your sister's name?"

"Keichelle. Keichelle Urmuz."

She painted a horrific picture as the prosecutor asked one question after another. Each inquiry elicited a more graphic scene. She and her sister, Keichelle, had been abducted by some soldiers. They were brought to a staging area in a military compound and processed. The next day they were loaded into a train cattle car with eighty other passengers of both genders and all ages. There were no bathrooms or clean water in the railroad car. People were crowded next to each other. They vomited, urinated, and defecated as they stood. The miasma caused her to faint. Her sister tended to her during their ordeal. They finally arrived in Auschwitz.

The prisoners were separated into different groups. Her cluster of women was forced to disrobe and was washed down in a large shower room with high-pressure fire hoses. They were not given towels with which to dry themselves. They shivered from the chill. Eventually, they were marched to the quartermaster's supply window and given clothing items, all of which were too large.

The prosecutor then asked Sandrine to roll up her coat sleeve. She turned her body from the witness stand toward the three judges and showed them the teal-colored numbers tattooed into her arm. One of the judges nodded his head.

"What happened at Auschwitz?" the prosecutor proceeded dispassionately. Sandrine related that initially she and her sister were placed in a separate building with other women.

"What did you observe about these other women?"

"They were like us."

"Can you clarify what you mean please," he maintained his composure.

"We were all twins . . . All identical twins."

"Just women?"

"Yes, just women."

She continued to explain that this group was given some sort of deferential treatment. For example, their heads were not shaved like the others she saw on the campgrounds. They were sent to a medical clinic where they were subjected to ocular treatments.

"Can you be more specific, Miss Urmuz?"

"They injected dyes into our eyes."

"What did that do to your eyes?"

"It changed the color of my eyes from green to blue."

"From green to blue. Was that a problem?"

"Not at first. But it caused me to get nauseous and dizzy. I used to lose my sense of balance."

"Anything else?"

"Yes, the color of my eyes kept changing."

"What color are your eyes now?"

"Grey," she took off her tinted glassed and pointed to her eyes.

He studied her face. One of her eyes remained half-shut. "What else happened to you at Auschwitz?"

"One night, after a month there, my sister Keichelle was dragged out of her bed by the guards."

"What happened to her?"

Sandrine broke down sobbing as she described the gang rape of her sister and how she was dumped back into the dormitory the following morning beaten and bleeding.

"Miss Urmuz, do want to take a break?" inquired the presiding judge.

She shook her head no and kept on narrating. She explained that when the sisters reported to the clinic that morning, the head doctor asked what had happened to Keichelle. Sandrine told him. The doctor was very angry and yelled out that the experiment was now ruined.

A few days later, she and her sister were transferred to the general population. They had their heads shaved and were given different clothes. The conditions were worse. People were moaning and suffering from broken bones, open wounds, malnutrition, and physical abuse.

During the next few months, they were raped and sodomized by the guards at least twice a week. Her sister died from the mistreatment. Sandrine herself was sterilized without an anesthesia.

At this juncture, the prosecutor laid the legal foundation

for medical records and photos of Sandrine. There were several shots of the scars around her pubic area. These were received into evidence without objection.

During the next few years in confinement, Sandrine was used as a sex object for the soldiers. She saw thousands of persons come and go at the concentration camp. They all suffered.

"What happened in 1945?"

"The Russians liberated us," she was almost done. She breathed out deeply and weakly smiled. "I was hospitalized for six months."

"And how are you now?"

"The doctors say that I have permanent disability on the left side of my body, that the headaches may go away over time, and that my body is fragile."

"Anything else?"

"Yes! I'm sterilized," she broke down again into tears. "I can never have a family!"

"Your honors, I think this would be a good time for our luncheon recess."

❧

Kulongoski assured Sandrine that she had done a great job. They ordered a goulash soup, but she didn't eat hers. She was too anxious and exhausted. She was warned that the defense was going to ask her some difficult questions in the afternoon. She should answer " 'yes', 'no', or 'I don't know.' " She was admonished not to guess or elaborate.

After lunch, they returned to the courtroom. Since there were 23 defendants, only one defense counsel was designated to cross-examine a witness in most cases.

"Thank you for telling us your story, Miss Urmuz," began the defense attorney with the roundish spectacles in a non-confrontational tone. "Do you personally know any of these gentlemen here?" he pointed to the defendants en masse.

"No."

"Have you ever seen any of these gentlemen before in person?"

"No."

"Um," he stroked his beard. "Let's go in a different direction. Are you Jewish?"

"I don't think so."

The defense attorney continued with similar questioning for about an hour and then he paused for a moment. He walked back to the defense counsels' table. His assistant handed him a file folder. He opened it and scanned it for a second.

"Miss Urmuz, are you suicidal?"

"What do you mean?"

"Have you ever wanted to kill yourself?"

She remained silent. She tried to look over to where Kulongoski was sitting, but the defense counsel was blocking her line of vision.

"Miss Urmuz, please remember that you are under oath."

She tried to mouth the words, but nothing came out. Her head bowed down and there was a faint answer, "Yes."

"I am sorry, Miss Urmuz, I couldn't hear you. What did you say?"

"Yes," her eyes gazed obliviously to the public spectators.

After a few more questions, the defense counsel moved that her testimony be stricken, "Your honors, this woman has never known or seen any of these gentlemen, she is not Jewish, and her mental state is very suspect . . ."

There was a blurring movement from the prosecutorial table. "Your honors, redirect?"

"Please."

The prosecutor approached the witness again and gave a friendly smile. "You have testified that you think that you are not Jewish. Did you wear the yellow armband with a blue Star of David in the camp?"

"Yes."

"Why?"

"Because my adoptive father was Jewish. And so was his sister."

"Did you ever practice the Jewish religion?"

"No."

"So why would you wear the Jewish armband?"

"For me, it was not about the Jewish religion. It was not even about the Jewish race. It was about the Jewish culture. It was showing respect for the kind of people who adopted us. So why not?" She was settling down and breathing more calmly. "It really didn't make any real difference. I could have easily worn a gypsy armband. As a practical matter, everyone in the camps was mistreated. Everyone."

She hesitated and then added, "Maybe the fortunate ones were those who died."

CHAPTER 24

THE MUGGING

Monday, July 8, 1974, San Francisco

The phone rang early Monday morning. Andrés had been in a deep sleep with a long flower patterned pillow propped over his head.

Although he was only half awake now, he still knew that off-hour calls were wrought with bad news. Somebody was in trouble or in the hospital. He reached for the phone.

"Hello," he said groggily, scratching his head.

"Hello, Andrés," the voice was speaking in a panic. "You have to come over right away!"

"Why? What happened?" he feared the worst. The adrenalin was awakening his brain, "Is your father all right?"

"Yes, but . . . no, uh, uh," Astrid was frazzled. "The police . . . the police must talk with you."

"What happened?" he was terrified. He hadn't done anything wrong. "When? Do you mean right now?" *Was something stolen from the house? What could they possibly accuse him of?*

"Bert is coming over to pick you up. Can you be ready in ten minutes?" he could hear her sniffle as she spoke.

"Okay," he was now resigned. *Damn!*

☙

He threw on some clothes. He looked at the clock. It said 8:15. *I could have slept in at least another hour. Christ*

Almighty!

Andrés closed the front door behind him and went out to the curb to wait, fixing his scarf and dragging along his sweater. The weather was overcast and slightly cool. He had forgotten to eat something this morning. He felt jittery and nervous. His mind raced trying to come up with a reason as to why the police would want to talk with him.

The Mercedes limo pulled up to the curb in front of him. Erik was not driving; Bert was. Bert stopped, got out of the limo, and started to walk over to open the door.

"Good morning, Andrés," greeted the valet who was garbed in his routine formal attire.

"Good morning," Andrés was apprehensive of this strange turn of events. "Do you mind if I sit up here with you?" he pointed to the front seat.

"Not at all," smiled Bert. It was the first time that Andrés noticed that the valet spoke with a French accent.

At first Andrés was too timid to ask what the police wanted. After a minute, his worry overcame him and he blurted out, "What's happening? Why do the police want to question me?"

"I have some tragic news. The police came over early this morning and told us that they had found Erik's body. He had been clubbed to death," the valet reported this in a cool tone. "They simply want to interview people who had been in recent contact with him."

"I didn't really have any contact with him," he hesitated for a second. "He just used to drop Astrid and me off at different places . . . for our cultural lessons."

"Oh, I wouldn't worry," Bert looked at him and it almost seemed that he winked at Andrés. "They are questioning the entire household right now."

Andrés did not know if he felt relief or not. He had not even remembered the chauffeur's name.

Ↄ

Astrid jumped into his arms as he entered the entryway. "Sorry about the phone call." She grabbed his hand. "Did Bert tell you what happened?"

He nodded.

"Oh, I see you are in good hands," the unshaven Schmidt exclaimed as he came out to the hallway and closed the door to the study behind him. He stared intently at the two. He seemed to be in a grumpy mood.

"Good morning, Andrés," Nan blubbered.

"Good morning," he returned the greeting quietly.

"Did you have breakfast?"

"Oh, I'm good, thanks."

Schmidt left the hallway, limping with his cane, without uttering another word. Astrid followed her father into the study.

Andrés was left standing alone. Fifteen minutes later the study door opened and Schmidt and Astrid walked past without looking at him. They were followed out by a middle-aged man with short black hair wearing a sport coat and tie.

"Mister Miramón?" inquired the police officer with the perfect Spanish pronunciation of Andrés' name.

"Yes, that's me."

"I'm Detective David Campos," he motioned for Andrés to enter the study. "This shouldn't take very long. Just need to ask you a few questions. It's just a formality."

In the room there was a short, muscular man who also was wearing a sport coat and tie.

"This is my partner, Detective Leland Leong."

Andrés moved the pillows on the sofa and sat down.

The two police officers alternated, asking him basic personal information, with Leong taking the notes.

There was a knock at the door and Nan walked in without saying a word carrying in a tray of coffee and sliced banana bread. She set it down on the coffee table and left.

The police officers were reluctant to indulge, but Andrés wolfed-down the food and drank like the starving student that he was. The other two soon joined him.

"So, Andrés, how well did you know Erik?" asked Campos.

"Not that well. He was like the chauffeur around here," Andrés grabbed a third piece of bread with his napkin and placed it on a white china plate. He was more concerned with the food than the interrogation.

"What are you studying?" immediately followed up Leong.

Andrés told him and then went on to ramble about the excursions around San Francisco that Erik had driven Astrid and him to.

"Do you know if he had any enemies?"

"No." The way that guy was built who would want to mess with him, Andrés thought.

"Andrés, how tall are you?"

"Five, eight."

"How much do you weigh?"

"About 140, I think?"

They were in the process of concluding the interview, when the door flew open. Two crew cut, muscled youngish men wearing black suits strutted into the room.

"We're taking over this investigation now," the beefy-sized intruder proclaimed with an air of authority.

"And you are?" Campos asked in a controlled tone, still

seated.

"We're with the U.S. Park Police. We were told that one of our employees was the victim of a homicide." The bravado had lessened.

"And who are you again?" verbally pushed Campos.

"I'm Polk and this is Campbell," he replied, trying to be professional. "We were assigned to this case."

"Who is this employee that you mentioned?"

"Erik Boehner," chimed in Campbell. "He did contract security work for the Sellarebu Pharmaceutical Laboratories."

Campos looked nonchalantly at Leong who acknowledged his partner ever so subtly.

"Well, the homicide we are investigating involves the chauffeur of this house," stated Campos. "And furthermore, the victim was murdered and robbed over a mile from here within the San Francisco City limits. We have exclusive jurisdiction here." He paused for effect. "However, if we discover anything related to your case, we will notify you. Just give me your business cards."

The faces of the two interlopers turned crimson. Campbell wanted to confront the San Francisco cops, but restrained himself.

"We're going to need to check this out with our supervisor," Polk was making his way toward the door and said glibly. "We'll be back."

Campbell was right at his heels as they escaped from the room. Andrés was stunned at the interchange that had occurred in front of him. He was then excused to leave, but not before grabbing another piece of banana bread.

"Well, Lieutenant Stone, who were those guys?" asked Leong. Leland was always casting his partner and himself in the television series, *The Streets of San Francisco,* which starred

Karl Malden and Michael Douglas.

"You do the background check on Erik Boehner. See if he has any next of kin," proposed Campos. "I'll find out who Mutt and Jeff are."

CHAPTER 25

THE WITNESS

January, 1947, Nuremberg, Germany

Sandrine was planning to go to Vienna after the trial. She had attended the tribunal proceedings almost daily. She listened in disbelief to the dozens of witnesses who had survived the atrocities at the various Nazi concentration camps. Sadly, from her own experiences, she knew that these accounts were true. *How could human beings act so inhumanely?*

Since the beginning of the trial, she had met on a regular basis with other victims who were also monitoring the adjudication. Jerzy, as she now knew him, was very supportive. He had a fierce passion for justice.

It was the thirty-seventh day of the adjudication. The prosecutor had finished presenting the portion of the case that recalled the testimonies of the victims. Now he was interrogating doctors and other experts about the treatment of the victims.

A dapper young man took the stand. He was clean-shaven and wore a tailored suit. He was sworn in.

"Please state your name."

"Augustin Teufl."

"What is your position?"

"Until recently, I worked as an apothecarist at the Frankfurt Hospital."

"Are you a doctor?"

"I have never received a medical credential."

"For whom did you work?"

"I reported to Doctor Freiherr and Doctor Magnussen."

"Your honors, before we continue, we want to advise the tribunal that Mister Teufl has been granted full immunity in exchange for his testimony."

"So noted. Please proceed with the witness."

Teufl elaborately explained that he provided medical materials to the physicians and doctors of the hospital. He had to prepare the correct dosages for vaccines, medications, and poisons. He also testified that he processed the applications for racial purity required for marriages.

Sandrine suddenly became alert. *What did he just say? Who is this person?* She tried to scrutinize the young man's countenance, but she was too far away and her eyesight was bad. She tried to revive the repressed memories of her and Zharko trying to get married more than five years prior.

"Mister Teufl, did you have other responsibilities?"

"Yes, I received and tabulated data from the Zwillinge Project."

"Zwillinge is the German word for twins, is it not?"

"Yes, that is correct. But in this case, it meant identical twins."

He went on to elaborate that at Auschwitz and other concentration camps, there were a multitude of experiments being performed on twins. He mentioned that one of the projects was to try to change the eye pigmentation to blue.

Sandrine cringed. This was Teufl! This was the person who was supposed to have helped her. This was Keichelle's friend. He had known that they were identical twins. No one else had really known or really cared. She pondered as to whether there was a connection between this man and the abduction of her and her sister. He appeared so innocent.

"Do you know why this type of experimentation was done?"

"Objection! This calls for a conclusion. This person is not qualified to state an opinion. Also, lacks foundation," cried out a defense counsel.

"Overruled!" gaveled the presiding judge. "Please continue, Mr. Teufl."

Teufl talked about the Reich's preoccupation with eugenics and *Arisierung*. He explained that the field of eugenics was the biosocial movement to improve the genetic composition of a human population with desirable traits. He described *Arisierung* as Germanization or Aryanization. This term referred to the forced expulsion and segregation of non-Aryans from normal life in Germany and its controlled territories. The Nazi Party, he concluded, wanted to establish an Aryan master race.

"While you were in Frankfurt, who was responsible for implementing this practice?"

"Doctor Freiherr and Doctor Magnussen."

There was a coughing sound from the defendants' table. An assistant handed one of the defendants a glass of water.

"Did you ever do any work for Colonel Rudolf Brandt or Doctor Eduard Wirths?"

"Yes, I received and tabulated data from them for the Seele Project. They were in charge of the Seele Project."

"Please describe this project briefly for the benefit of the tribunal."

Teufl depicted a highly elaborate and scientific experiment of trying to identify and manipulate the human genes thought to constitute the soul of a human being. Different chemical cocktails were injected into human embryos. The most successful cases were based on a laudanum formula. He delivered his testimony with such self-assurance that everyone seemed overwhelmed.

"What is laudanum?"

"Simply defined, it is a tincture of opium. It is reddish-brown and has a bitter taste."

"Mister Teufl, can you enlighten us on who the subjects of the Seele Project were?"

"They were inhabitants from the Reich's colonization and occupation in Togoland, Cameroons, Tanganyika, German East Africa, Burundi, and Rwanda."

"Were these subjects sent to Auschwitz?"

"To my knowledge, no," Teufl opined smugly. "The subjects, with whom I dealt, resided in laboratory clinics in the Frankfurt area."

"Were these subjects Aryan?"

"No," there was a grin on his face. "The majority of them were from Herero Bantu tribes."

There was a loud rumbling of shock and distaste throughout the room. The presiding judge banged the gavel to restore order.

"Please clarify what this project had to do with Germany's eugenic policy."

"It didn't," Teufl made a pregnant pause. "The Seele Project was intended to create a military android."

The court broke into pandemonium. Several defendants jumped up and started to shake their fists at Teufl. The terms "traitor" and "coward" were being thrown at the witness. Soldiers rushed forward and restrained the unruly parties.

The judge pounded his gavel without much success. He then called for an hour lunch break. The foreign correspondents overran the telephones trying to contact their home offices.

"Jerzy," Sandrine clutched at his lapel. "I think I know this man. I think that he is the one responsible for sending my sister and me to Auschwitz.

He gave her a silent, stoic look.

 og

Later in the afternoon, a defense counsel representative began his cross-examination.

"Given that you have fortuitously been granted immunity by the prosecution, isn't it true that you were an active participant in all the actions that the defendants have been accused of?"

"No, I was simply a mid-level employee," he gave the interrogator an icy stare. "I was merely following orders."

The questioning continued for the rest of the afternoon. The histrionics of the prosecution and the defense erupted from time to time.

Sandrine looked intently at Teufl when he finally finished giving his testimony and was excused in the late afternoon.

"Jerzy, now I am sure this is the man who betrayed my sister and me to the Nazis," she emoted.

"Do you have any proof?" Kulongoski asked expressionless.

"No," she was anxious. "Well, yes. I know it in my heart."

og

The muggy summer heat overwhelmed the city of Nuremberg. Finally, on August 20, 1947, the trial ended.

Seven of the 23 defendants were sentenced to death and nine were given prison terms ranging from ten years to life.

When Sandrine heard that seven had been acquitted, she cursed. "I can't believe that those demons will not be punished."

Kulongoski took a deep breath and gave her the standard spiel that justice had been served.

"And as for Teufl," she blurted out angrily, "how does that guilty bastard walk away untouched?"

CHAPTER 26

MORE QUESTIONS

Monday, July 8, 1974, San Francisco

Schmidt was sitting down on the couch and leaning on its armrest. Next to him was Matilda dressed in black. Campos was finishing up his second cup of coffee.

"Just a few more questions, Mr. Schmidt," said Campos craning his neck toward him. Campos had recalled Schmidt back into the study. "We need to clarify a few more things."

The older man shook his head. He had a blank expression on his face. Matilda wrung her hands as she looked over at her brother-in-law.

"Did Erik Boehner do more for you then drive you around?"

"Well, he took care of me," Schmidt said hesitantly.

"What do you mean took care of you?" prodded the detective.

"Oh, he is too proud to say it," interjected Matilda. "My brother-in-law sometimes has trouble walking and getting around. Erik helped him."

Schmidt glared at his sister-in-law. She just ignored him.

"When did you hire him?"

"He started working with us almost a month ago, I think," Schmidt replied.

"Do you know where he worked before coming here?"

"Well, he worked for Sellarebu Pharmaceutical

Laboratories."

"What kind of work did he do for Sellarebu?"

"I'm not sure."

"When did you hire him?"

"Well, I didn't really hire him. He was provided to me by the company that I work for."

"And Mr. Schmidt, what company do you work for?"

There was silence. Schmidt's eyes were blinking and looked glassy.

"I work for the Sellarebu Pharmaceutical Laboratories."

"The same company that Erik worked for?" Campos voiced as he was becoming more intrigued.

"Well, sort of," Schmidt was not volunteering much information. "I work in the international division for this global enterprise. I don't know that much about Mister Boehner."

"What kind of security work was Mr. Boehner providing for you?"

Schmidt looked at Campos as if he was a child caught with his hand in the cookie jar.

In a soft voice, he slowly answered, "We are an international company and we have many competitors who want our secrets. Sellarebu provides us protection against them."

"Detectives, we have tried to be very cooperative," broke in Matilda in a gentle manner, "but he is getting very tired."

"Oh, we apologize for taking up so much of your time this morning," Campos started to stand up. He closed his notepad. "Just one more thing. We understand that Mr. Boehner resided here on the premises."

"Yes, he lived in the basement of the adjoining building," Matilda bleakly contributed. She did not observe Schmidt giving her a serious gaze.

"We are going to have to seal his room off for a few days and have some of our lab people come here and examine his lodging."

"Is this really necessary, officer?" piped up Schmidt. "What purpose could it serve? You said that this was a robbery. The robbery did not take place here." The older man was becoming more and more agitated.

"Unfortunately, it is necessary, Mister Schmidt," calmly responded Campos. "It is our standard operating procedure in homicide cases."

"In that case, I will have Nan escort you down to the rooms," obliged Matilda. "Is there anything else we can do for you?

"No, but thank you for your time and patience with us. We know that you are upset about what happened," Campos and Leong were making their way to the door. "By the way, do you know if Mr. Boehner had any next of kin?"

"No," Matilda gave them a sweet, but fake, smile, "but I'm sure that Sellarebu would have that information. I will have Nan meet you in the entry way right away."

Left in the foyer, Campos directed Leong to call in the lab personnel so that their scientific investigative staff could immediately come to the house.

"Hey, Leland, what does your gut tell you?"

"Yeah, something smells" acknowledged the junior partner. "And it's not the banana bread."

A moment later Nan approached them and escorted them through a corridor and down a set of stairs.

ଔ

Schmidt was in his bedroom alone. He was propped against the pillows. His feet, without shoes, were on the bed.

"Hello, Arnold," he yelled into the phone, "I have been trying to get a hold of you all afternoon! Where have you been?"

"Don't panic, Johann," Neumann tried to calm him down.

"Did you know that Erik was killed?"

"Yes," said his colleague impassively.

"What in hell are we going to do?"

"Nothing. I'm working on it as we speak."

"Nothing! This whole thing can explode in our faces!"

"I'm trying to get the feds to take over the case."

"What the bloody hell good will that do?"

"They have as much to lose as we do. Maybe more."

"So?" Schmidt carped.

"I've warned you that we have to cooperate."

"But we don't want the police involved!"

"I'm coming over tonight."

ଓ

Around five o'clock in the afternoon, Campos and Leong left the Schmidt residence after having thoroughly examined Erik's living quarters. The seagulls were flying overhead with mock laughter. Pine scents emanated from the nearby forest.

"Some interesting memorabilia," said the senior partner has they walked to their black and white.

CHAPTER 27

GOING BACK

Tuesday, July 9, 1974, San Francisco

Andrés and Astrid had agreed to still meet on Tuesday. They had originally planned to take the ferry to Sausalito, but Astrid's father wanted them to stay closer to home. Schmidt had been edgy that morning when they took off. Bert drove them to the North Beach area. It was a clear day with the slightest hint of a breeze. He had problems maneuvering the limousine through the streets of San Francisco. He didn't know the most expeditious ways to go from point A to point B, and became very jumpy around the buses and double-parked vehicles. Bert finally dropped them off at a park.

The young pair stirred up the pigeons as they walked across the lawns. Wet blades of grass stuck to their shoes. Most of the benches were occupied with homeless people drinking beer in brown paper bags, women with children in strollers conversing, and couples having little picnics. Somebody was playing a Jefferson Airplane song on his portable radio.

"How is everyone holding up at your house?" Andrés inquired as they continued to stroll looking for a place to sit and chat.

She reached for his hand. He took hers. "Okay, I think."

"What's going to happen now?"

She did not reply at first. Then she softly said, "I don't know."

They passed people lying on old army blankets reading books or taking naps, the jock in his sweat suit throwing a Frisbee to his border collie, and children playing on the swings by the pine trees.

"Andrés, can we get a coffee?" she said in a neutral tone.

"Sure," he was looking across Columbus Street at the Italian restaurants, bakeries, and delis. "Hey, do you want to check out the Caffe Trieste? Remember when we hung out over there the last time?"

She nodded. She seemed slightly distraught.

They jaywalked across the street and a few minutes later they were ordering their cappuccini and biscotti. They sat down at an old wooden table with initials etched all over its surface. There were yellow-toothed smokers next to them playing chess, gesticulating animatedly, and swearing in Italian. The two tried to slide away as far as possible on the seat, but to no avail.

"I'm really sorry that I had to call you yesterday morning," her eyes seemed sad. "The police surprised us."

"No problem," he said nonchalantly. "It wasn't your fault."

She peeled off her jacket and hung it behind her. Andrés did the same.

"I don't think Nan liked the way he treated the maid and the cook."

"Who? Erik?" Andrés seemed to think this was irrelevant. "He wasn't a real friendly guy. He just did his job. No crime in doing that."

"You are right, I suppose," she acquiesced. "But sometimes I felt that he didn't like taking care of my father. He would make snide remarks."

"It sounds like almost everyone I know who works," he

taunted, "except for being with you, of course."

She finally laughed.

The portly waiter brought over their order. There was a hiatus in the smoking next to them. A game had just finished and players were changing seats. A man with a gold tooth assumed one of the playing positions. A frizzy-haired old man wearing a brown beret occupied the other place.

"I thought things would be different here," she sighed.

"Ahh," Andrés was busy dunking his biscotti into his cappuccino, oblivious to everything else.

"Well, in Santiago we always had a guard at the gate and a security detail that patrolled the colonia."

"You're kidding!" Andrés was half-surprised.

"No, really," her face was serious. "You don't want your house broken into. But that was not what disturbed my father. He was afraid that I could be kidnapped and harmed."

"Wow! That's heavy duty."

"When I was little, I would be driven to school every day. My driver would be waiting for me when school was over," she was reminiscing. "When I was older, I went to boarding school for two years. After that my father and my aunt brought me home to study. I had private tutors. But I missed my friends at school. I haven't had many friends in my life, Andrés."

She reached over and put her hands around his neck. She pulled him forward. She gave him a kiss. He did not resist. She licked her lips. She could savor him. He tasted like coffee and cream. She held on to him tightly.

"I wouldn't worry about it," he stuttered.

"Will you always be my friend?" she asked, her eyes penetrating his.

"I hope so." He reached out and ran his hand through

her hair. "Hey, does your family have any relatives or friends in the Bay Area?"

"I don't think so," her brows knitted. "My father works with Mister Neumann at the hospital. That's all I know."

The noise in the establishment started to pick up again and more clouds of cigarette smoke lingered around them.

Andrés reached for the envelope that he had received earlier that morning. He was ready to pay the bill and leave.

"Andrés, do you want to know something strange?" she pondered for a moment. "I just remembered that Mister Neumann came over to the house very late last night."

"Hmm."

"I had almost forgotten. He and my father were in the study. I could hear them arguing for a long time. And this morning my father and aunt were yelling at each other. I don't think that I have ever seen my Aunt Matilda cry before."

"Bummer!" Andrés got up casually and walked over to the cashier and paid the bill.

⊗

They returned home early. Schmidt and Matilda were waiting for them in the study. There was a Manuel De Falla orchestral cantata playing as background music on the stereo.

"A glass of sherry, my boy?" offered the elderly man in an amiable tone.

"Sure," Andrés replied meekly.

"My sister-in-law and I have some news for both of you," he took a sip of his drink. "We have to take care of some important business back in Santiago. Matilda is leaving for Chile on Thursday."

Both Andrés and Astrid were taken aback.

"After much discussion," Schmidt glanced over to Matilda, "we are going to let you decide, Astrid, if you want to go with your aunt."

"Is it really necessary that she has to go, father?"

"Yes," Schmidt nodded.

"Auntie, would you be disappointed if I didn't go with you?" she implored moving over toward Matilda. She gave her aunt a pleading look.

"Well, I really don't want to go, but it is imperative," Matilda glared at her brother-in-law. "Of course, I would prefer that you accompany me, but you have only recently arrived. You need to be fully prepared to start school in the fall." She had spoken stoically with her hands folded on her lap.

"We both agree that you are a young woman now," her father was very serious. "We need to learn to trust you. We won't always be around."

CHAPTER 28

PHOTO ALBUM

Friday, July 12, 1974, San Francisco

The sky was blowing puffs of clouds as Andrés made his way to class. There were fewer than twenty students in the seminar room. The instructor was dressed in a brown herringbone sport coat and khaki pants. He went over some basic course information and encouraged them to seriously start working on their senior theses as soon as possible. He warned them that it would take more work than they might think. Andrés had been doing fairly well since he didn't have a full time job and had plenty of free time. Their assignment for the week was to go to a library.

"Hey, man," hailed one of his classmates. "How was your trip? I didn't think that you would come back."

"It was sweet," Andrés winked. "Saw a lot. Did a lot."

They shot the breeze as they walked over to the University Center and checked out the notices and ads on the bulletin kiosks. Still, no one had taken the baby turtles that were being offering for free.

His acquaintance departed. Andrés heard his stomach growl. He was left debating whether to go to the school cafeteria or to the grocery story. He had almost caught up on his back rent with the landlords and was now eating a little better.

"How's it going, love bandit?" snickered a voice behind

him.

Andrés whirled around and saw Judy grinning from ear-to-ear. She was wearing a short plaid skirt with a tight powder blue sweater squeezing her body.

"What's up?" he replied halfheartedly.

"Same old stuff. Hey, where is your chickie poo?"

Andrés shrugged his shoulders.

"She didn't look old enough to know how to pee," scorned the longhaired girl. She pulled out a box of Shermans and lit one.

Andrés did not respond.

"Hey, did you know they opened up a new Thai place just down Fulton?" she batted her bright brown eyes.

He nudged his head negatively. He knew that he should just walk away, but she was looking good to him. She could be fun at times.

"Hey, guess what, hotshot! You are taking me to lunch there," she grabbed his arm and they began strolling down the street.

The brightly decorated place was a mom and pop hole in the wall eatery. One of many scattered around the university. Judy ordered the yellow chicken curry. He asked for the chicken pad see-ew with fried noodles.

"What have you been you reading?" he asked slowly trying to connect with her.

"I'm doing 'The Lost Estate' by Alain-Fournier."

"Never heard of it," he frowned. "Obviously French."

"I just started it. Hans Christian Anderson meets 'The Great Gatsby'."

The wife of the restaurant owner brought their orders over along with bowls of white rice and chopsticks. The meal was spicy, but underwhelming. Andrés thought that his dish was a little greasy.

Judy and Andrés played nice. They were non-confrontational during their tête-à-tête.

He paid the check and they exited. A woman with a black scarf wrapped around her head was pushing her little grocery cart down the street muttering to herself.

"Hey, you have to come over to my place," she said in a semi-sultry tone, not expecting any resistance. "I have something I want to show you."

He did not respond, but simply marched along side of her for three blocks until they reached an old Victorian building trimmed in gold, purple, and green. The front door was made of oak and was extra wide. Inside, the landing smelled of mold. They walked up to the second floor.

He took off his coat and sat on the paisley-patterned purple and black couch. She walked over to her stereo and picked up an album.

"Thought you might get off on this," she gleamed.

"Far out!" he took it from her. It was Joan Baéz' latest album, 'Gracias a La Vida.'

She withdrew the 33 from its jacket and put it on the stereo.

The vibrato of the anti-war folk singer sent goose bumps up and down both their backs.

"You don't have any weed, do you?"

"No," he answered. A cat crawled on top of him and purred.

"She likes you," Judy scooted closer to him. She stroked his hair. He did not resist. He was in tune with the music.

She took his hand and led him to the bedroom.

෬

It was dark as he was returning home. The stars were out

and dogs barked as he passed by. He was hungry again. The lunch did not really sit well with him. He kept burping. A middle-aged man was walking a poodle with a pink collar.

Judy was a self-assured person who knew what she wanted and knew how to get it. He was feeling a little guilty. He didn't consider her a girl friend. He wasn't leading her on. Andrés kept trying to rationalize this arrangement.

What am I going to do with Astrid? He ruminated. *She is really young. I made her father a promise that I would not take advantage of her. I don't want to mess up. I really don't want to lose this job. I need the bread.*

He finally reached his house. He grabbed the mail from his mailbox. As he walked to his door, he noticed a large manila envelope on the rattan chair situated on the porch. He noticed that his name was hand-scribbled on the outside.

Andrés sighed. *Astrid is a very nice girl. The poor thing has no friends. Her aunt is like a dragon lady. I know that Astrid likes me. I don't want to pretend to like her. But I did tell her that I was her friend. Damn girls!*

He walked inside his apartment and dropped his mail and the manila envelope onto his little table. He scrambled three eggs with a little milk and cheese and toasted two pieces of bread.

He casually perused the mail that was mostly ads that he readily discarded.

The room was finally warming up. He made himself some chamomile tea.

Andrés was yawning as he grabbed a knife and cut open the large manila envelope. He pulled out an old blue photo album. There wasn't any note attached. He wondered who had delivered it to him. It seemed strange.

As he started to sip his hot tea, he opened up the album.

He started to leaf through the pages. His eyes dilated. He bent over to get a better look. He saw old photos of twins of all ages with double black cherubic angel tattoos on their shoulders. He was horrified at what he saw.

Reluctantly he turned the pages. Each new photo was more shocking than the prior. Disfigured children. *Oh, Jesus!* Castrated males. *Oh, f__king Christ!* Women with their wombs cut open. *Mother f__ker!*

He ran into the bathroom and threw up.

CHAPTER 29

THE LIBRARY

Saturday, July 13, 1974, San Francisco

Nan served Andrés a cup of coffee as he waited for Astrid to finish getting ready. He had worn the same clothes as he did the day before. There were dark circles under his eyes. He had not slept well.

Schmidt peeked into the waiting room.

"Good morning, my boy," he walked in swaying from side to side using his cane. "How are you?"

Andrés feigned a smile and replied, "Fine, thanks."

Schmidt sat down next to Andrés and waited until Nan left the room.

"You'll have to excuse me. I have to leave in a few minutes. Some kind of emergency at the lab," he chuckled. "But we need to chat first."

Andrés put down his coffee. His hands were clammy. *He is going to read me the riot act!* Andrés knew that he shouldn't have gotten so friendly with his daughter. She was that man's only child. Andrés needed the job! He could beg for a second chance.

"You know that Matilda had to go back to Santiago. She should be back in a couple of weeks. She has been so conscientious in helping raise Astrid . . ."

Andrés now thought that it was Matilda who wanted him terminated. The two had probably decided that before she left.

"I know that Astrid likes you."

The young man knew that he had screwed this up. He would have to look for a real job now.

"I need you to keep an extra eye on her. She is so naive," Schmidt shook his head in exasperation. "Please don't let her wander off by herself, especially in isolated places in the city."

Andrés felt like he was getting a reprieve. He was speechless, but uttered, "Yes, sir."

"My boy, you'll have to excuse me now," he hobbled out of the room.

Thump. Thump. Thump. Andrés could feel his heart pounding. He felt that it was going to burst through his chest. The last 24 hours had beleaguered him. He leaned back on the couch and closed his eyes.

"Hey, *dormilón*, are you asleep?" ribbed Astrid. "I'm ready. How about you?"

∞

The pair walked down congested Union Street. The skies were blue. They decided that it would be a nice day to take a stroll, rather than a bus. Astrid had bought herself some jogging shoes and was getting used to walking up and down hills and the hard concrete sidewalks. Today she was even wearing a pink pastel velour running suit.

Although the weather was clear, the air was cool. It helped Andrés wake up. They passed dry cleaners with dirty windows, apartment buildings with laundry on the railings, and Asian restaurants with signs in Chinese characters. They finally stopped at a coffee shop that had a big jade plant by the front door, next to a water bowl placed on the sidewalk for dogs. There were people smoking and reading newspapers at the three small outdoor tables.

When Astrid came back from using the unisex bathroom, there was a large steaming cappuccino waiting for her.

"Thank you, *mi corazón*," she gave him a warm smile.

The odor of grilled onions and burning grease emanated from the kitchen.

He felt bad about her unrequited affection toward him. "Hey, have you heard from your aunt?"

"Yes," she sipped her creamy beverage. "She called us the other night. She arrived safely. The weather is cold, she said. I'm glad that I didn't go with her. She is taking care of family business. Hopefully, she will be back within two weeks."

"You know I'm surprised that she didn't make you go with her. She seems very strict. I don't know what she thinks about me. She does remind me of Sister Mary Ascension, back in fourth grade, who used the ruler on me."

"You probably deserved it," she punched him on the shoulder.

"No way!"

A young Russian woman came into the café with a crying baby. The mother was carrying groceries and a diaper bag in addition to the child. Andrés wondered how the poor woman was going to drink her coffee. *Bummer!* He felt sad. He was reminded about the photo album that was mysteriously delivered to him and the graphic pictures of the tortured women and children.

Andrés sank back into a pensive state. He was still despondent over the photos. He became more and more apprehensive about his dilemma. *Should he share the pictures? If so, with whom? Why was the album given to him?*

"Astrid, I want to show you something," he started to pull the photo album out of his backpack. "I think we need to keep this a secret between us for now."

She looked at him with puzzled eyes. "Okay."

He moved from his side of the table to hers and together they started to flip through the pages slowly.

"Oh, my God!" she cried. "This is the worsest nightmare!"

"Worst," he corrected her. She was so innocent. "I'm sorry. Maybe I shouldn't have shared these with you. I'm sorry."

"No. No, it's all right," her face was somber. She sniffled. "I'm just shocked. How can human beings be so cruel?" A tear crept into the corner of her eye.

He put his hand on top of hers.

What he did not realize was that Astrid was reading the captions to the photos that were in German. She understood what they said. She was totally mortified.

"Where did you get this?"

"I don't know. I found it on the porch last night," he started to put on his jacket. "Hey! I have an idea. I have to go to the library anyway."

They left and walked over to the Golden Gate Valley branch library that was a few blocks away and asked the librarian where they could find information about Nazi concentration camps.

They were initially directed to the World War II history section. It was as quiet there as in a funeral parlor. They spent an hour looking through thick and dusty tomes that gave very descriptive accounts of Auschwitz, Dachau, and Treblinka. The black and white photos were very graphic. A few of the books were in German and Polish. One was in Romani.

A grey-bearded man with curly sideburns and a big black hat kept looking up at them from his table that was strewn with all sorts of loose-leaf papers. It was obvious that he was eavesdropping on their conversation.

"Geez, the Nazis would have killed everyone in San Francisco. They wouldn't have liked anyone," contributed Andrés.

"I'm just glad that some survived."

"For some, the survival was worse than death," the elderly man was suddenly in front of them. "They felt guilty that their families and loved ones died and they did not."

Andrés and Astrid were speechless. They nodded their heads.

"You may want to go over to the Judaica section. It has a decent collection on the Holocaust." The old man turned around and walked back to his table.

∛

The pair was mentally exhausted by the time they arrived back at the house. The day had felt like a study session cramming for final exams. They had taken the bus back and walked up the steep concrete stairs that they used as a shortcut to the house.

"Oh, Astrid, I'm so glad that you are home," cried Nan.

"What's wrong?" Astrid had become alarmed.

"You're father is in the hospital," Nan was clutching her apron. "We don't know what his condition is. Bert is with him right now."

Astrid grabbed her purse that she had just set down. "Come on, Andrés, we have to go see my father."

Andrés did not argue. "What hospital is he at?"

"At Letterman," Nan said tearfully. "Something happened at the lab."

CHAPTER 30

THE ER

Saturday, July 13, 1974, San Francisco

A black nurse with an Afro directed Astrid and Andrés upstairs to the coronary unit. The hall reeked of bleach and other hospital smells. It was late and an orderly was pushing a meal cart into one room and pulling another one out. Eventually, Astrid and Andrés spied Bert standing outside a door.

Astrid rushed up to him. "What happened?" she blurted.

"He had some pains in his chest and felt dizzy. They rushed him immediately to the emergency room. He was there all afternoon," Bert reported. "He's resting right now."

Astrid immediately hurried past him leaving Andrés behind. Her father was in bed with an intravenous saline drip line inserted into his right wrist. Schmidt's eyes were closed and his mouth was open. His face looked ashen. He was breathing laboriously. Tears came to her eyes. She positioned herself next to the bed and softly stroked his right foot.

His eyelids started to open up. "My darling Astrid," he eked out. "I'm glad to see you."

"How are you?" her voice was in a panic. "What happened?"

"Just some routine stuff . . . You don't need to worry . . . I'm fine," he talked to her in spurts.

She was not used to seeing her father in such a disabled

state. She recalled that when he had had a major stroke years before, he had told her that he had accidently fallen. Until then he had been in fairly good shape although he was not much of an exercise buff. He had suddenly grown old. His physical condition aged him by at least twenty years. Schmidt had difficulty walking and his hair turned white before it started to fall out. Soon thereafter, he was confined to rest for a month and Matilda took over the entire household. This time Astrid feared it was much worse.

"How are you, Mr. Schmidt?" Andrés had just entered the room and stood between Astrid and a rolling tray table.

"Can you get me some water?" his eyes pointed to a yellow plastic water pitcher on top of the tray.

Astrid poured a little water into a plastic cup and held the straw for her father.

"I just had a little discomfort in my chest . . . It's gone now . . . The doctors ran some tests. They want to keep me here for observation . . . My own private hotel suite . . ." his face was now brightening up. "Even with room service."

A hospital aide in cerulean scrubs rolled in with Schmidt's dinner. It was chicken noodle soup with saltine crackers and a small carton of apple juice. Astrid spoon-fed him the broth with the crackers crumbed into it. She used the paper napkin to wipe his mouth between bites.

He slurped up the soup and then closed his eyes for a moment. Astrid could see that he was exhausted.

"Papá, is there anything that we can do for you right now?"

He made a feeble attempt to respond. "I had to fill out some papers this afternoon . . . You have some kind of durable power of attorney . . . You need to read it . . . Where is it?" he gasped. "Call Bert in."

Seconds later the valet came in, "Yes, Mister Schmidt?"

"Where are those papers you helped me sign today?"

"I'll get them, sir," Bert opened up a drawer at the bed stand and retrieved the documents. "Here there are, sir."

"Give them to Astrid," he started to say. "Wait . . . you need to have copies made. Now . . . right now. Try the nurses' station."

Andrés perceived that Schmidt wanted to be alone with his daughter. "Bert, I'll go with you."

Schmidt nodded. Bert and Andrés left the room with the latter closing the door behind them.

"Astrid, my dear, I will be all right . . ." he was trying to maintain control between laboring breaths. "I do not want any surgery . . . I do not want any anesthesia . . . no medical procedures at this hospital. Nothing! Promise me that!"

Her head nodded. She looked up at the monitor. She did not understand what the numbers and graphics meant. She felt like she was in a daze.

"If I need any kind of surgery . . . even the most minor type . . . have them transport me to the USF Medical Center . . . do you understand, my dear?"

"Yes, Papá," a tear rolled down her cheek. She stroked his left hand. It had some sort of hospital wristband on it.

"At home . . . in the bottom drawer of my armoire . . . underneath my sweaters is a key chain," he seemed to be fading. "It opens up the file cabinet in my closet."

The door opened and the aide retrieved the food tray. The father and daughter remained silent while this task was being performed, and until the worker left.

"You'll find envelopes of money and a ledger. The ledger will show you how much each staff person is to be paid . . . They are paid only on Fridays. I should be back home by then . . . but if I'm not . . ."

"Shouldn't I call Aunt Matilda right now and have her come home?"

"Heavens no!" he was getting agitated. "Not right now!"

"Two more things. These are very important," he was struggling to continue. "Have Andrés stay at the house until I return . . . We will pay him appropriately when I come home."

Astrid could not believe her ears. Aunt Matilda would strangle Johann if she found out. It would certainly make Astrid feel better if Andrés were around. Too many confusing thoughts were inundating her mind. She felt a headache coming on. She and Andrés had not eaten much all day.

"And my dear," he inhaled deeply and squeezed her hand tightly. "Trust nobody . . . absolutely nobody . . . Do you understand?"

"Yes," she murmured.

"Nobody!"

The door opened again and a grey-haired nurse came in. "Time for your medication, Mister Schmidt."

There were three little tablets, each of a different color, in a small plastic cup. She gave him each of the pills one at a time and he had to take a sip of water in order to swallow each one.

"These will help you sleep," smiled the veteran.

Andrés and Bert returned.

"You really should let Mister Schmidt get some rest," said the older woman tactfully. "He will probably have some more tests done tomorrow."

"Bert," Schmidt interrupted as he motioned to his valet. "Andrés will be staying overnight at the house until I return . . . take him home to retrieve some of his things."

"Yes, sir."

"And Astrid is in charge of everything."

She looked surprised. Her father had always treated her like a child. Now she was supposed to be the responsible grownup.

"I hope this is not a problem, Andrés," it was more of a statement than a question. He was fading quickly. "Remember what we talked about." His voice seemed to drift.

"Yes, sir," Andrés was overwhelmed by the request. "I mean, no, sir. I don't see any problem. I can stick around the house."

The trio departed in order to let Schmidt go to sleep.

They headed first to Andrés' apartment to pick up some clothing and toiletries. Andrés left the mysterious photo album there.

"Bert, I want you to come back to the hospital tomorrow morning and look after my father," Astrid issued her first directive. "We will join you after mass."

CHAPTER 31

THE NIGHT

Sunday, July 14, 1974, San Francisco

He saw a monster as he peered into the mirror. Andrés had had a terrible night at the Schmidt's. Astrid and he had arrived back at the house around midnight on Saturday. It was too late to have had dinner and everybody had been too tired to even snack.

The biggest challenge was Astrid. She had tapped on his door around 2 a.m. She crawled into his bed next to him. He didn't own a pair of pajamas so he was just in his undershorts.

"Astrid, what are you doing here?" he asked annoyed. "You know that you can't be here."

"I'm afraid," she pleaded. "Aunt Matilda is not here. Neither is my father. You are the only one."

"That's fine," he was vexed by her immaturity. "You are going to get me in trouble."

"No one is going to find out," she offered. "No one is going to tell."

"I promised your father that I would behave with you."

"I know that. But I'm eighteen. I'm going to go to college," she was emboldened. "I'm a woman."

"You have to leave."

"Oh, pleeease . . . Just five minutes," she snuggled closer to him.

The denial never came out of his mouth. She pressed her

chest against his rib cage. She smelled like vanilla. Her hair was so soft as it fell over his torso. Her head rested softly on him. Astrid breathed deeply.

Andrés wanted to push her off. Instead he was being aroused. He felt the heat. It was difficult to maintain self-control.

He awoke a few hours later. She was gone. He fell back to sleep.

Then in the early morning hours he had to use the bathroom. Andrés got up and slammed into the dresser. His toe felt like it was broken. He was not used to the unfamiliar setting.

After a quick shower, he trimmed his beard. Astrid was at the breakfast table when he hobbled down the stairs. Bert had already departed for the hospital.

"Good morning," Nan greeted him with a friendly smile. "Coffee?"

He nodded and she poured. He dumped some cream and sugar into his cup.

A few minutes later, a fruit, yogurt, and granola parfait was served to him and Astrid, in what looked like ice cream sundae dishes. *This is really awesome,* he thought as scooped up the cereal mix, *having dessert for breakfast!*

"How did you sleep, Andrés?" Astrid said with a coquettish grin.

"Okay," he bobbed his head as he kept eating.

"Are you coming to church with me this morning?"

Although he was raised Catholic, he hardly ever went to mass.

"I didn't really bring the right clothes."

"That's no problem. We can give you one of father's sweaters. That'll be good enough."

Nan brought them each a cheese omelet with wheat toast. Andrés slopped butter and boysenberry jam onto the bread. He scarfed down the viands without another word.

"We normally go to the ten o'clock mass," she said. "We'll have to walk."

"That's cool by me," he remarked. *She is worse than a baby sister,* he thought, although he was an only child himself. He knew that he could not let her walk to church unescorted. Mister Schmidt would have a conniption fit over that. He couldn't recall the last time that he went to mass. As for confession, he wouldn't even think about it. He thanked Nan for the food and told Astrid that he was ready to go any time she was.

A half hour later they walked out the door. Astrid was wearing a charcoal grey plaid woolen skirt with a black sweater. She had a thick striped belt around her waist. Andrés was wearing brown corduroy pants and an oversized olive green sweater that belonged to Mister Schmidt.

Astrid wanted to walk hand in hand down Green Street, but Andrés was walking too fast. There was hardly any vehicular traffic and very few people on the sidewalks. They passed several neoclassical residences with gold trim; red, white, purple, and orange bougainvillea hedges; and political bumper stickers, signs, or flags in the windows.

"Andrés, something is not right," she huffed as they rushed along.

"Like what?"

"With my father."

"He'll be okay," Andrés tried feebly to reassure her.

"No, I mean, I think someone is threatening him."

Andrés applied the brakes and she stopped also.

"What do you mean?"

"I had to open my father's mail this morning. Yesterday's mail . . . To see if there was anything important," she paused for a moment. She was out of breath. "I found an angry note from Neumann demanding that father share something with their clients."

"Like share what?"

"I don't know."

"I'm sure it's just business stuff. Old Neumann doesn't look like the friendly type anyway," he tried to appease her.

They proceeded along and joined fellow parishioners as they approached the beautiful façade of Saint Vincent de Paul Church. It was a bricked structure with three Roman arches over the portals and colorful stained glass windows. There was a large tower in the back of the church.

Astrid and Andrés ran up the concrete stairs. They entered and found some empty places in the back pews. Little silver-haired ladies with handkerchiefs tied around their heads made up the majority of the churchgoers. Astrid pulled a black bonnet out of her large purse and put it on.

A priest with a heavy Irish brogue welcomed his flock. The mass began and the faithful participated in all the refrains. The church organ at times overwhelmed the rite. Andrés listened attentively to the sermon.

"And according to Matthew 22, verses 37 to 40 . . ."

Andrés was feeling morose from the prior days' events.

"Love thy neighbor as thyself . . ."

He was also feeling guilty about how shabbily he had treated Astrid this morning. He knew that her father was ill and that she was too young to be able to cope with everything. Her father trusted him and Andrés didn't want to show any disrespect or ingratitude. He needed to cut Astrid a little slack.

Astrid did not take Communion. The mass ended and people shook hands with one another.

"Thanks for coming to church with me," Astrid's face was glowing. "Sorry about last night. I know I'm a spoiled child."

"No problem," he felt bad for her. "Where are you going now? To the hospital?"

"Yes, I need to see my father. I'll probably send Bert home. Poor man."

"I gotta go home for a while and grab some more clothes and my books. What time should I catch up with you?"

"Anytime. I'm just going to be with my father."

"Shall I hook up with you at the hospital?"

"Sure, if you don't mind carrying your things over there."

"Sounds cool."

He found Astrid a cab and directed the turban-donned Sikh driver to the hospital. He handed her two five-dollar bills to pay for the taxi.

"See you later, alligator."

"Thanks, Andrés," she waved goodbye.

Andrés trekked slowly toward his apartment. He felt a little relieved now. He said good morning to the man in the wheelchair who just came from the grocery store. A hummingbird zoomed around the garnet penstemons.

He finally arrived home and changed clothes after a quick shower. Andrés concocted a salami sandwich and washed it down with some old orange juice that tasted bitter.

For the next few hours he did his weekly laundry and finally returned to his lodging. There he packed an old brown grocery bag with a set of clean clothes. He tossed his notebook and other materials into his backpack. Andrés then remembered he had to retrieve his mail.

He grabbed the advertisement for plumbing needs, a

throwaway weekly marketing newspaper, and a letter without a return address.

Andrés started to open the letter.

CHAPTER 32

SHARING

Monday, July 15, 1974, San Francisco

The clock by his nightstand said 9:05. Andrés had overslept. He rushed to get ready, even though he was still drowsy. Finally, he ran downstairs. Nan greeted him with a coffee cup.

"Good morning, Andrés," Nan smiled as she poured him some coffee.

"Sorry. I overslept," he added cream and sugar.

"Astrid and Bert have already left for the hospital," the Schmidts' maid informed him. "She will see you later. She said not to worry."

Andrés thanked her. In front of him were two soft-boiled eggs, bacon, and toast. He was slightly embarrassed, but got over it after eating a few bites.

A half hour later he was on his way back to his apartment. He had some homework that he had to complete for his class on Friday.

His place looked like a closet compared to the Schmidt's lodgings. He sat at the table writing out drafts until he got hungry. He made himself a grilled ham and cheese sandwich that he washed down with apple juice.

Andrés finished most of his assignment and decided to go to the hospital.

cx

Astrid looked bushed when Andrés finally entered Schmidt's room that afternoon. The little makeup that she wore had dissipated from her crying. Schmidt was asleep. She sat at the foot of the bed continually rubbing her father's feet.

The youngsters did not speak. They did not want to wake up her father. Schmidt finally woke up when the nurse's aide came in around five o'clock. The wheels on the meal trolley made an earsplitting noise as it rolled in, one wheel was definitely askew. Again Astrid fed her father some chicken noodle soup.

She declined later on when Andrés asked her if she wanted to go to the cafeteria for something to eat. He was hungry, but sucked it up.

They finally departed late at night after a nurse gave Schmidt his medication. The nurse had taken the patient's vital signs before she gave him the tablets and suggested to the pair that they should go home and get some rest.

It was past ten when Nan cleared the dinner dishes from Astrid and Andrés. She had prepared a hearty beef stew for them. They had arrived home late from the hospital. Poor Astrid had not eaten all day.

"Thank you, Nan," expressed Astrid. "We won't be needing anything else tonight."

She and Andrés went into her father's study and she closed the door behind them. He became nervous.

"What I couldn't tell you at the hospital is that they have decided to keep my father there a few more days," she was reporting to him with tears in her eyes. "I talked to the doctor and he says that father has a little bit of fluid in his lungs. He wants to keep him there as a precaution. He doesn't want my father to catch pneumonia."

In the study Andrés now reached for her hand as they sat

down on the couch.

"You must be totally fried."

"I am," her eyes half-closed as she snuggled up to him.

"I need to show you something," he said earnestly.

"What is it?"

He grabbed an envelope from his back pocket and pulled out the note. It was handwritten and had a twin black angels logo printed at the top of the page. The word "Zwillinge" underscored the symbol.

"Somebody wants to meet me tomorrow at the Caffe Trieste," Andrés said in a tense tone.

"Who?"

"Don't know who it is."

Astrid took the note and slowly read it.

"What are you going to do?" her forehead fretted.

"I guess I'll go."

"By yourself?"

"Sure. You have to go see you father. The note says come alone."

"But what if something happens to you?"

"That's why I'm going to give you this letter. For safekeeping." He handed it to her. "If I don't come back in one piece, call that detective guy . . . What was his name? Do you still have his card?"

"I have it someplace. I think his name was Detective Campos."

CHAPTER 33

TORNA A TRIESTE

Tuesday, July 16, 1974, San Francisco

Andrés arrived at the Caffe Trieste at about ten minutes before eleven. He had left Astrid at the house. Bert was going to drive her to the hospital to see her father later on.

He was still full from the great breakfast of French toast with real maple syrup that Nan had prepared. So he only ordered a macchiato. An elderly man, wearing a brown narrow brim Trilby hat with thick black-framed glasses and reading the local newspaper, was seated at a table next to him. The steam rising from the espresso machine sounded like a locomotive. The smell of strong coffee overwhelmed the room.

An Asian woman carrying an umbrella and pushing a baby stroller ordered a cappuccino to go. A muttering homeless person toting two vinyl suitcases grabbed a caffè americano. Andrés looked at his watch. It was now five minutes past eleven. He kept looking at the door.

"Would you like the newspaper?" inquired the patron next to him. He spoke with a strange accent.

"No, thanks," Andrés remain fixated on the entrance. He only had a swig of coffee grit left.

"Have you seen this magazine?" the stranger boldly placed it in front of Andrés.

Andrés was perturbed by the rude behavior until he saw

the publication was an old Stern magazine with a beautiful blonde girl portrayed on the cover. It was from 1947.

"Look at page fifty."

Andrés suspended his resentment. He paged through the photos and ads until he came to a featured story. He couldn't understand anything. It was all in German.

"Look at the photos. Do you recognize that man?"

There was something familiar about the person in the article. Andrés couldn't readily recollect what it was.

"Who are you?"

"George. George Kulongoski."

"Are you the person who sent me the note?"

The older man nodded. He was smallish is stature and sported a brownish-grey chin beard. His nose seemed to be too small for his face. His sunken eyes looked like two black holes.

"What do you want from me?"

"You are a college student, correct?"

"Yeah. Why do you want to know?" Andrés was getting testy.

Kulongoski ignored the counter question. "I need you to go down to Stanford. Go to the Hoover Institute. Research this man," he pointed to a black and white photo of a clean-shaven young man with his dark hair parted down the middle and wearing a dark suit.

"Who's this guy?"

"Augustin Teufl."

"I don't even know this dude. Why should I?"

"Do the research and then you will know."

"If you know all this stuff, what do you want with me?"

"You will find out."

Andrés was confused and angry. *Who is this jerk? Why is*

he telling me what to do?

A couple of guys wearing midnight blue jogging suits and knitted caps came into the café.

The barista gave them a coquettish smile.

"Meet me back here on Friday," ordered Kulongoski. "Same time."

"What makes you think I'll do it?"

"You will. After you do the research, you will understand."

"Why don't you simply tell me what the hell is going on?" Andrés had raised his voice.

"Next Friday," Kulongoski suddenly got up and left the establishment.

Andrés was stunned. He still had the magazine in his hands.

He knew that Astrid spoke German. He would show her the magazine.

He walked down two blocks to the bus stop, passing a dozen newspaper stands along the way. He had a strange feeling that someone was following him. Andrés turned around. Nobody was around except the two guys from the café. At the bus stop he found himself next to a purplish-grey haired elderly woman with very few teeth.

A quarter of an hour later he hopped off the bus and was making his way back to his apartment. He jaywalked across the center of the busy street. Out of nowhere raced a black Dodge Monaco sedan in his direction. Andrés assumed that the car was going to slow down. Instead the muscle car sped up. He was in the middle of the street. The vehicle was bearing down on him. He couldn't move.

Suddenly, a white delivery van slowly pulled out of a loading zone along the street. The black car swerved to miss it and its wheels screeched for a nanosecond. Andrés jumped back just in time. The smell of burning tires filled the air. The wheels of the Dodge squealed as it peeled out and swung wide, barely making the left turn.

"Asshole!" Andrés flipped off the errant driver. "Up yours!"

The windows of the Dodge were tinted. Andrés hadn't seen the driver. He didn't recall if there was a front license plate, but he did get a quick glimpse of its grill emblem. It looked like the symbol of an eagle.

"Grrr! Frigging City drivers!"

☞

That evening found the smell of caramelized onions wafting through the house. Andrés had returned to the Schmidt home after finishing his Friday assignment and getting some more clean (relatively speaking) clothes. After washing up, he joined Astrid for a late dinner.

"How is your dad?"

"Better," she sipped her sparkling water. "He asked about you."

She related her long day with her father and his constant napping. Astrid was concerned about his health. She had never seen her father look so pale. And so old.

Andrés had devoured his meal and was going to share his experience at the Caffe Trieste, when Nan rushed in.

"Sorry to interrupt, Astrid," the maid pointed outside the dining room. "You have a telephone call."

"Excuse me, Andrés," Astrid got up from the table. "I'll be right back."

Andrés cut another piece of the apple tart and began on it.

"Would you like a coffee while you wait?" inquired Bert coming into the room. "Cream and sugar?"

"Sure," Andrés reached out for the cup, but before he had an opportunity to drink it, Astrid charged back into the room.

"My aunt Matilda just called," she exclaimed frazzled. "I had to tell her about Papá."

"Is she flying back?"

"She's in the middle of some important business for my father," Astrid rambled. "She said that she couldn't return until it's finished."

"How did she sound to you?" Andrés put his hand on hers trying to calm her. "She probably was more worried than angry."

"A little of both. She was angry with my father for not calling her immediately. She called him a stubborn old man," she sighed and tried to relax. "I'm going to have to tell my father now. He doesn't need any more stress."

"When are you going to see your father again?"

"Oh, I don't know. Tomorrow?" she ran her hand through her hair. "I'm too upset."

"I'll come with you," he gave her hand a squeeze.

"You're so sweet. I need to do a few things right now. Meet me in the study in twenty minutes . . . maybe thirty minutes."

Andrés sauntered into the study and opened up a newspaper. He knew that a half hour meant at least 45 minutes. He went right to the Sports section. The headline story was about Dizzy Dean's passing away from a fatal heart attack in Reno. Andrés used to play baseball when he was a kid and remembered the Saint Louis Cardinal pitcher well. From the Sports pages, he drifted over to the Comics.

Forty-eight minutes after her exit from the dining room, Astrid returned. She had changed her clothes. She was wearing black jeans and a powder blue cashmere sweater.

"Okay," she announced. "Where were we?"

He dropped the newspaper onto the coffee table.

She drew up an afghan blanket on top of her.

Andrés began telling her about his meeting at the Caffe Trieste.

Her eyes closed ever so slowly, then opened. Within a minute she was sound asleep on the sofa.

Andrés picked up the newspaper and continued to read it where he left off. After he was finished with it, he decided to go to bed.

He adjusted the blanket on top of her, turned off the study lights, and left her on the sofa.

Andrés had made a commitment to go see Mister Schmidt the next day. He was still rattled about his strange meeting with Kulongoski. Why should he go down to Stanford and do research? He had more than enough to do for his own project.

CHAPTER 34

COUCH TOMATOES

Wednesday, July 17, 1974, San Francisco

Astrid was acting scattered at times. She was totally stressed out. She was exhausted, both mentally and physically. She and Andrés had only the briefest conversation on Tuesday night after his enigmatic meeting with Mister Kulongoski. She had fallen asleep in the study. He did not see her until the following morning.

"I'm sorry that I was not a good hostess last night," Astrid had apologized as the two sat for breakfast. "My mind is *muy preocupada.*"

"No problem. We're cool."

"This is yours," she handed him an envelope that contained his weekly stipend. It was awkward for both of them. She did not want to appear haughty or inconsiderate nor consider Andrés a paid-for commodity. He, in turn, did not want to feel like a gigolo. He thanked her and put the envelope into his back pocket without opening it. With that out of the way, they continued with breakfast.

The soft-boiled eggs came after the yogurt parfaits. Andrés dipped the ends of his toast into the yellow liquid. Nan poured him more coffee.

"So, how was your meeting yesterday?" Astrid inquired. "I'm glad that you're back."

"It was really bizarre . . ." he narrated the odd happenings at the Caffe Trieste. He showed her the magazine. She read the article but did not volunteer the translation. She remained silent.

Neither did he mention the crazy driver incident on his way home. "I don't think I'm going to go down to Stanford. Why should I?"

"Well, it's your choice. We can't do our regular lesson anyway," she was sounding impassive. "I'm going to spend the day with my father. I worry about him."

"But why did the guy pick me?" Andrés was still preoccupied by the encounter with Kulongoski.

An hour later Bert dropped them off at the passenger loading and unloading zone of the hospital. There were several patients sitting in wheelchairs being discharged and this area was very busy. The skies were overcast and a moist mist blew in from the northwest.

Schmidt was still recuperating at the hospital.

The nurses knew Astrid and Andrés by their first names now.

She greeted her father with a smile. "How are you feeling?"

"I want to get the hell out of here!" his voice had an edge that was normally rare when he talked to his daughter.

"Let me talk to the doctor again," Astrid tried to smooth out the situation. The doctors had told her that they were concerned about her father falling into such a weakened state that he would be more susceptible to respiratory attacks.

"Tell the doctor that I am okay and want to leave this place."

"Yes, Papá."

"And how are you, my boy?" Schmidt turned his attention to Andrés.

"Fine. Thank you, sir."

"I am tired of being cooped up in this place," the old man tried to make light of it. "This place is full of human vegetables."

Andrés excused himself to go to the bathroom.

"They need to keep that son of a bitch Neumann out of here," Schmidt groused. "Astrid, remember what I told you."

Astrid then told her father about her conversation with her Aunt Matilda. This only aggravated him more. His face had become more and more sallow as the days went by. His speech patterns at times were unintelligible. She was really worried about him.

Andrés returned to the hospital room.

"This place is worse than hell," Schmidt complained with a faint smile. "There is nothing on television except terrible news and insulting game shows for couch tomatoes."

Andrés almost burst out laughing, but controlled himself. Couch tomatoes. Couch potatoes. *Who cared?*

Schmidt dozed off and on during the day. Approximately every two hours a nurse would come in and check his pulse and vitals. Other aides came in to replenish his drinking water, empty out the urine bag from the attached catheter, provide medication, or chat with the pair.

Andrés and Astrid went down to the cafeteria for lunch. They had sloppy joes and orange sodas.

"I wanted to call my aunt and have her come home right now, but my father won't let me. She would know what to do."

"What could she do that you are not already doing?" He gently put his hand on top of hers. "You're doing fine."

"You're probably right. Anyway, my father would be really angry if I did," she was now resigned. "I know that I am spoiled and need to grow up. But I love my father."

"I am not spoiled, but I still need to grow up," he mocked and they both tittered.

That night when they again came home late, Andrés told Astrid that he had decided that he needed to go down to Stanford the following day.

"I only wish I could go down there with you, Andrés. I hear the campus is very beautiful. You need to take me down there sometime." She reached over and embraced him. She then gave him a passionate kiss.

CHAPTER 35

HOOVER

Thursday, July 18, 1974, San Francisco

On their way to the hospital that overcast Thursday morning, Bert and Astrid dropped Andrés off at the Caltrain station on Fourth Street. He rarely took the commuter train down the San Francisco Peninsula. The only time he ever went down to the Palo Alto area was to drink and play shuffleboard at the Dutch Goose. His friends would pile into a '58 Chevy Impala and spend the weekend night cruising or boozing. They would try to pick up Stanford girls, but usually met with little success.

He climbed up the stairs of the train car and found an empty row. There were several riders who were wearing Giants jerseys or warm up jackets. A few brightly clad athletic types hauled their bikes aboard. He spied a foxy brunette a few rows away snapping her gum.

The train bounced up and around the tracks. The backyards of buildings and houses exposed a multitude of untold tales. He was tired and wanted to sleep. The ordeals of the last few days had emotionally drained him.

∞

He took a shuttle from the Caltrain station to the university grounds. The sky down the Peninsula was blue and the weather was perfect. The Stanford campus was like a mini-Camelot with its expansive lawns and classic buildings.

Dozens of people from all over the world were walking about. Joggers and bicyclists whizzed by him. He wandered around looking for the Hoover Institute. The first person he asked replied in broken English that he was just a visitor and was lost also.

There was a young brunette in a red tank top sitting on an oversized beach towel in the ovular grass area in front of the Quad.

"Excuse me. Do you know where the Hoover Institute is?" He looked at her. She was gorgeous. *Beautiful and brainy!* He reflected.

She pointed to the large tower to their left. He thanked her and made his way to the building.

As he entered, he saw old paintings and antique furniture. It reminded him of a stately mansion that he once visited. He looked at the directory next to the old gilded elevator doors. A couple of floors higher found him at the research reception desk.

"Are you a student here?" queried the middle-aged librarian with horn-rimmed glasses.

"Not here," he pulled out his USF student identification from his wallet and presented it to her.

"That's fine," she directed him to the main card catalog room. He looked at the Stern Magazine to ensure that he had the correct spellings.

He found several entries and wrote them down on his notepad. He then tried to find the different sections of the library. He rode the elevator up two more floors. He entered a marbled hall with large oak tables lined down the center. The sources in English were easy to locate. However, the foreign language sources were not readily evident. The air seemed stuffy and there was no real air conditioning.

The hardbound books were dusty and written in small print. The indexes were valuable and Andrés was able to take some preliminary notes. He found out that Augustin Teufl was born in 1922 in Vienna; that he worked at a hospital in Frankfurt, Germany, in various capacities; and that he was a chief witness for the prosecution in the Doctors Trials in Nuremberg. Teufl had testified against a host of Nazi doctors involved in eugenics, war crimes, torture and the extermination of non-Aryan groups, and medical experimentation on different subject groups. The photos of Teufl were those taken at the military tribunal. The photos were all in black and white. There was no further information on him after 1947.

Andrés decided to take a lunch break and left the building. He eventually found the Student Union and grabbed a couple slices of pepperoni and cheese pizza. Eye candy passed his table. He was in heaven. He grabbed a tall cup of coffee before returning to the Hoover Institute.

His backpack and the library books and files were still on the table when he returned. There was no one else in the hall, except a Korean student wearing a Stanford Band tee shirt who was replenishing the bookshelves. She looked like a high school student.

Andrés began to peruse the materials. He began with the WWII files in manila envelopes. Some were duplicative of the information in the other books. His list of bibliographic sources seemed endless.

"Do you work here?"

"Yes," said the skinny student. "Do you need some assistance?"

Andrés jumped at the opportunity and gave the youngster his list. A minute later they were walking up a stairwell to the next floor. There was an entire section on the Nuremberg Trials way in the back. It was dark, dank, and dusty. One by one the young woman pulled the files from the archives until a half hour had elapsed.

Finally, the young woman excused herself. "Sorry, I have to go to class."

"Thanks," Andrés saluted her. "Hey, what are you studying?"

"I'm doing a double major. Pre-law and computer engineering."

"What a trip!" Andrés was overwhelmed. *A lot of brainiacs here!*

Andrés came over to a well-lit area and set down his materials that now covered two tables. Andrés started going over the files. He realized that most of the documentation was in German, Russian, or French. He pushed those to the side and just focused on the English ones. Fortunately, there were English transcripts of the Nuremberg trials. The information was repetitive of what he had already read. However, there was a salient reference that kept creeping up.

It was getting close to four o'clock when Andrés walked back down the stairs and found his backpack and the other books. He did another search for the name Kulongoski. Bingo! A Jerzy Kulongoski had done research on war crimes and medical experimentations in concentration camps for the prosecution in the U.S. Nuremberg Military Tribunal against the Nazi doctors. Kulongoski and Teufl were connected!

But what does this have to do to me?

❧

It was past nine o'clock by the time Andrés finally arrived from his day at the Hoover Institute to the Schmidt house. He had to ring the doorbell because did not have a house

key. Bert who had dark circles under his eyes amiably greeted
Andrés. On the dining room table, Nan had left a plate of
sandwiches, cut into quarters. It seemed that everyone had
retired early.

CHAPTER 36

HANGING

Friday, July 19, 1974, San Francisco

The following morning found the smell of bacon wafting through the house. It awoke Andrés. After washing up, he joined Astrid for an early breakfast.

"How is your father?"

"Better," she sipped her coffee. "I want him to come back home."

She related her long day with her father and his constant napping. Astrid had talked to her father's doctor. They were still doing more tests. The early indications were that Schmidt was in stable condition.

Andrés devoured his breakfast and was going to share Thursday's experience at Stanford, when Astrid excused herself to finish getting ready.

Andrés took coffee and went into the study to read the newspaper. He could get used to this type of life, he thought.

She reappeared in the study wearing black jeans and a powder blue cashmere sweater. She wore some orange monarch butterfly earrings.

"I'm ready," she announced.

He grabbed his sweater and dropped the newspaper onto the coffee table.

They said goodbye to Nan. In spite of his protestations, Nan was going to have Andrés clothes laundered that day.

"You'll have to tell me what happened yesterday down at the Hoover Institute," Astrid requested as they jumped into the limousine.

Bert drove them toward the hospital. On the way over, Andrés told her about his research on Teufl and also about finding out who the mysterious note writer was.

"Who is this person?" she asked.

Andrés briefly described Kulongoski to her and the role he played in the Nuremberg trials against the Nazis. Two minutes later Astrid was let off at the hospital to see her father.

Cʑ

Bert continued the drive and gave Andrés a ride to USF where he was to attend his weekly seminar. He stumbled into class a few minutes late, but no one seemed to care.

During class Andrés was still contemplating what he had discovered at the Hoover Institute. He had decided to confront Kulongoski and find out why this old man had latched onto him. Andrés was not sure what he should do with the photo album and the other materials. Maybe he should just give them back. He certainly didn't want them.

After class, Andrés just missed the bus going toward North Beach and now he was forced to wait at the bus stop with an Asian woman and her two toddler children. It was a beautiful, warm day with the morning mist having burned off. The odor of rancid grease from a nearby restaurant could be smelled for blocks.

Eventually, he arrived at the Caffe Trieste huffing and puffing. He was out of shape. He was five minutes late. He scanned the place. The same old Italians were playing their card games and kicking up a fuss. Andrés' stomach was bothering him. He felt bloated. Maybe he was getting nervous about his meeting. Against his better judgment, he ordered a cappuccino and sat down at a large table.

There was a newspaper nearby that someone had discarded. He went right to the Sports. Not much new there.

The front door of the café swung open and a tall, slender cinnamon-skinned woman glided in with her hippie longhair boyfriend. He wore the traditional red bandanna around his head. Her down-to-her-butt black hair was braided with red, white, and green ribbons. She wore a loose fitting black leather vest and cutoff jeans that made Andrés obsess on her.

"Hey, dude," the beau came over to Andrés table, "can I steal a couple of these chairs?"

"Sure. Go for it."

What a stone cold fox she was! His eyes were dilated with stardust. It took him a few minutes to gather himself and refrain from staring at the electrifying Venus. His body tingled. His hormones were starting to kick in.

Even the Italians in the corner had stopped their bellowing. *Marone!* The celebrity and ogling lasted for at least twenty minutes. That was when the couple left.

Andrés regrouped his thoughts. Kulongoski had still not showed up. He went for the Comics section and experienced a few chuckles. He did not dare attempt the crossword puzzle. Finally, at a quarter past twelve, he decided that Kulongoski was a no-show and left the café after buying a ham and cheese panini to go.

The weather was still warm and the sidewalks were filled with more pedestrians. He caught the westbound bus and as his reward, he was serenaded by a wailing baby for the entire ride. After he disembarked, he went into a corner liquor store and bought an orange soda. He munched on his sandwich as he entered the Presidio, on his way to the hospital.

Schmidt's eyes were puffy and his mouth was agape.

"How are you, my boy?" he mumbled. The old man had not been wearing his green tinted glasses in the hospital.

"Fine, sir," Andrés replied. He did not see Astrid in the room.

"Don't get old. I haven't had a decent meal in almost a week," he cackled hoarsely. "And heaven knows how long I've been constipated."

They chatted, with the young man doing most of the listening. Schmidt thanked Andrés for taking care of his daughter and staying at the house.

"Oh, you're early!" said a feminine voice. "I wasn't expecting you until late this afternoon," said Astrid as she entered the room.

The trio made small talk, with Astrid trying to assuage her father's grousing. In the afternoon Schmidt took a nap. Astrid and Andrés escaped to grab a coffee at the cafeteria.

"How was your meeting with Mr. Kulongoski?"

"The jerk never showed up!"

Astrid excused herself and dashed off to the ladies' room.

Andrés spotted a newspaper. He had read half of it earlier. He really hated the news. Everyday there was a story about "Tricky Dick" Nixon and the Watergate scandal. The editorials rang out about governmental leaders lacking moral compasses and acting outside of social norms. The main banner headline said that the OPEC had ended the oil embargo. *What embargo? Why should I even care? I don't even have a car!*

He continued reading a few more articles while he waited for Astrid to return. A heading that read "*Authorities Fail to ID Hanging Body*" caught his attention. His eyes quickly scanned through the story about the local police discovering a man, clad only in his underwear, strung up in an apartment in the

Western Addition neighborhood of San Francisco. It looked like a robbery gone wrong and had become a homicide. Law enforcement was seeking the public's assistance in trying to identify the victim.

There was a police photo of the deceased at the bottom of the article. Andrés was stunned.

"I'm back, Andrés."

CHAPTER 37

THE BOOKS

Saturday, July 20, 1974, San Francisco

During breakfast, Andrés finally decided to share with Astrid what he had read in the newspaper the previous day. He had wanted to tell her earlier, but he did not want to upset her further. He needed some time to be sure before he acted.

"Astrid, I need to tell you something about what I saw in the newspaper yesterday."

Andrés told her that although the victim of the burglary and homicide had a contorted facial expression, he had recognized Kulongoski's distinctive beard.

Astrid gave him a strange look. She seemed horrified!

He continued to tell her about the strange set of events that seemed tangentially related to them. He wanted to call the police immediately, but Astrid put her hand on his forearm.

"Let's be sure before we call," she advised. "I think I remember seeing that symbol of the two angels before."

"What are you talking about?" He gave a puzzled look. "I don't understand."

"In your photo book," she stared back at him. "Those ones."

"Where? Which ones? Where have you seen them before?" Andrés was perplexed.

"I think in my father's books or papers."

"What does it mean?"

"I don't know," she put down her buttered toast.

"We could ask your father."

"I don't want to worry him," her green eyes seemed so persuasive. "He has to think about getting well first."

Nan walked into the room.

"Anything else for you two?"

The two nodded their heads "no." Nan removed some dishes. Andrés and Astrid remained drinking their coffee. Andrés was also finishing up a banana.

"What time do you want to run over to see your dad?"

"A little later," she paused. "We could look in my father's library first to see if we can find anything."

"Doesn't he have a gigantic library?"

"Yes, but we only have a small collection here. Most of father's works are in our library down in Santiago."

"How many books are we talking about?"

"I don't know. Thousands?"

∞

The library at the Schmidt house had twelve floor-to-ceiling bookcases filled with literature, science journals, art books, and other esoteric subjects in a multitude of languages. Astrid knew that her father spoke many languages fluently, but didn't know exactly how many. She herself could speak English, French, and German, in addition to her native tongue of Spanish.

There were Ritter and Holbein vanitas-type paintings and Dali prints interspersed among the bookshelves. Three standing lamps stood guard over the leather reading chairs.

Andrés started at one end of the room, she on the other. The young man was mesmerized as he pulled out a Victor

Hugo novel bound in leather, written in French. He could spend a decade exploring this treasure trove.

Meanwhile, Astrid was slowly pouring over some medical and pharmaceutical books.

"I must have seen the symbol when I was a child," her brow furrowed as her fingers walked along the bindings. "Now, angels, where are you hiding?"

She was flipping through the pages of a tome on biotechnology that she could not understand. The formulae were complex and the graphics were convoluted.

"Excuse me, Miss Astrid," Bert had entered the library like a phantom. "What time would you like to go to the hospital?'

She paused. Her mind had been lost in thought. "Oh, in about fifteen minutes."

"Very good. I'll be at the car waiting for you," Bert left the room as silently as he had entered.

"Hey, Andrés, how are you doing?" she yelled over to the other side of the room.

"Your father has some really awesome books," he had moved over to the natural history books and was perusing a few field guides for birds around the world. The kingfisher photos intrigued him. "I have never seen such freaky creatures."

"I have to finish getting dressed," she put back the books she had pulled out. "We can continue looking tonight."

"Sure," he was moving on to some art books.

CB

The visit with Schmidt was uneventful. He was in a cantankerous mood. His eyes were swollen and he complained about having dry mouth and difficulty swallowing.

The good news was that the doctor had told him that he might be released as early as the upcoming Monday.

The young pair came home for a late supper. Nan served them a leg of lamb with green beans and baked potatoes. Astrid picked at her food. Andrés had second helpings of everything, especially the chocolate chip ice cream.

"Religion!" she blurted.

"What about religion?" he said with the spoon just about to enter his mouth. "We're going to church tomorrow, right?"

"Angels can be religious symbols," she pushed her ice cream dish away from her and turned directly toward him. "We should be looking in my father's books on religion."

"Sounds awesome," he resumed inhaling the ice cream.

Minutes later they were combing through the Catholic, Judaic, and Islamic books in Schmidt's library.

"We're not talking about specific angels like Gabriel," she pointed to a chapter on archangels. "Why two angels instead of just one?"

"I don't remember anything about angels," he grabbed another book. "I think that there are several types of angels."

"Are there any famous myths about angels?"

"Dante's *Inferno?*" he didn't want to sound ignorant. "I don't know. All I really remember about the logos is that most of them were both black, but a few were black and white."

"Were there two angels?" she tried to understand.

"They were the same," he was thinking, "but maybe mirror-images?"

"I don't understand, Andrés!" she gasped exasperatedly.

Nan came back into the room carrying another of cup of ice cream.

"Nan, thanks," he gave her a charming smile. "You're the

best. By the way, could you please bring me a blank piece of paper? I already have a pen."

Five minutes later Andrés was drawing some rudimentary renditions of the angels.

"It probably symbolizes something with the Archangels Michael and Lucifer."

"Do you mean the struggle between good and evil?" *Being a Comparative Literature major came in handy every once in while,* he grinned.

"Yes," her face lit up.

Astrid excused Nan for the remainder of the evening when the latter came in to check on them.

Andrés and Astrid laughed and giggled for the next hour. They were just being silly because they were punchy from all the tension.

Finally, Andrés started to put the books away, especially those they had pulled from the upper shelves. Astrid suddenly was engrossed in some sort of German manuscript that was bound with string.

∝

Two voices whispered in the darkness on the other side of town. "Jerzy has been killed!"

"Do you think they are on to us?" said the other, with a hint of fear.

"I don't know," there was a pause, "but I think we should assume they know about us, just to be safe."

"Then we need to contact Sandrine."

CHAPTER 38

AMEN

Sunday, July 21, 1974, San Francisco

The fog was heavy and the air was damp. Andrés did not have a jacket when Bert dropped Astrid and him off at Saint Vincent's for Sunday mass.

Astrid had not been very talkative since the night before. She seemed to be preoccupied at breakfast time.

Earlier, after their morning meal, Andrés had called the police station looking for Detective Campos. The police detective had previously left his business card at the Schmidt residence when he was investigating the Boehner matter. Campos had the day off and Leong would be back in the office in the afternoon. Andrés felt nervous about calling the police, but he knew that he had to do it.

The mass began and the priest gave his sermon to the congregation that was clad in coats and other winter wear in the middle of summer. Andrés tuned out the history lesson on Jeremiah's trial in Jerusalem.

Bert returned around eleven o'clock to pick the pair up. He dropped Andrés off at his apartment before driving Astrid to the hospital to see her father. Normally, she would have given Andrés a little kiss or hug, but today she didn't. Andrés wanted to ask her what the problem was, but he figured that she was just in a funky mood.

He was thinking about other things. On the positive side,

Andrés didn't mind that his laundry was being done at the Schmidt house. He now had time to catch up on his studies. He knocked on his landlord's door.

An over-aged preppie-looking man wearing a white cardigan cable knit tennis sweater over a pink button down shirt opened the door.

"Well, hello, stranger," he beamed. "Haven't seen you for a while."

"What's happening, Maurice?" Andrés pulled out an envelope from his pants pocket and extended it toward his landlord who readily accepted it.

They chatted for a few minutes. Andrés only had a balance of $110 that he owed for back rent.

Eventually, Andrés went down to his apartment after picking up the mail. His place was cold, but he did not want to turn on the heater. Both of his plants were on life support. He watered them anyway.

For lunch, he scraped off the white mold that was starting to spot the cheddar cheese and made himself a sandwich.

Andrés kept procrastinating. He read his mail, even the ads. He called his uncle and aunt in San Antonio. What he really wanted was to take a nap.

Finally, with a herculean effort, he started to attack his thesis. Astrid had insisted that Andrés borrow the Neruda books from her father's library. He started to write down the bibliographic information for each work. For the Spanish version of *Twenty Love Poems and a Desperate Song*, Andrés had to utilize his dictionary to translate several of the words.

In the late afternoon, he took a break. He grabbed a glass of milk. Luckily, it was still good. Andrés remembered that he needed to look for the album that the murdered man had sent him. He thought that he had left it on top of the table, but it wasn't there. For the next twenty minutes, he looked high and low, but couldn't find it. *I don't think that I left it at the Schmidt house*, he grimaced.

Andrés went back and found his place in the book of poetry. *"Entre los labios y la voz, algo se va muriendo . . ."* [Between the lips and the voice, something is dying.]

☙

"We have to act quickly," the voice calmly instructed over the phone. "We only have a very narrow window."

"Okay."

"When is he going to be released?"

"Probably tomorrow," uncertainty could be heard. "One doctor said tomorrow."

"The rendezvous will be at Stern Grove."

"Okay. Make it between nine and ten."

"In the parking lot. Bring the car all the way to the back."

"Okay," the dripping of sweat could be heard over the phone.

"If something goes wrong, call me again at this number as soon as possible. I would strongly recommend using a different public phone."

"Yes, I know. I know."

"And lastly, no more rogue activities. JI is not happy with you taking out that neo-Nazi wacko without permission. You have compromised the whole operation. We have been working on this for years." There was the bark of a dog behind the voice.

There was contrite silence. Bert hung up and walked over to the car. He had a pickup to make.

☙

The dog barked again.

"There, there, Amen," Sandrine petted him. "Do you

want a treat?"

The huge black, lupine beast bared his teeth. His tongue jetted out. She threw him some jerky treats that were devoured in nanoseconds.

"Good boy!" she stroked his back. "Mommy needs to brush you."

She opened the door to the old and weathered white Chevy van. Amen jumped up onto the passenger seat.

"Why are there so many idiots out there, Amen?" she started the vehicle. "Why can't they all be like you?"

She slowly pulled away from the curb.

"It looks like tomorrow will be the day. Huh, boy?"

The ebony dog looked at his master and saw a woman with silver grey hair parted in the middle, wearing an old drab violet-colored crocheted woolen shawl. She had one eye half closed and was bent over like a willow tree. She could have passed for Janis Joplin's mother with her paisley skirt and leather sandals.

"Revenge will be ours, Amen."

PART III - MACCHIATO

CHAPTER 39

MISSING

Monday, July 22, 1974, San Francisco

The police officers arrived at the house right after Astrid and Andrés had finished their breakfast. The young girl had been too nervous to eat much because of the impending arrival.

Earlier that morning, she had called her aunt who tried to pacify her. Although the family had had advantageous relations with the Pinochet government, one could never be overconfident when it came to the authorities. Matilda hoped to return to San Francisco within the next two weeks.

Campos and Leong were invited into the study. Nan offered them coffee and they both accepted. They also helped themselves to the walnut orange coffee cake.

"We appreciate you wanting to help, Andrés," led off Campos who was wearing a grey tweed sport coat and a narrow royal blue tie. Leong had his notepad open and was sitting in a velvet chair between Astrid and the other two.

Andrés nodded his head in acknowledgement.

"I remember that you told us you are a student at USF," the detective was trying to bond with the young man. "I'm glad that I'm not still in school," Campos laughed.

Nan came in and inquired if anyone needed anything else. Leong said no and asked her to please close the door behind her.

"Andrés, please tell us what you know."

Andrés slowly began to narrate the arrival of the album and the meeting with the old man at the Caffe Trieste. Astrid's eyes never left Andrés face. She seemed distraught.

"And where is the album now?"

"That's the thing. I don't know," Andrés was getting unnerved. "I thought that it was at my pad. But I couldn't find it. It's not here either. I already checked it out."

"And what did this album contain?"

"It had all these gross photos. They looked like people in a torture chamber."

"Can you be a little more specific, Andrés? I know that this is difficult. Just try your best."

Andrés described several examples of the maimed victims in the German concentration camps. He also mentioned the dozens of photos of lookalikes that had twin black angel tattoos on their shoulders.

"Were these old photos?"

"Yes. They were in black and white. Many of them were faded."

Andrés got emotional when he talked about the castrated males and the women with their wombs mutilated. Tears flowed from Astrid's eyes.

"And you say that you can't find the album?"

Andrés shook his head no. He grabbed his coffee cup, but it was empty.

"And you said there was also a letter."

"Yeah. It told me to go to the Caffe Trieste."

"And you went?"

"Yes."

"But you don't have the letter either?"

"No."

"And you went to see a person that you didn't even know because he sent you a letter?"

"Yes," Andrés felt stupid. *How lame am I?*

"Did you get this person's name?"

"George," Andrés eyes flittered upwards as he strained to remember. "It sounded like George Kulongoski or something like that. I couldn't really be sure. He had an accent."

"What kind of accent? New York?"

"No, I think it was some sort of European accent."

Leong looked over to Campos. There was some kind of secret communication between the partners.

"Was the letter typed?"

"No. It was handwritten. The writing was kind of messy."

"This person asked you to go down to Stanford and do some research about someone named Teufl?"

"Yeah. I think this guy Teufl was a witness in a trial against the Nazis."

"What kind of trial are we talking about?"

"It was in Germany someplace. My notes are also missing."

This time Campos glanced back at Leong. He tried not to roll his eyes.

"We're almost done. A few more questions," Campos seemed incredulous about Andrés' rendition. "Tell us why you think you recognize the photo in the newspaper."

"It just looks like the guy I met with in the café. You know, they both had the same kind of beard."

"Any other similarities?"

Andrés couldn't think of any. He was mentally exhausted.

Campos thanked him for his cooperation. The officers stood up.

"We'll follow up on this," said Campos straightening out his coat. "We'll let you know what we find." Campos knew that they probably wouldn't.

"Excuse me," a soft voice popped up. "May I say something?"

The faces of Campos and Leong turned to Astrid.

"Sure," Campos sat back down.

"Andrés showed me the album and letter," she was wringing her hands. "I couldn't go to Stanford because I had to be with my father."

"You didn't meet the man at the Caffe Trieste, did you?"

"No, I was at the hospital with my father."

The two police were not aware that Mister Schmidt was currently in the hospital. Questions jumped into their heads. *Why was Andrés living in their house now? Why was the girl trying to protect him?*

"The letter had the symbol of the double angel on the bottom," she parenthetically added.

"Sorry, Astrid, can you clarify what that means?"

"There were black angel tattoos on some of the concentration camp victims. The ones that Andrés was talking about in the album."

"Do you know what the symbol means?"

"I'm not sure," she started to speak with a little more confidence. "The album had the double angel symbol with the word 'Zwillinge' on the cover page. I think some of the tattoos were black and white angels."

"What does that mean?"

"Twins. Zwillinge means twins in German."

"That's it!" interrupted Andrés. "I remember now. The

photos in the album had twins with these tattoos."

"The letter had a twin black angels logo," reiterated Astrid. "On the bottom."

Campos and Leong were now trying to decipher the relevance of any of this. *Had they wasted their morning with some overly imaginative youths?*

"One more thing," Astrid pulled out two books from underneath the coffee table. "Here are two books describing the Nazi twin experiments at Auschwitz. They also have pictures of the angel symbols."

Leong took one of the books and started to leaf through it.

"Where are these books from?"

"From my father's library."

"Hold on a second. I need clarification. Andrés you said the angel symbols were all black."

The boy nodded his head affirmatively.

"And, Astrid, you said the angel symbols were black and white."

She in turn nodded her head.

"Well, which is it?" Leong asked in a somewhat forceful tone.

"Well, I only remember these books having both angels being black," responded Andrés, feeling like he was under the third degree.

"What about the letter?" pressed the detective.

"I don't exactly remember," Andrés turned his head toward Astrid.

"Andrés is correct," corroborated the girl. "But the album was different. It had some black and white angels."

Leong was going to ask another question, when Campos made a halting sign with his right hand toward his partner.

"These books also talk about Teufl and his role in the experiments," Astrid emphasized, her eyes fixed on Leong. "Detective, how good is your German?"

Astrid was annoyed at the detectives' seeming reluctance to believe them.

CHAPTER 40

ONE MORE DAY

Monday, July 22, 1974, San Francisco

After the police had departed, Nan came back into the study.

"Bert called while you were meeting with the police," Nan said in an even tone. "They are not going to release your father today . . . I'm sorry."

Astrid sighed heavily. Tears dribbled down her cheeks. Her mouth was partially open. She was speechless.

Andrés put his arm around her. She leaned into him.

"It'll be all right," he tried to assure her. "Why don't you go lie down for a while? We can go to the hospital later on."

Astrid's head nodded weakly as Nan picked up the remaining dishes.

ത

It was too early to have lunch and Campos and Leong were still full from the morning snack. There was the smell of stale cigarettes and vomit as they entered the police station. A dozen pink telephone messages were impaled on a metal holder awaiting them. They sat at their desks drinking brown dishwater brew disguised as coffee.

"Hey, Leland, check this out. Another restaurant burned down last night," Campos held up a new incident report that was lying in his in-box.

"Let me guess, partner," Leong mocked. "It was on

Broadway and the place has been near bankruptcy for the last three months."

"Damn, you're good!" they both laughed. "Let's see what the arson team finds out."

David Campos had served in the Marines and had gone to college on the G.I. Bill. He had majored in Criminal Justice and Forensic Science at San Jose State. He had been a detective for five years. He believed that most criminals were not evil, just weak or stupid.

His partner, Leland Leong, had been raised in the Inner Sunset District of San Francisco. As a youth, he was involved in a neighborhood gang until he was caught for stealing cigarettes. His parents did not speak to him for an entire year because of the shame that he had brought upon the family. Eventually, he straightened out and went on to earn his college degree at Berkeley. Both detectives were married and had children. They had many things in common, especially their hatred for politicians and used car sales persons.

"Hey, Leland, didn't you take some language classes at Cal?"

"Yeah, but I don't remember anything except the cuss words."

"What did you think of the books that the Schmidt girl showed us?"

"They were books about the Nazi concentration camps. They reminded me of the stories that my parents told us when we were little. The ones about the Japanese invading China and subjecting them to torture and other inhuman acts."

There was a pregnant silence.

"Hey, do you have the lab report on the Boehner case?"

Leong handed him the buff-colored manila envelope. Campos used his rusty letter opener and pulled out the information.

About a quarter of an hour later, Campos disrupted the serenity.

"Hey, Leland, this says that Boehner had a blue green swastika tattooed on his left arm."

"Okay, so Boehner was probably a charter member of the Aryan Brotherhood. He worked for the Schmidts," Leong stroked his chin. "Hmm, the vic we found hung may have been involved in some anti-Nazi activities, at least according to the boy friend. I think that's what the Andrés kid was trying to say. Nuremberg? I'm not getting the connection. If you believe the dorky boy friend, Boehner was somehow involved also. What are we not getting?"

"Crap!" Campos suddenly exclaimed and went around to Leland's desk and pointed to the toxicology report. "Boehner was killed by a lethal injection. The note here says it is very quick acting and normally difficult to trace."

"So it was not a beating or mugging," Leland's hand moved to rub the back of his stiff neck.

"That's not all. Check out the notation," he leaned over Leong's back. "This type of lethal injection is the pet drug of the Mossad." *Crap! How were the Israelis involved*, he wondered.

捣

After the inquisition by the detectives, Astrid had gone to the hospital. Andrés went back into the Schmidt library. He was looking for history books, especially those focused on World War II. Most of the ones that he found were in German or Spanish. He picked up a large book that had tons of illustrations. He looked mostly at the photographs, but could not find any more double angel tattoos. There were some things about post war trials in Nuremberg, but he couldn't understand them. He pushed the book aside. He would show it to Astrid later on.

"I brought you some sandwiches," Nan put down a tray of small open-faced ham and cheese on ryes, baby dill pickles, barbequed potato chips, and a soda.

He thanked her. He could definitely live here. This was the life. He looked around the library. The old books. The beautiful paintings. There was even a vase of yellowish white freesia, purple lilacs, and pinkish hydrangea. Unconsciously, he inhaled the floral perfumes. *These flowers probably cost more than I make in a week,* he pondered.

Astrid came home earlier than expected.

"Father is ready to come home," she smiled at Andrés. "He says that he will walk home tomorrow if he has to."

They talked about his condition and what needed to be done in the upcoming weeks to restore him.

"I am afraid that he is not going to get around much without his cane or his wheelchair," she shared. "He hates his wheelchair. He doesn't want to be an invalid."

They had a moderate dinner of a green bean salad, chicken Kiev, and roasted potatoes. The wine was a nice Russian River chardonnay.

After the dessert of cherries and vanilla ice cream, they retired to the library. Andrés showed her the book that he had been studying earlier in the day.

"I am sorry that I didn't tell you about the books with the angel tattoos last night," she was hesitant in her tone.

"No problema."

"What type of monsters could do such things to other human beings?"

She picked up the book that Andrés had found and read it. She explained the Nuremberg trials to Andrés.

"I think they made a flick about it a long time ago. I was too young to remember it," he said. "We need to go to the movies. This last week has been so stressful."

"Sure. That would be nice."

Nan entered the room making sure that she made enough noise, just in case. She asked if they wanted something else.

Surprisingly, Astrid blurted out, "We'll have two Baileys with ice."

Andrés had no idea what she ordered.

"Did you say that you talked to your aunt this morning?"

Astrid told him about the tenuous political climate in Chile at the moment. Andrés remembered that he had experienced some unusual events when he was down there. He didn't realize how much undue influence ITT (International Telephone & Telegraph) and the CIA had over Chilean politics and the economy. The word down in Chile was that the U.S. government had supported the military *coup d'état* and the assassination of President Salvador Allende.

Nan returned with the drinks.

"Oh, man, this is totally awesome. It's like a milkshake." Andrés was oblivious that this was an alcoholic drink and that Astrid was under age.

Nan had left the bottle of Bailey's and an ice bucket with them before she departed.

"Do you have other relatives down in Chile?"

"The only one left is my aunt Matilda. There were only two girls. A few cousins, but everyone else has passed."

"How come there are no photos of your family around here?" he asked.

"Father does not allow them. He took the death of my mother very hard," she poured them a second drink. "Do you want to see a photo of my mother?"

"That would be awesome."

"Okay. Let's go," she grabbed his empty hand and they proceeded to walk upstairs to her bedroom.

Andrés felt a little strange as he entered. He knew that he shouldn't be there alone with her. She patted the bed and motioned for him to sit. He didn't trust her. She pulled a photo of a fair-skinned young woman with straight black hair dressed in the fashion of the day. He really didn't trust himself.

"What was your mother's name?"

"Carmen Grossman. Her father was German and her mother was Chilean."

"Who was older, your mom or your aunt?"

Astrid started to choke. Andrés let her sip the rest of his drink.

"Andrés, hold me. Hold me tight."

"Astrid, I probably shouldn't be here right now."

She kissed him softly on the mouth. He reciprocated.

"Astrid . . . Astrid . . . but I promised your father."

"Don't worry. I'm not going to tell."

She rose from the bed, locked her door, and turned off the light.

"Astrid, I can't."

"Oh, yes, you can."

"Your father is coming home tomorrow!"

"That's why it has to be tonight."

He groaned as she touched him. "Oh, my God!"

CHAPTER 41

GONE

Tuesday Morning, July 23, 1974, San Francisco

The sunlight shone through the bedroom window. Andrés had to go to the bathroom. He tried to roll out of bed to his right, but there was a half-naked body blocking him.

Oh, man! I screwed up! Andrés lamented. His head ached. He jumped out of bed from the other side and sneaked out of the bedroom without using the bathroom. He silently tiptoed down the hallway to the guest room where he was staying during this interim period at the Schmidt house.

He took a quick shower and was debating on whether to go back to his apartment or wait for Schmidt to return from the hospital.

It was already eight o'clock when he finally walked down the stairs.

"Andrés," Nan looked at him with hawkish eyes. "I have a cup of coffee ready for you at the breakfast table."

He feebly muttered thanks.

"You look a little tired this morning," she glibly observed. "Bert has already left for the hospital to pick up Mister Schmidt."

❦

"We gave you an extra day," shouted the gruff voice over the phone. "Did you get anything out of him?"

"Unfortunately not," the voice hesitated. "We even tried

the Soviet SP-117 drugs. That didn't even work."

"We are paying you a lot of f__king money to get us that information. You haven't given us squat."

"Don't worry. You'll get the information."

"And if you don't?"

"We will. We have their phones tapped. We are thinking of snatching the daughter."

"Oh, this is just great! We don't want the f__king FBI involved! Damn it! Don't f__k this up!"

The ire sizzled throughout the office. Neumann and his cohorts cringed at the ranting and raving.

"We have recruited some former Stasi agents," Neumann offered. "They know how to get results."

"We don't give a damn what you are doing! You are being paid for important intel vital to our government. Just get the f__king report! By Friday, do you hear?"

The clang of the phone hanging up at the other end startled the listeners.

Neumann's aide pressed the speakerphone off and asked. "Who are the Stasi?"

"They are the former secret service police of East Germany. They are bad asses," barked Neumann at his secretary. "Get a hold of Vera and Tanya."

"What should I tell them?"

"That I have a lucrative assignment for them. A $25,000 contract each, if they get results by Thursday."

ভ

"I'm really sorry about last night," Andrés whispered.

He and Astrid were alone in the study. They had not conversed much when she had joined him earlier for breakfast. He had kept looking askance at her. Andrés had trouble eating the scrabbled eggs with goat cheese and sundried tomatoes.

"I'm not," Astrid retorted. "Don't worry about it."

"But I promised your father!"

"I'm a big girl now. I can make my own decisions."

"But he might find out. I could lose . . ." He wanted to say "my job" but restrained himself.

"I'm not going to tell," she stared into his eyes and then kissed him on the cheek.

"Well, I couldn't be the only virgin going to Mills, could I?"

Andrés was now feeling even worse because he had deflowered his patron's daughter in a direct breach of his vow.

"Promise me this," the young man said in a panicky tone. "Promise me that you won't tell anyone."

"Okay. I promise," then a mischievous grin appeared on her face, "except my girl friends back home."

❀

He had raced to his apartment after his encounter with Astrid. Sweat was seeping from his pores. Andrés had to escape from the Schmidt house. *What kind of game was that girl playing?* He passed a bald, ruddy-faced man walking his two yelping terriers. The air smelled of burning garbage. *I'm such a frigging idiot!*

After retrieving his mail, he flew into his apartment, almost tripping over his old bike that had a flat tire, and immediately crawled into bed. The house was cold and started to reek of mold because the heat had not been turned on. He pulled the Pendleton blanket over his head and fell asleep.

❀

Early that morning the green Mercedes slowly pulled into the back of the parking lot of Stern Grove. There were only a few cars around. An old white Chevy van flicked its headlights on and off. Bert pulled the limo up next to it.

There was very little conversation between Bert and the woman as they transferred Schmidt into the van. The big black dog looked on.

Just an hour earlier, Schmidt had finally been discharged from the hospital after signing a stack of papers that he was oblivious to. Bert had helped dress him. Schmidt had lost weight during his hospital stay. A nurse had settled him into a wheel chair and waited for Bert to pull the limo up to the passenger loading and unloading zone. Bert helped Schmidt get seated into the back of the limo as the aide left.

"Here drink this," Bert handed his passenger some orange juice.

Moments later Schmidt was unconscious from the spiked libation.

At this moment the woman was giving Bert final instructions. "Let's walk over here." They found themselves in a densely wooded area.

She pulled out a 9mm luger pistol from her leather handbag.

"Get down on your knees," she commanded.

"Please, don't do this!" he pleaded.

Whoosh! The pistol cracked him in the back of the head.

"G__ damn it! That hurt!" his hand found warm blood.

"We have to make the attack on you and the abduction realistic," she said in a patronizing tone. "If you hadn't acted so impetuously with Boehner, this would not have been necessary."

଼

Andrés was lying on his bed taking notes on the Neruda books. He had his funky pillow propped underneath his bearded chin. He had opened up a window slightly to air out the place and had lit some scented candles to get rid of the stale odors.

The phone rang and he picked up.

"Andrés, are you coming over tonight?" the voice seemed to be shaken.

"Sure. What time is it?"

"It's past six."

"Oh, man, I didn't realize it was so late. Sorry, chickie-poo."

"Andrés, my father hasn't come home yet."

"Maybe he's caught up in paper work. You know how bureaucratic hospitals can get."

"I called the hospital. He checked out just after ten this morning," she said nervously. "I'm worried."

"I'll be right over."

"And Bert is not back."

CHAPTER 42

ANOTHER ABDUCTION

Tuesday Evening, July 23, 1974, San Francisco

Astrid pushed the food on her plate around with her fork. She could not eat her dinner. Her eyes were swollen sockets. Andrés tactfully tried to cheer her up without any success.

"I think that God is punishing me," the white sleeve of her blouse was wet with black mascara, "for the sin I committed last night."

Oh, man! What a bummer! For sure, she is going to rat me out to her father. I'm going to be screwed!

Even Nan seemed worried, which was not her custom. Andrés suggested that if Schmidt and Bert were not home by nine o'clock, they should call the police. The other two seemed to agree.

○ℰ

Per prior arrangement, Bert had called Nan at eleven o'clock that Tuesday morning.

"Schmidt residence."

"Nan, this is Bert," he recited by memory the script of the conspiracy. "Is Mister Schmidt there, by chance?"

"No, he's supposed to be with you," she replied dryly. "What? He's not with you?"

"No, Mister Schmidt has been kidnapped. Somebody knocked me out."

"Did you report this to the police?"

"I'm coming home right now to call them. My head is killing me. I can't see straight."

"Shall I tell Astrid?"

"Not until I'm home."

"Do you want me to call a doctor?"

"No, I'll be all right. See you soon."

Nan heard the click as Bert hung up the phone. A second soft click sounded just as she returned the receiver back to the cradle.

Now, it was past nine thirty in the evening and Bert still had not arrived. Nan was wondering what had gone wrong. She couldn't tell Astrid. That might disrupt the plan.

She was relieved when Andrés finally called Detective Campos.

☙

"Leland, that young kid Miramón called," the detective was unrolling his shirtsleeves and pulling off his tie.

"What's up now?" Leong asked impatiently.

"He says that Schmidt didn't come home from the hospital," putting on his sports coat. "He says that Schmidt and the valet left the hospital at ten this morning."

"That's strange," Leland started to straighten out his desk and put away some files. "What did you tell him?"

"The usual. To wait 24 hours and then file a missing person's report."

"Sounds good to me. Let's get the hell out of here." He went over to the stained coffee maker and turned it off.

"Anything on Kulongoski?"

"Not yet."

☙

Bert had driven slowly back to the Schmidt home after the transfer that morning in Stern Grove. Everything seemed to be going according to plan. Bert would report the attack and the abduction to the local police who would be looking for a gang of kidnappers. His cohort did not tell him what she was going to do with Schmidt. Bert had no regret for killing Boehner. He nonchalantly accepted the rebuke for the death. One less savage in the world.

It started to sprinkle as he entered the Presidio. He turned on the windshield wipers but they only streaked his windshield.

Bert was less than a quarter of a mile from the house, when he saw a blue Chevy sedan with Nevada license plates parked along the side of the road. It had its emergency blinkers on. A woman wearing a black leather jacket and tight jeans stood next to the car. She seemed to be looking at a large map. He slowed down.

More out-of-towners lost in the Presidio. This was a common occurrence. She had shoulder length raven black hair with trimmed bangs. He saw another woman, a shorthaired blonde, who came around the back of the car and flagged him down.

I just want to get home, he thought. *My f__king head is killing me.*

Against his better judgment, he stopped the limousine behind the Chevy. The dark haired lady waved and started walking toward him with the map dangling from her right hand. She looked attractive in a masculine sort of way. She was built like a serious athlete. He rolled down his window.

"Are you lost?" he yelled out at her.

"Yes," said the husky voice approaching the driver's side.

"We are looking for buried treasure," she laughed. "Actually, we want Schmidt."

"What . . ." he was about to hit the accelerator when he

felt the hot pains in his right leg. The blonde had sneaked over to the passenger side, quickly opened the door, and shot him twice with her silenced Mauser.

"Who . . ." he weakly blurted out before he fainted from shock.

The two women opened the driver's door and dragged him out of the Mercedes toward the back of their car leaving a trail of blood. The blonde popped open the trunk of the Chevy. They grabbed a blanket, wrapped it around him, and threw him in the trunk.

They jumped into the sedan and sped away.

ᘓ

Neumann pushed the speakerphone function and dialed the number.

"Have you got the information yet?" demanded the irritated recipient of the call.

"No, not yet," replied Neumann obsequiously. "It's just a matter of time."

"Time that we don't have. And neither do you if you don't want to be deported back to Chile. We're sure that Pinochet would like to have a little chat with you and your company."

"Now, wait, let's not get hasty," protested the silver-haired Neumann who was sweating bullets. "Were you the ones who kidnapped Schmidt today?"

"What the f__k are you talking about? You said that you had some Stasi agents going to kidnap the daughter." The phone seemed to be glowing red.

"Don't worry. We have Schmidt's valet," Neumann tried to pretend that he was not frightened. "We will persuade him to tell us where Schmidt is."

"Unbelievable! F__king unbelievable!"

"This gives us a great cover when we find Schmidt. He

has already been kidnapped," there was a feigned laugh. "The daughter will probably call the police tonight."

"You better have our information by Friday, or by God, you'll pay the price. Do you understand?"

❧

"Andrés, I just called my aunt and told her what happened."

Andrés became unnerved. Had she confessed to the aunt about their romantic encounter?

"She is trying to catch a flight back here tomorrow."

He would have to be a man and face the consequences of his actions.

Astrid was feeling better. Nan had brought her some chamomile tea with some little cucumber and cream cheese sandwiches that she had readily eaten.

Andrés tried to discuss esoteric things so that she would be distracted. Andrés talked about his aunt and uncle in Texas. He mentioned wanting a pet cat, but unfortunately, he was allergic to the feline hair.

"Astrid, tell me about your mother."

"What do you want to know?"

"Was she a twin?"

"How did you know?"

"I didn't really," he pondered how to diplomatically ask the next question. "I was just wondering why you don't resemble your aunt."

"What do you mean?"

"Were they identical twins?"

"Why, yes," there was more than a hint of curiosity in her responses.

"Haven't you ever thought it was strange that your physical features are not the same as your aunt's?"

"Like what?"

"Your hair is reddish, hers is black. Your skin is olive. She is fair-skinned. Your eyes are green, hers are brown."

"That doesn't mean anything."

"You really don't even resemble your father."

"What are you saying?" her voice started to get huffy.

"I don't know what I'm saying," he tried to backtrack. "I'm just trying to connect the dots."

"What dots?"

He had to explain the idiom to her and eventually she calmed down.

"Your mom's name was Carmen Grossman, correct?"

"Yes."

"May I ask a favor of you?"

"Okay," her forehead crinkled. "What is it?"

"We need to make a long distance call to Chile."

"Are you serious?"

"Yes."

"When?"

"Right now. We need to check something out."

CHAPTER 43

WE'RE BACK

Wednesday, July 24, 1974, San Francisco

Astrid tossed and turned. She was unable to sleep most of the night. She was awakened by a call from her aunt who told her that she was catching her flight in thirty minutes. Aunt Matilda asked if Bert could pick her up at the airport. Astrid lamented that Bert had not returned home the night before either.

"Don't worry, child," the voice took control. "I will be home soon. Just pray."

God is punishing me! She sulked.

 catch

It was slightly before dawn when the Presidio security service pickup truck noticed a car parked on the narrow road blocking part of the street. The security officer turned on his Kel-lite and walked over to the rear passenger side of the limousine. He shined the light inside the backseat and did not see anything. He approached the front passenger side. He could hear the crickets singing to one another. It was not unusual to find young teenage couples making out anyplace in the Presidio. But this was not the case.

There seemed to be some dark stains on the tan leather front seats, but he couldn't be sure. He noticed that the car keys were still in the ignition.

He went around the back of the Mercedes and went up

to the front driver's side. He noticed some small pools of dark liquid. For the most part they looked dry. He was careful not to step on them as he peered inside the car. The patrolman stopped and put the flashlight between his knees as he put on his gloves. He carefully opened the driver's door. There were dark cherry color stains on the seat.

"This is car 31. Have a 10-37. Come in . . ."

ജ

The incident report was bounced to the night watch commander who was going off duty in less than thirty minutes. He did not want to deal with a suspicious car report that would take all morning to complete. He immediately called the security person directly and told him to secure the area, and also to wait for the city police whom he was going to call before going home. After calling the local law enforcement office, he put in a courtesy call to the liaison officers Polk and Campbell whom he thought would be coming in later that morning. He left the office ready to go home and get some sleep.

ജ

A blinding light was spinning over his head. There was a voice yelling at him, but he couldn't hear it.

Electric shocks emanating from his genital area caused convulsions throughout Bert's body.

"You are going to die anyway, you shit-stinking pig," the former East German swimming champion warned. "You're not going to need this part of your body every again. Tell us now and I will make your death quick."

He moaned in agony.

The grey walls closed in on him. Bert was strapped to a medical bed. There was an intravenous drip line that fed into his left wrist. The leg with the bullet wounds was bandaged up, but blood was seeping through.

His head slumped over. There was no sound.

"Wake up, you wimpy eunuch," the blonde injected another dose of methamphetamine into his right arm. "Stay with me you piece of crap!"

ℭ

Leong and a brunette woman dressed in an emerald green pantsuit interrogated Nan in the library. Nan had told the officers that Bert had called the previous morning and said that he had been beaten up and that Schmidt had been kidnapped.

She was very impassive while the police officer was asking her questions. She did not want to volunteer too much information for fear of undermining the clandestine mission that she was a part of.

The background information on Bert that she provided the two investigators had been prepackaged to minimize suspicion.

At the same time in the study, Astrid was sobbing and begging Campos to go find her father. Andrés was not allowed to be with any of them. He was left sitting at the dining room table.

The doorbell rang. There was no one to answer it. Andrés finally went over and opened the front door when he heard some heavy pounding.

Two muscular men in tight fitting dark suits pushed their way in without being invited.

"Hey, who are you?" yelled Andrés in an intimidated voice.

"Where are the cops?" the taller one demanded.

"And I said who are you?" the youngster was trying to be brave.

"We're in charge of the Schmidt kidnapping," said the other suit. "Now where are they?"

"Okay, man. I'll get them. Just chill."

Andrés left the two in the entryway and walked to the study door. He knocked. Someone inside yelled something and he entered.

Minutes later Campos came out and told Andrés to get Leong.

Campos sauntered slowly to the foyer.

"Good morning, gentleman," he greeted them. "I hear you want to see us."

"Yeah, we're taking over the kidnapping investigation now," said the junior partner.

"Let's see if my memory is working," Campos was facing the two. "You are Campbell and you are Polk. Is that correct?

"Yeah, and we are taking over the case," Campbell informed the detective.

"You know, I must have misunderstood you the first time we met," retorted Campos. "I thought you told me that you were U.S. Park Police."

"We are," said Polk in a cavalier tone.

"Well, it seems that you also work for the Department of Defense," countered the policeman.

Leong emerged from the library with the woman investigator, Nan, and Andrés. Leong rushed over to his partner's side.

"So what?" smirked Polk. "So now we have jurisdiction on the kidnapping and we need you to back off."

"Why's that?" asked Campos in a seemingly ingenuous tone. "It's my understanding that if there is a kidnapping it belongs to the local jurisdiction."

"Why?" Polk was getting haughty and gesticulating.

"Because of 18 USC 1201. Because Schmidt is working here as an international consultant for Sellarebu with us. You should know that by now."

"Who's 'us'?"

Polk hesitated for a moment. "That's classified," he now appeared smug.

"Unfortunately, no one has officially reported that Schmidt was kidnapped," Campos was playing a gutsy game of chess with the DOD agents. "Have you received a ransom demand?"

"It doesn't matter. Bert Reynolds, the valet, was kidnapped," rebutted Campbell. "And he is an employee of the Presidio."

"And the Mercedes was found on Presidio grounds," augmented Polk.

"I'm sorry to inform you gentleman," said the detective, "as far as Mister Reynolds is concerned, all we may have here is a missing person."

"But we were told there was blood," said Polk with a reddened face.

"Ah, yes, our crime people are investigating to determine whose blood it is," Campos smiled. "We should know within a few days."

"You can't do this!" expressed Campbell in a hostile manner.

"If we need to make nice with the feds, we have Grace O'Malley of the FBI working here with us," pointing to the professionally dressed woman with bulky piano legs standing next to Nan and Andrés who had been observing the contest. "If you have objections, you can contact her boss, Director Kelley."

൦൮

"Bert, I feel bad that she has been hurting you," the black haired woman said softly to the bloody lump of flesh flopped on the bed. "It doesn't have to be this way. We already know who you work for."

The two Stasi women had been alternating being with Bert for the last twelve hours. Tanya would torture him until he passed out and then revive him with methamphetamines. Vera would give him two or three oxycodones to relieve the pain and try to placate him with promises of freedom.

During the course of the tortures, Vera had discovered a black and white double angel tattoo on Bert's left upper arm and blue-green numbers on his forearm. As former Stasi agents, they knew that he had been imprisoned in a Nazi concentration camp.

"The JDL [Jewish Defense League] really doesn't care about you at all," she wiped the sweat and blood from his brow with a hand towel. "Even the Jewey Defense knows that you're all expendable," she hissed.

೦೩

"Hey, Kemo Sabe, how did they find out about Schmidt and Bert?" Leong lingered over a cup of bitter coffee in the office.

"Don't know. Probably, a coincidence," Campos winked. "Anything yet on Kulongoski?"

"Yeah, the report was sitting on my desk this morning."

CHAPTER 44

THE HOSPITAL

Wednesday, July 24, 1974, San Francisco

"This is a really a bad trip," Andrés was shaking his head after the police left. "What a bummer! I think we need to do something about it. We need to help find your father."

"What can we do?" Astrid responded with a quizzical look on her face.

"I don't know," His hands went to the top of his head. "Do you want to walk to the hospital?"

"What are we looking for there?"

"I don't know. But, I think it wouldn't hurt to check some things out. This sucks!"

It took them over a half hour to walk to Letterman Hospital. They went up to the private hospital room where Schmidt had been during his stay. The halls smelled of Pinesol and were filled with abandoned wheel chairs, patients ambling with their walkers with hanging saline solution bags, and visitors carrying flowers and stuffed animals. The pair talked to one of the nurses who had not been on duty when Astrid's father had been discharged. The attending physician was nowhere to be found.

"Now where, Andrés?"

"I don't know. You told me that your father worked here at the hospital, right?"

"Yes, but I don't know where exactly. Erik and Bert were

the ones who used to drive him over here."

"Let's try the Administration office or the Personnel office."

After studying the hospital directory, they took the elevator up two floors and walked to another wing.

There was a little old lady with grey wavy hair and Eve Arden glasses who was the receptionist to the Administration office. Her small mouth exhibited sharp yellowish teeth. She sent them to another wing. Andrés had stolen a few chocolate kisses from her candy jar.

The Personnel office was located in the opposite direction from where they had exited the elevator earlier. They were instructed to wait. Astrid picked up a People's magazine and started to read an article about Rock Hudson and Carol Burnett. A balding man with a scraggly beard dressed in a white smock with a blue and gold striped tie approached them.

"I'm Donald Tabard. How can I help you?"

"We're looking for my father," Astrid started. "Johann Schmidt. He's a doctor here."

"Do you know in which department?" he asked politely.

"Pharmacology," she admonished herself for not knowing exactly where her father worked. "He is with Sellarebu Pharmaceutical Laboratories."

"I'll check. It'll take me a minute."

Andrés had left to use the restroom. When he returned, Donald Tabard was telling Astrid that he couldn't find the name in the directory.

"But it has to be here somewhere," she insisted. "He works with a Mr. Neumann."

"Sorry, don't know him either," he retorted indifferently.

Disheartened they went to the cafeteria in the basement.

They ordered cold drinks and Andrés grabbed a honey bran muffin which the two shared, 80-20. They talked about what they would say to Aunt Matilda. Astrid was afraid that she might be sent back to Santiago.

"Wait here for a sec," Andrés jumped out of the plastic chair wiping his mouth with a white paper napkin.

Astrid observed him walk over to a table where three African-American staff in tan smocks were laughing in the corner.

"Excuse me, friends," Andrés interjected breaking up the ongoing conversation, "I need to ask you a question."

The three men were surprised, but nodded that they were cool.

"Weren't you one of the helpers who used to bring meals to Mister Schmidt?" Andrés directed his inquiry to a caramel-skinned individual. Andrés thought that he had remembered the man's brownish Afro.

"That would be me, young fella," he gave Andrés a million dollar smile.

"We're trying to find him," Andrés explained. "He was discharged yesterday."

"That sounds about right," the meal orderly remarked. "I haven't seen him for a few days."

"Did you see who used to visit him?"

"Let's see now," his eyes looked up to the left. "Let's see if I can remember. There was you and your cute little lady friend sitting over at the table back there. For a while there was a dude who looked liked a bodyguard. Haven't seen him in awhile. There was his doctor, the nurses, and the rest of the medical staff. And let's see. There was also a short guy who looked like some type of valet or driver."

"Anyone else?"

"One night when I was picking up the patient's food tray, there was an older guy hassling him. It was none of my business, so I didn't pay much attention."

"What did this person look like?"

"About your height. A lot heavier. They were arguing so I pretended not to notice," he pulled his right ear. "And I think this guy wore a monocle, one of those single lens things. My grand uncle used to have one. My uncle Jeremiah."

"Do you know where the research facilities are here?" Andrés continued.

"Over the years, they have closed most of the research facilities here at the hospital. They're crying no money," he put his hands behind his head and yawned. "Others just moved to the lab behind the hospital."

Moments later Andrés related the fruits of his questioning to Astrid.

"I think the person with the *monóculo* is Neumann, my father's business partner."

"Do you want to check it out?" said Andrés already yanking her arm toward the back door exit not giving her an opportunity to decline.

The building behind Letterman Hospital had a bunker design with narrow slits. Four uniformed soldiers guarded the front door. Nonchalantly, Astrid and Andrés walked into the double glass doors to the receptionist.

"Yes, may I help you?"

"We are looking for my father," she responded to the request. "Johann Schmidt."

"I don't know if he is in today," the receptionist said haughtily. "He doesn't come in everyday. I haven't seen him for a while."

"May we go to my father's office?"

"Sorry, you don't have security clearance to do so."

The two were puzzled. They decided to give up for the day.

"I did see Sellarebu Pharmaceutical Laboratories on their directory," Astrid mentioned to Andrés. "What do you want to do now?"

"I don't know."

Astrid's head started to fall forward and her face contorted. Andrés thought she was going to break down. He knew that she felt powerless.

"Hey, brat, we need to kick back and chill." Then an idea crossed his mind. "Let's jet over to the movies." He knew it would be awhile before they heard back from the detectives.

From the lobby of the theatre, Andrés called Campos and related to him what little they had found out. The detective thanked them for the information.

♋

"Well, so far we know that the valet drugged Schmidt and handed him over to an old lady who drove a white van."

"Are you serious?" Neumann tapped his fingers impatiently on his desk. "Do we know why?"

"We think it has something to do with their ties to Germany," Vera opined. She mentioned the six numbers tattooed on the inside of his Bert's forearm.

"Was he Jewish?"

"Don't think so," Vera mused with a smile. "He wasn't circumcised. That is, until we got to him.

Vera and Tanya grinned evilly as Neumann stared at his provocateurs.

"Do we know anything else about him or this lady?"

"We think that the valet was some type of foreign agent," Tanya contributed. "We have to assume that this old lady works for the same organization. Her name may be something that sounds like Sandrine. We are checking with our contacts."

Neumann was interrupted by a phone call in his office. The two Stasi women lit up cigarettes. When he finally got off the phone, he was in a foul mood.

"What did you do with his body?"

Tanya replied innocently, "He smelled like shit. So we gave him a bath."

"An acid bath," cackled Vera.

Neumann turned his head. He knew they were without equal in obtaining vital information, but working with sadomasochists was not his favorite pastime.

"Do we know where the old lady took Schmidt?"

"It couldn't be far," suggested Tanya.

"And why is that?"

"First, we haven't heard anything about it in the intel circuits," pondered Tanya. "If the old lady is acting alone, it is unlikely that she could move Schmidt around easily. It makes more sense that someone else will be picking up our man. Some group like the JDL or Justice International."

"If that's the case, we have a day or two at the most," contemplated Neumann.

"Oh, there was one other thing that we discovered."

"What's that?" solicited Neumann.

"On his arm, there was a black and white double angel tattoo."

CHAPTER 45

A HUNK OF BURNING LOVE

Thursday, July 25, 1974, San Francisco

The phone rang at the headquarters of the Anti-Defamation League in New York City.

"Hey, Fats," yelled the middle aged bald man with palsy. "It's for you."

"Sasha, stop calling me that," threatened the petite ebony-skinned woman "or my foot is going to invade one of your orifices."

Fátima Luzzatto had been raised by her mother in Brooklyn. She was tough as nails. In her junior year of high school she went to the prom with a senior who tried to put the moves on her at his cousin's apartment. When he failed to stop, she bit part of his ear off. The boy's father was a local rabbi who was unaware that his son was dating. The father brought criminal charges against the girl. In order to avoid prosecution, she enlisted in the U.S. Marines where she served for four years. The son was sent to work at a kibbutz in Israel.

"*Ciao, bella,*" the detective was reflecting on the passionate fling the two had had at a joint FBI/local police training in Chicago in 1966 before he was married. "This is David Campos."

"Why you sack of crap!" she greeted him in a brown sugary tone. "You finally call me after all this time. How is my Latin lover?"

She was drop-dead gorgeous and had always been pursued by dozens of men. Her mother had been a slave in Axum, Ethiopia, until Fátima's father rescued her. He was part of the Italian invasion of Abyssinia in 1935. The poor soldier was bewitched by this queen of Sheba and brought her back to Napoli. Her parents later emigrated to Brooklyn with the one-year old Fátima in 1946. Her father died a year later.

"Fine," David smiled to himself. "Still fighting the battle between good and evil."

They made small talk about what was happening in their personal lives. She had been unable to continue in the law enforcement field because of her diabetes. At the moment Fátima was ignoring her co-workers when they tried to interrupt her with other phone calls.

"Okay, you love monster," she was tapping a pen on her desk. "What the hell do you want? You didn't call me up for a quickie."

The detective asked her if she had any information on a George Kulongoski or if she knew what the significance of the double angel tattoos was.

"I don't know. I have a source here at the JDL I can ask," she started to say softly. "*Yeb vas,* Sasha! I'm still on the phone, asshole!"

"Thanks, cara," he sighed exasperatedly.

"You owe me, stud muffin," Fátima teased. "Next time you're in town, I'm going to make you moan and groan until you call 'mama'. I'm gonna set you on fire."

There was brief silence at his end of the line.

"Just kidding!" she jumped back in.

Campos pondered whether or not she was really joking.

ଔ

Aunt Matilda had been sitting at the breakfast table since early morning. Her eyes were bloodshot and it appeared that she had not changed her clothes from the day before.

Nan had prepared a light breakfast for Matilda while they waited for the youngsters to wake up.

"Do want anything else, madam?" Nan picked up the soft-boiled eggcup and toast plate.

"No, thank you," Matilda replied mechanically. Her airplane connection from Miami had been delayed several hours due to a light rain in the Bay area. The taxi from the airport had arrived only a few hours before.

"If you want to rest or bathe, I can call you when they come down."

"Thank you, but no."

Matilda had been trying to sort out the events that had occurred during her absence. She was perplexed about why her brother-in-law had been abducted and his valet was missing.

About a quarter to eight, Astrid and Andrés hurried down the stairs and joined Doña Matilda. There was a big hug with matching tears between the women. There was even a little warmth shared between Matilda and Andrés when he kissed her on the cheek.

"Auntie, we have so much to tell you," exclaimed Astrid.

"Let's wait until after your breakfast," Matilda was once again exercising control.

After the morning meal, the three sat down in the study.

"Firstly, I want you to know how sorry I am for leaving you both in this difficult situation," the aunt was rubbing her hands. She looked intently into their eyes. "I feel awful for not being here. But there were things to be done back in Santiago that seemed important at the time. Now, I'm not so sure."

The two looked on quietly.

"And you, Andrés," she shifted her weight toward him, "Thank you for protecting my niece. *¡Gracias a Dios!* I hope that it hasn't inconvenienced you much."

His face reddened. If she only knew what they had been up to, he would have been drawn and quartered.

"Let's start from the beginning," Matilda started the interrogation.

Andrés took the lead, nervously tapping his heel on the ground, and explained the events that had occurred after Erik, the chauffeur, had been killed just before Matilda had left. Astrid explained that Schmidt might have had a heart attack, but they weren't sure.

"Why were the police involved?" inquired the aunt. She had just finished experiencing the reach of Pinochet in Chile with daily government harassment and was glad to be back in the States. She did not trust the military or the police.

Andrés did not tell her about the murder of Kulongoski. Astrid told her that the police were curious about her father and where he worked.

Astrid excused herself and left the room to go to the bathroom.

Matilda motioned to Andrés with an open palm and offered him more coffee.

"Ma'am, I need to ask you a question," he tried to assert himself. "Are you a twin?"

"Why, yes?" she answered raising her head giving him a surprised look. "Why do you ask?"

"Identical twin?"

"Yes," said Matilda, her pupils dilating. She responded in bewilderment, "How did you know?"

ଔ

Neumann was on the phone talking to a former colleague back in Dresden, Germany.

"The number began with XZ," he reported. "They think the remaining numbers were 8942 or something like that."

Forty minutes later the phone rang. The German collaborator had called back. There was a brief conversation between the contact and Neumann. Finally, he hung up and looked at his cohorts.

"They think that his real name was Hubert Gniewosz," Neumann stroked his chin. "Now we need to find his twin sister."

CHAPTER 46

SHANA MADELA

Thursday, July 25, 1974, San Francisco

Detective Campos was scanning his telephone messages while sipping his second cup of black coffee for the morning. Leong was out of the office conducting an interrogation on a prostitution ring case.

The two had read the report on the death of Kulongoski. There were now more questions than answers. It seemed that a trace of a promethazine truth serum was found in his blood that strongly suggested that someone had tried to extract information from the victim.

His extension rang and he picked up, "Detective Campos."

A deep Eastern European accent slowly began, "Ah, Detective, maybe it is not such a good idea that I should be talking to you. But what can I say? Your shana madela would cause problems if I didn't."

Campos assumed that it was the unofficial call from the Jewish Defense League that he was waiting for. The speaker confirmed that Kulongoski had been working for Justice International, a global group that worked to bring perpetrators of Nazi war crimes to justice. The voice also mentioned that Kulongoski had been part of the prosecution team in the trial against Nazi doctors who conducted experiments on and mutilated concentration camp inmates.

The detective was horrified with the atrocities, but he was uncertain as to how everything was linked together in this case.

"Do you know who Augustin Teufl is?" the detective queried. "And how is he involved in all of this?"

"Maybe you should ask, who doesn't know of him?" the voice answered in a sardonic tone. "He was a material witness against the Nazi doctors. And it seems that he was given some sort of immunity. Can you imagine? It was widely believed that he spearheaded many of the inhumane experiments himself."

"The experiments on twins?"

"Yes. Those too."

"Did they have special tattoos?"

"Yes, double angels."

Campos had two homicides and two possible kidnappings. He had Nazis and neo-Nazis. He had Europeans and Chileans. *What was the common thread?* And then there were those guys from the Department of Defense.

"How do I get back in touch with you if I need more information?

"You don't," the voice asserted. "On the other hand, your khaverte Fátima will make such a big deal. Okay, you win. I will call you back on Monday."

"Thank you."

"Zoy zany mit mazal!" [Good luck!]

ॐ

"¡Madre de Dios! Nan, it seems that we are losing everyone in the household," bemoaned Matilda. "I feel terrible about being absent during this tragic period."

"Yes, madam."

"We no longer have a chauffeur. But, we really don't need

one since the police impounded the limousine," remarked Matilda who was now pacing in the study. "We don't have Bert who attended to Mister Schmidt and did all the little extra duties. Nan, I think we need some extra help around here. Someone to assist in purchasing the groceries and transporting Astrid."

"Excuse, madam, but we don't have another car."

"*¡Ay Dios mio!* You are correct," replied the matron acting surprised. She paused for a moment. "I will secure another."

What am I going to do about my brother-in-law? Doña Matilda was ruminating. She had to admit to herself that she could only pray. And what was wrong with that?

Nan's eyes were scouting the room for tasks that had to be done. She was not really being attentive. She had distractions racing through her head as well.

"I am thinking about asking young Andrés to assume some of these tasks." Doña Matilda had shifted gears. "What do you think, Nan?"

Nan knew how friendly Astrid and Andrés were becoming. But she knew that Astrid was a coddled child who normally got her own way. She also felt sorry for Andrés. She knew that he was struggling and could use the money. He had always treated Nan respectfully.

"I think that your idea has been well thought out," Nan said tactfully.

"Great! Let's see if he can begin tomorrow," Matilda was now in her planning mode waving a pen in hand with her eyes reaching for the chandeliers. "You write down the grocery list. I'll get a car. I still have to pay bills . . ."

附

"Well, have you got the information yet? Do you know where that damn report is?" carped the voice to Neumann.

"You only have until tomorrow."

"Here is what we have so far. Schmidt was kidnapped by his valet. The valet used the alias Bert Reynolds," Neumann was narrating what he and his Stasi associates had accomplished in the short time.

"Okay, I know all that crap," the voice at the other end of the line was ill-tempered. "What about the report and the research?"

"The valet delivered Schmidt to an old woman in a white van in a San Francisco park. He didn't know where Schmidt was being taken."

"Oh, great! That means you imbeciles don't know where he or the f__king research reports are."

"Excuse me," interjected Neumann. "But before we go into name-calling, just remember that the valet was vetted by your Department of Defense boys and was cleared. The valet's real name was Hubert Gniewosz. He was not Jewish. He did not work for the Jewish Defense League. Your boys dropped the ball."

"This is a total ass wipe fiasco," steamed the DOD official. "Heads are going to roll when I find out who screwed up."

"We think that this valet guy may have been working with Justice International, but we're still double checking."

"How in the hell does that get us Schmidt?"

"We have not heard any chatter throughout the network related to Schmidt. We are assuming that if there is a transfer, it will take place within the next few more days."

"I told you that you only have until tomorrow," stated the voice menacingly. "We're ready to send you back to South America first class."

"That won't be necessary. Let's be honest. The United States does not want the world to know its dark and dirty secrets."

"Screw you! You wouldn't be able to pull it off."

"My associates know who you are, where you live, and how often you defecate. They have been working very hard and want to be paid. In fact, I have offered them a bonus," Neumann was playing his poker hand. "I am glad that you have removed the arbitrary deadline. You will have results very shortly."

"Why, you ballsy son of a bitch!"

"Another thing. I want you to do another background check on the Schmidt maid. We think that she might be the valet's sister. Twin sister, if you understand me correctly. I hope your boys didn't screw up there also."

"I can't believe this crap. I'm going to kick some serious ass."

"And remember, don't forget to send us the money," Neumann added. "You have until tomorrow."

CHAPTER 47

THE STABLE

Friday, July 26, 1974, Half Moon Bay

During the early morning a fine mist had drifted in. A foghorn sounded in the distance. The coastal highway down to Half Moon Bay was devoid of much traffic. The hunched-over older lady made her way slowly over the gravel path from the little cottage to the enormous stable out back. The large structure had once been a horse stable for the Peninsula's weekend riders. Now it was largely abandoned, but it still smelled of old hay.

Sandrine was carrying a bucket of water and an old cottage cheese container half-filled with milk. The black lupine dog pranced behind her. She struggled to open the rickety wood door that was about to fall off its hinges.

"*Bleib!*" she commanded her dog to stay. Amen had been trained as a land mine detection military canine. He was injured in an incendiary explosion when he was still a young pup and had to be released from the service. A friend of hers who was a K-9 handler gave him to Sandrine as a companion dog. She renamed the animal "Amen." He was a well-behaved dog that could stare at a rare steak placed in front of him without pouncing upon it. He was her best friend.

The interior of the old wooden stable was lined with six stalls on each side, in various stages of disrepair. The loft overhead in the back was scattered with a potpourri of old farm machinery, broken crates, and dozens of scurrying rats amidst bales of hay.

It was now daybreak and a crumpled figure was rocking slowly back and forth in the third to last stall on the right. An old horse blanket covered the decrepit old man who had his right hand shackled to a post.

She opened the gate to this stall.

"Take off the blanket!" she ordered.

Schmidt kept on rocking. His hair was straggly. He was half-catatonic.

"Your blanket will get wet."

The blanket slipped from his shoulders. He was naked from head to toe, wallowing in his own excrement. The miasma was overwhelming. He pushed the covering away with his grimy feet.

Splash! The water had been flung on him in a split second. He gasped for air. His free arm wiped away the moisture from his face. Droplets dribbled down from the end of his nose. His bloodshot eyes squinted.

"I'm never going to give you the information," he weakly asserted. "You might as well kill me now. I'm not talking."

She ignored him as she had done since the day they had arrived at this Justice International safe house. She barely fed him and only bathed him with buckets of cold water. He had been handcuffed to the stall and was left to foul himself.

Sandrine placed the plastic container of milk within his reach. He strained as he tried to reach it. Finally, using his left foot, he pushed it next to him. He followed his impulse and tried to guzzle down the liquid.

A white stream of liquid was suddenly propelled from his mouth.

"F__king sour milk!"

No exercise. No conversation. Bad food.

She started to leave.

"I have nothing to say to you!" he convulsed in a bewildered tone. "Nothing . . . I said nothing! Do you hear me?"

In the afternoon, Sandrine brought Schmidt two pieces of moldy white bread. The rats were successful in absconding with almost half of the ration, but he didn't care as he gobbled up the morsels.

"I'm still not giving you the information," was his mantra.

And again, she turned around without responding to him and walked out the door. Sandrine was not sure why he kept saying the same thing over and over. She just assumed that he was demented and she really didn't care.

Amen greeted her. His tail wagged happily. She gave him a friendly pat on the head. With only a silent hand signal, she instructed him to go inside the stable. He obeyed and situated himself in the stall opposite that of Schmidt's.

The white van made its way slowly down the Pacific Coast Highway. *How much longer do I have to babysit this pissant? I should just kill him and make everyone happy,* Sandrine thought angrily.

The pier at Half Moon Bay was nearly empty. Most of the fishing crews had gone home. She found a pay phone behind a greasy seafood hangout. Sandrine called her contact at Justice International.

"How are things going?" hastily inquired her section leader back on the East Coast.

"Okay," curtly replied Sandrine. "What did you expect?"

"Just want to make sure that everything is still good."

"Everything is all right. When is the pickup?

"Sunday or Monday."

Sandrine wanted to scream. Everybody had damn bureaucracies.

"We had a complication," continued the section leader.

"And what's that?"

"Our agent, Bert, who turned our target over to you, was kidnapped right after he made the delivery," there was a pause. "We are assuming the worst case scenario."

"That the neo-Nazis got him?"

"Yes."

"And that he is going to talk?"

"Yes," there was no emotion in the response.

"Well, he doesn't have much to tell. His story is that he was mugged and coerced into turning over the target to an old lady in a white van in a public park parking lot."

"At least the transfer was successful."

Sandrine was starting to sign off. "I will call back on Sunday, at 1 o'clock my time."

"That's the plan," the reserved speaker concurred. "By the way, you do know that Jerzy Kulongoski was murdered last week."

It was like a knife had pierced her heart. Sandrine hadn't heard about the tragedy. He had befriended her after the trials and was her initial sponsor into Justice International. *Those bastards! Schmidt was not long for this world!*

CHAPTER 48

THE CON

Friday, July 26, 1974, San Francisco

It had drizzled throughout the morning but Matilda sent Andrés to the store anyway to buy some groceries. Astrid insisted on accompanying him.

The phone rang and Nan picked it up in the hallway.

"Schmidt residence."

"This is a call for Nan Hill please."

"This is she," Nan replied smartly. She rarely received any communications at the Schmidt house.

"Well, hello, Angnieszka," cackled the husky female voice.

"Who is this?" Nan was now perplexed.

"Never mind who this is!" shouted the voice. "Where is Schmidt?"

"I don't know," Nan panicked. "I don't know what you are talking about."

"Listen very closely," sneered the unidentified caller. "We have your brother."

"I don't have a brother."

"Don't lie to us or things will get very bad for Hubert," warned the voice at the other end of the phone. "Do you have a matching tattoo also?"

"What?" Nan could not breathe.

"We know all about you and the camps."

Nan did not know how to respond. She had now been compromised as an agent working with her brother. She had undergone weeks and weeks of training but nothing had prepared her for this. Her forehead was breaking out with beads of perspiration, droplets streamed down her body. This caused her maid's attire to cling to her skin.

"Here's the thing. We want Schmidt. If we don't get him, we will torture your brother. The German concentration camps will seem like a California beach vacation," the caller was deliberate. "Do you understand?"

Nan slowly nodded her head.

"Do you understand?" the voice barked.

"Yes, but I don't know where Schmidt is."

"You better find out or we'll start sending you pieces of your brother through the mail. We might even start with his manhood. We will call you back tomorrow at the same time."

ငဢ

"Aren't you missing class?" Astrid asked, wearing her damp tan raincoat as they pushed the shopping cart around the produce section of the Safeway supermarket in the Marina District.

"Yes, but your aunt asked me last night if I would help out around the house until Mr. Schmidt or Bert come back."

"Andrés, I am very worried," the young girl said with dismay. "What if something terrible has happened to my father and Bert?"

"I know. I'm worried, too," Andrés said shaking his head. He was also thinking about the chauffeur and Kulongoski. *Stuff happens!* "This is a total bummer."

"What else did my aunt say to you?" pressed Astrid. "Are you supposed to be my bodyguard or something?"

"Chill, princess, me a macho bodyguard? No freaking

way!" protested her companion. But after a slight pause, he blurted out, "No, just your babysitter."

She slugged him on his left tricep as hard as she could, "You brat!"

He raced the grocery cart through the fruit section as fast as he could. They both started to giggle in their chase. They needed this release of frustration and tension.

ॐ

"Yes, the maid fell for it," laughed Tanya. "Stupid cow."

"Hey, have you heard from your fed friends about the money?" Vera questioned Neumann. The call had been placed from Neumann's office and he had witnessed the ruse.

"Yes, they are even greedier than we are," Neumann asserted. "Their arrogance and self-righteousness are pathetic."

ॐ

Just minutes before, Nan had hung up the phone. The little mascara that she wore was running. She was hurrying out of the hallway, when she ran into Matilda.

"For heaven's sake, Nan, what is the matter?"

"Nothing, madam," she said as she slipped away to her room.

Nan fell upon the bed and began sobbing. Her face was buried in her pillow. Her gray hair was splayed about. How did they find out that she and her brother "Bert" were secret agents for Justice International? Her brother must have talked! He had probably already been tortured.

Nan, formerly known by her Polish name, "Angnieszka", could still physically feel the pain that she was subjected to after the French had sent her to Auschwitz. The French were collaborators with Nazi Germany in sending Poles, Czechs, Jews, gypsies, homosexuals, and other groups to the concentration camps. She and her twin brother Hubert had identical black and white angel tattoos on their arms along with their exclusive XZ numbers courtesy of their Nazi doctor tormentors. They were subjected to inhumane torture and experimentation. Luckily, they were put back into the general prison population because their medical value had lessened because they were not identical twins.

Nan knew that Bert would tell them everything eventually. Their anti-torture training didn't prepare them to last for more than a few hours. Her brother was not a coward, but she knew that he could not survive another onslaught of suffering. She needed to save him.

There was no phone in her room, only an intercom speaker. She snuck into the library. She knew that Matilda seldom went in there.

Cautiously, Nan called her Justice International contact. No one answered. There was only an answering machine. Nan didn't want to leave a voice message. She hung up. Five minutes later, she called again and met with the same result. Finally, after four attempts, there was a metallic sound and a hoarse voice spoke.

Security codes were exchanged and finally the contact asked, "Why did you call?"

"I need to save my brother. They have him," the anxiety poured out. "They are killing him."

"What do you want us to do? Shut down the entire operation?" there was a cold tone in the questions.

"My brother is one of us. We need to save him."

"Yes, he is one of ours. A valuable agent, but he knew the risks. And so do you."

"Please," Nan pleaded. "Couldn't we give them what they want in exchange for my brother's life?"

"You have to f__king kidding me!" The weeping must

have touched the JI operator. "Shit! I'll kick this upstairs. No promises. Call me back in exactly an hour." The phone was slammed.

⋙

The room smelled of burnt coffee and stale cigarettes. A few uneaten glazed donuts were scattered on the desks throughout the department.

Leong had underlined passages in the Kulongoski file with his thick yellow marker.

"It looks like Kulongoski worked for an organization that pursues war criminals who avoided prosecution, after his stint in the Nuremberg Trials."

"What's the name of this group again?" Campos was scribbling more notes down.

"Justice International," his partner answered. "Gracie has Interpol contacts that have been assisting us."

"That's what I was afraid of," bemoaned Campos bouncing his pen on his desk. "The captain will want to turn the case over to the CIA."

"For all we know, the CIA could be part of this mess."

"Let's ask the captain to hold off a few more days," Campos knew that they were getting close. "We'll tell him that we are working closely with the FBI."

"You mean Gracie?"

Campos winked at him.

⋙

At exactly sixty minutes from the prior conversation, Nan made the call.

"The bosses are not happy with the request," admonished the JI contact, "and especially not with you."

"He's my only living relative!"

"The company has spent a lot of time and money

implementing this project. And you, at the last minute, want to abort the plan."

"The target is an old man now. He is of no worth. He'll die before long."

"Remember the greater mission that you and your brother believe in," lectured the hoarse voice. "That injustice will not be tolerated in this world. So many have already sacrificed their lives for justice."

"What about justice for my brother?"

"Here's what we are willing to do," the tone was matter-of-fact. "We are going to make contact with the agent who has the asset in play. We will ask for a value assessment at this point. As we have said before, we are making no promises. Call us back Sunday morning at 10 o'clock. I hope you know what you are asking."

αβ

"Do we just wait and see what happens now?" said Vera to Neumann after relating to him the gist of the wiretapped phone conversations between Nan and Justice International.

"What if they say no to her?" Neumann whined. "We'll have nothing."

"Not so fast," interjected Tanya. "Judging from the conversation we just heard, we still think that Schmidt is somewhere close."

"Maybe we should kidnap the maid?" proffered the Sellarebu executive.

"It wouldn't do any good," opined Vera. "She doesn't know anything and her brother is already dead."

"Well, how about the daughter?" Tanya smirked.

"Let's think about that," pondered Neumann.

CHAPTER 49

BACKGROUND CHECK

Saturday, July 27, 1974, San Francisco

Andrés enjoyed driving the old Plymouth Valiant that Matilda had procured for the household. Astrid was constantly feeling distraught and did not want to be cooped up in the house. She would make up excuses so that she and Andrés could escape from the house. This day, they drove over to North Beach. They needed some comfort food after all the emotionally charged events that had recently taken place. Astrid had her caffè mocha and he had a macchiato with a chocolate biscotti. The aroma of the coffee beans gave them new energy as if they could absorb the caffeine just by breathing the perfume deeply. Andrés teased her and tried to make her laugh. The old men in the back were still playing their scopa, the popular Italian card game and smoking black tobacco cigarettes.

"Andrés, why would anyone want to kidnap my father?"

"I don't know," he looked puzzled. "Normally, kidnappers are after a wad of dough."

"Dough?"

"Money, honey."

"But we haven't heard from anybody," she whimpered. "Aunt Matilda says that we must pray and be patient."

"Does your father have something valuable that someone might want?"

"Like what?"

"A big old diamond? A Picasso painting?" Andrés was brainstorming a list. "A secret formula for making chocolate that does not melt?"

"How come your thoughts start with your head and end up with your stomach?" she pointed her finger as she accused him.

He glanced at his inexpensive Casio runner's watch. "We better split. Your aunt will get uptight if we are out too long."

As they jaywalked across Columbus Street on the way to their car, someone in a black car with an eagle symbol grill emblem and darkened windows was taking photographs of the pair.

⌓

"Hey, David," his partner yelled out. "This case is taking some crazy turns. It's so strange. I don't know what to make of it."

"Now what?" Detective Campos raised his eyes from the pile of papers stacked in front of him.

"Schmidt did not exist before 1945."

"What do you mean?"

"Grace sent over some Interpol files on Schmidt and Reynolds. They did not exist prior to 1945 for Schmidt and 1946 for Reynolds."

"Crap!" snapped the partner. "This sounds like a WWII spy novel. We probably can safely assume that Schmidt and Reynolds are not their real names."

"Do you think that the DOD knows all about them and has been sandbagging us on these cases?"

"I don't know," pondered Campos. "Something is wrong. Maybe the captain is right and we should dump the case back to the feds."

"We could go out to the Schmidt house and ask a few more questions."

"Sounds good," his stomach was gurgling from all the coffee he had drunk.

"Do you mind if we stop and eat lunch at that little Cuban restaurant in the Haight before we see the folks?"

ଓ

The phone rang and Nan rushed to the coffee table to pick it up.

"Well, Agnieszka," the cold voice asked. "What have you found out?"

"Nothing," she stammered. "But I'm still working on it. Honest."

"It's too late," Tanya had a devilish smile as she goaded Nan. "We are going to send you a piece of your brother. We just haven't decided if it is going to be his hand or his manhood."

"Please don't hurt him!" Nan cried out. "I need more time!"

"There is no more time," was the frigid retort.

"Please!" wailed Nan. "I'll do anything you ask. Anything."

"Anything?" Tanya winked at Vera. "Anything is a big commitment."

"But first I want to talk to my brother before I promise to do anything."

There was derisive laughter at the other end of the line.

"You want what? Just for that, we're going to send you his hand and his shriveled up pouch! You want to make demands?"

"I'm sorry! I'm sorry!" Nan was out of control with her constant sobbing. "I didn't mean it. Please don't hurt him!"

There was a pause. A new voice came on. It was fresh and perky. "Agnieszka, we don't really want to hurt you or your brother, you understand. We just need to find Schmidt. He has something very important that we need. Your brother will not be touched if you keep your word. You'll get to join him, I promise. Will you keep your word no matter what is asked of you?"

Nan turned her body around as she saw Matilda walk by. She struggled to pull herself together.

"Why, yes, you can count on it," Nan said in a pretended tone as Matilda stared at her. "Excuse me, madam, this is the flower shop."

Matilda gave Nan her old nun teacher look, but walked on.

"Very good, Agnieszka, quick thinking," praised the friendly provocateur. "Now let's talk about what we need from you."

☙

After lunch Andrés suggested to Astrid that they go back into her father's library and look for anything that could be important. Astrid grumbled and said that they had already done that.

Nan cleared the dishes and the two went to the library.

He climbed up on a library ladder and searched through the tomes on the upper shelves. He found nothing except dust that caused him to sneeze occasionally.

Astrid went through her father's desk without any success.

Matilda surprised them as she entered the room. They related their theory to her that the kidnappers were searching for something of value that Schmidt had, but the pair didn't know what it was. They did not share about Andrés' folder with all the Nazi tortures and experiments, or anything about

Kulongoski with her.

Matilda was silent throughout the narrations by her niece and Andrés. Nan popped her head into the library and asked if anyone needed anything. Everyone said no.

"Have you been successful in the library?" the matron asked.

Astrid told her that they had found dozens of medical reports in German. She clarified that most of the materials were about medical procedures done on twins. While she had read them, she did not really understand their significance. Matilda gave a startled glance over to Andrés who maintained a poker face.

"Have you checked the file cabinets in your father's office?" Matilda asked.

"I did, but I didn't find anything," sighed Astrid. "But on the other hand, I don't know what we are looking for."

"What about your father's safe?"

"What safe?" questioned Astrid sheepishly.

"The one in your father's bedroom," described Matilda. "It is behind that hideous still life painting."

Moments later Astrid and Andrés were twisting and turning the knob on the rectangular wall safe. No one seemed to have the combination.

"Where would father have written down the codes?"

They searched high and low and even went back to her father's office. No luck. Finally they gave up.

Astrid wanted to take tea in the study when the doorbell sounded. She went over to the front door and looked out the peephole.

"Sorry, to bother you," the visitor said.

CHAPTER 50

PAIRS & STRAIGHTS

Sunday, July 28, 1974, San Francisco

The air was sweltering and the interior of the church was like an oven. Sweaty bodies pressed against one another during the mass. Babies were crying from the overbearing heat and their mothers quickly took them outdoors. Andrés had his head hanging over the church missal. He couldn't locate the proper passages as the priest continued the mass. He had driven Astrid and her aunt to church that morning. He enjoyed driving the gutless sedan around the City. Back in San Antonio, his uncle had given him an old pickup when he graduated from high school. It kept breaking down and it was not real cool for dating, but Andrés cherished that truck. He had to sell it when left for college in California. He couldn't afford the upkeep and didn't need the distraction. Public transportation in San Francisco was awesome anyway. Plus, he could always fix up his bike, if he had to.

"*Ora pro nobis,*" the priest looked over his congregation with his hands held apart. Doña Grossman insisted that they go to the mass recited in Latin rather than the one in English because it was more fitting to God in her eyes.

Andrés could overhear the black-veiled Astrid and Matilda praying for the safe return of Schmidt with their crystal rosaries in hand.

After the church service, the three went out to brunch.

The aunt had given Nan and the cook the day off, but Nan declined, saying that she wanted to stay around the house in case there were further developments in the abductions.

Matilda had asked Andrés to choose a place to eat. On the one hand, being a former nun, she was a frugal eater; on the other hand, living with Schmidt, she was used to having every type of food imaginable. Andrés picked the University Café, eminently well known by his fellow USF students for serving unlimited muffins with breakfast.

The place was full with the after-church crowds. If the restaurant had a downside, it was that service was very slow. It took forever to get one's order. This lent itself to a conversation about Detective Campos' visit to Doña Matilda the day before. She reiterated that he was concerned about her brother-in-law's disappearance. He had asked her some questions about Schmidt's background and business dealings. She had told him about her sister's marriage to Schmidt and her death in childbirth.

"Did he ask you if you were an identical twin?" asked Andrés putting down his blueberry muffin.

"No," she looked quizzically at the youth, "but he had a lot of questions about Johann's company, Sellarebu . . . SPL. I really couldn't answer most of them."

"They have no leads yet?" inquired Andrés between bites.

"No," she hesitated. "He asked me if anyone had sent a note or made a call to us. I told him that I have not received anything. Have you received anything, Astrid?"

"No, tía. I think he is also afraid that they may have to turn the case over to the FIB."

Andrés knew that Astrid meant the FBI, but he wasn't going to correct her. Instead, he went for another muffin. This time it was carrot raisin.

"I did tell him that the people from his company had been bothering him the last few weeks about some information they wanted."

ᚱᚱ

Nan had wanted to make sure that everyone was out of the house before she made her call to Justice International. Earlier she had searched all of the Schmidt household's rooms, desks, and drawers, but had found nothing that seemed important.

Now Nan was antsy. It was ten o'clock. She dialed. She let the phone at the other end of the line ring a dozen times. She hung up and redialed. Still no answer. She swore under her breath.

Five minutes later, she was successful in getting a human voice.

"Well, we've talked to his custodian and told her the situation."

"Great!" Nan's heart leaped with hope. "When can you tell me where he is?"

"That's the bad part."

"What do you mean?"

"He's going to be terminated."

"How can that be? He was supposed to be transferred someplace!" Nan was panicking.

"Our agent was told about your situation," said the sympathetic voice. "She says that the subject is no longer an asset. He just needs to be terminated."

"Wait! I just need to talk to the agent and explain," Nan pleaded. A tear ran down her cheek. "I only need a few minutes with the agent! Please! Only a few minutes! I need to find out where Schmidt is! It could save my brother!"

"We'll get back to you," the other side hung up and there

was a solid dial tone.

ଓ

"*Scheisse!*" screamed Tanya as she dialed the phone number of the Schmidt house. "We have to act quickly. It sounds like some agent has gone rogue."

"Schmidt residence," Nan answered in a grieving voice.

"Well, where is Schmidt?" yelled the caller.

"I haven't found out yet," she babbled.

"We told you what would happen to your brother if you didn't keep your promise," Tanya smiled malevolently at Vera.

"I'm still trying," Nan supplicated. "I need more time. Just a little more."

"Fine, have it your way. But for now we are not going to kill your brother," terrorized Tanya. "We are going to film him being cut up into little pieces. Then we are going to send copies to the media. How does that sound, bitch?"

ଓ

The trio was greeted by Nan when they returned to the house. Matilda asked her to open some windows because of the heat. The aunt then went to her room and retrieved some memorabilia.

Moments later, Matilda was showing Astrid and Andrés old, faded photographs of herself and her twin sister.

"These were taken in 1946. Carmen and I were just ten years old. Father was new to this country. I mean to Chile, when he met our mother."

"You two are so cute!" beamed Astrid. "You made quite a pair."

"Ah, your mother was the gregarious one. Always smiling and making people laugh," Matilda's head twisted upwards trying to recall her youth. "I was the shy one. I didn't speak much."

"You know, I don't really see a resemblance between Astrid and you," tactlessly remarked Andrés.

Astrid and her aunt looked at each other and then at Andrés. There was a pregnant silence. He felt uncomfortable.

"I just meant that since your mom and aunt were identical twins, you should look a little like them," he was backpedaling quickly.

"I better get going," advised Doña Matilda. "I have to make sure that everything is in order. Astrid, did you have to write any checks?"

❧

There was a pounding in Doña Matilda's head. Her eyes hurt. Her sight seemed blurred. Her brother-in-law was missing. The household was in turmoil. What else could go wrong? She knew that she had to remain calm and put up a strong front, at least for the sake of the two youngsters.

They were so naïve, she thought. Their imaginations were running away from them with the rantings about "twins" and other crazy notions.

Doña Matilda knew that prayer was her preferred way of dealing with adversity. She believed in the power of prayer. She would ask God to help her and her brother.

❧

Minutes later, Andrés was escorting Astrid to Schmidt's bedroom toward the painting that he thought was rather ugly. They decided to try once again to open the wall safe. He looked over at Astrid as if to ascertain if she had found out the combination.

"I asked my aunt if she knew the combination," Astrid shirked. "But she didn't . . . Sorry."

"I have an idea. Try 22-22-22."

She turned the knob back and forth, but the safe did not

open. He suggested 33-33-33 and 11-11-11; both attempts were also unsuccessful.

"How about my birthday?" she contributed.

They both were excited, but this failed also.

"I feel that we are close," he wiped his sweaty hands onto to his brown corduroy jeans. "I'm going to try 33-22-11."

The last tumbler clicked and the safe swung open. They both jumped up and down; and clapped each other's hand.

"I'd rather be lucky than smart," he smirked.

She started to pull out materials from the safe and placed them on her father's bed. They looked incredulously at the trove. There were dozens of medical reports written in German. After combing through the documents, they came upon a folder entitled "Zwillinge." Their eyes opened wide. They were in shock.

Astrid translated some pages and told Andrés that they described the medical treatment of twins. The black double angel tattoo symbol was displayed prominently throughout.

"Should we show this to my aunt?" whispered Astrid with angst.

"And to the detective?" asked Andrés.

CHAPTER 51

THE RENDEZVOUS

Sunday Night, July 28, 1974, Half Moon Bay/San Francisco

It was nine o'clock that night when the telephone rang at the Schmidt residence. Nan had been pacing restlessly between the kitchen and the hallway after dinner. There was still the lingering garlicky smell of lasagna that Andrés was sent out to purchase from Vito's Italian deli. She couldn't eat.

"Okay, you got your wish," the voice said to Nan. "If you want to see the target, you must come tonight."

Nan carefully wrote down the directions on a piece of paper. She repeated them back.

"And one more thing, come alone."

☙

Thirty minutes later she was driving the household Plymouth Valiant down Highway 1. The windows were rolled down because of the heat. The air conditioner didn't work.

"Thank you for coming with me," Nan said to her passenger.

The traffic on the coastal highway was sparse. The twilight was bordered by the sun setting on the horizon, expanding into heliotropic strata. She drove on the slow side because her vision was not good at night. Finally, she passed the abandoned gas station.

"We're looking for an old mail box on the right hand side of the road," she advised her companion.

The ocean side of the highway was an overrun grassy plain. At times the blue luminescence of the waves breaking onto the shore could be seen.

"I think I see it," said the passenger pointing. "Over there!"

They approached the sandy dirt side road and the car slightly skidded as they took the turnoff without braking. Then, going very slowly, they bounced up and down the pitted, eroded track for at least a mile.

⟪

"I think they're stopping," cautioned Vera who was riding on the passenger side of the black utility van that was tailing the Valiant. She pushed back her raven hair.

They had intercepted the phone conversation between Nan and her JI caller. They were about two hundred yards behind Nan.

Suddenly, the road dust was being kicked up in front of them as the Valiant turned off the main highway.

"Let's park here," Tanya said as they pulled off to the side of the road.

"Okay. No one is going to notice," Vera pointed to her knapsack. "I'm ready. I have the goodies"

⟪

Finally, after bouncing up and down like a pogo stick in the car for several minutes, Nan spotted an old shack next to a dilapidated stable. A white van was parked next to the corral fence. Nan flicked her headlights three times before making her final approach.

As she parked in front of the stable, an old woman and a black dog met them. Nan and her companion got out of the car and started to walk over the loose gravel toward the shack. The dog very subtly kept himself between his mistress and the strangers.

"I said to come alone," snarled the haggard lady as she turned her back waving the two forward. "Oh, crap! It doesn't make much difference now."

They entered the shack that had no furnishings. It was full of dirty paper plates and empty tin cans. It reeked of urine.

"I'm sorry that I can't offer you anything," she motioned for them to sit down on some old wobbly wooden crates. "I'm Sandrine. We'll be leaving tonight anyway. Me and Amen. Just the two of us."

Nan and the other person chose to remain standing.

"I just need to speak to him for a few minutes," blurted out Nan. "He has information that some people want."

"For this, you risked the success of the mission?" Sandrine dismissed her. "He deserves to die and he will."

"No, if I get the information from him, they will let my brother go!" she pleaded.

"Oh, you are the sister of the jerk who killed one of those neo-Nazis," reproached the older lady. "That is what screwed up the timetable and forced us to change the plan. You have a lot of nerve being here."

"For the sake of my brother, please!" cried Nan. "I need him alive!"

Nan's companion had remained silent. She had wrapped a long black cape around herself.

"Your brother is dead!" coldly stated Sandrine. "Those people use every trick in the book. You are such a fool! You should have known better. They wouldn't have used you if you brother were still alive. Such a bloody cow!"

Nan fell onto the ground wailing.

"Couldn't she just see him for a few minutes," said the voice of the companion softly. "What harm would it do?"

"And who are you?"

"I am Matilda Grossman," she calmly replied. "The sister-in-law of Johann Schmidt."

"Oh, great!" retorted Sandrine sardonically. "Just f__king great!"

Moments later, the three women walked out of the malodorous shack, crunching on the pebbly path toward the stables. The smell of sagebrush was sweet to their noses. They could hear the pounding of the surf down by the cliffs. Several stars were budding in the dark blue skies. Sandrine carried a lantern and the other two shared a handheld candle. Amen led the way in. The interior of the stable was pitch black except for a small glimmer of light on the back wall. They proceeded toward the third to last stall on the right. There was hay piled shoulder-high around the area. A lone figure seemed to be sunken in the mulch.

"Wake up!" screeched Sandrine kicking the prostrate shape with her foot. "You have company."

There was an unnatural moan from the body.

"This is judgment day," crowed his custodian. "I vote that you should die for the millions of people you have caused to suffer. For your crimes against humanity. For your immorality. For your betrayal."

Sandrine held her lantern up to Schmidt's face. He was forced to close his sunken eye sockets and shied away. He howled as the manacle dug into his skinny wrist.

She looked askance at Nan. "Go ahead. Ask him."

Nan walked forward with the candle and looked at the pathetic figure. Matilda hid herself back in the shadows.

"Please, Mister Schmidt," Nan appealed. "Please tell me what those people want. I need to save my brother."

Schmidt shook his disheveled head from side to side.

"They will kill him if I don't give them the information!" Nan bellowed. "You don't want me to lose my brother, do you?"

Sandrine jumped forward toward Nan. "I told you that your brother is dead, you dumb bitch!" she hissed. "I lost my sister because of this beast. I can't believe that you really want to keep this monster alive!"

"Johann," said the soothing voice that approached him. "What have you done that people want to execute you or extract information from you?" Matilda looked at this poor person through the eyes of a former nun. "Is the wrong so wrong? Is the price too high to make it right?"

Schmidt's eyes slowly opened up. It seemed that he recognized the presence of his sister-in-law. Slowly his head raised itself and began to move. It fell up and down in a languid manner.

"Don't you get it? There is no Schmidt! This devil sent my sister and me to Auschwitz along with thousands of others," wailed Sandrine. "My sister and I were subjected to vile medical experiments. We were tortured. We were mutilated. We were raped. We were pissed on. My sister died because of him. I would have died too if I hadn't been rescued by the Russians. This piece of shit deserves to die!"

There was a loud sigh. It was from Matilda. "Are you a twin?" she inquired of Sandrine in a cautious tone. "An identical twin. *Eine Zwillinge?*"

"*Ja*. How did you know?" Sandrine nodded in surprise. "I still have the black double angel tattoo and my concentration camp numbers."

Sandrine pushed up her tinted glasses that revealed steel grey eyes and then rolled up her sleeves. There was an XZ number tattoo on her left arm and black twin angels one on her right forearm.

Amen barked.

"*Geh rein*!" Nan pointed to the stable opposite them. The animal promptly obeyed and went over to the back of the stall. "*Braver Hund*!"

"Johann, is this true?" Matilda questioned him in disbelief. "Who are you really?"

Her question was met with silence.

☙

It was getting dark on that Sunday evening. Polk was adjusting his red, white, and blue striped tie in the waiting area of Sellarebu. The door sprang open and Neumann motioned the two DOD agents into his office.

The SPL executive offered them a drink. Both declined.

"You know that the Stasi agents are right now on their way down to recover Schmidt," Neumann stated as he leaned back in his high leather chair. He had discarded the jacket of his three-piece suit. His forehead was beaded with drops of sweat that he tried to wipe away with his white monogrammed handkerchief. He fiddled with his monocle.

"Yeah," strutted Campbell. "We're wondering why you sent those two dykes to get Schmidt. We could've done it."

"Drew, I appreciate your enthusiasm and cooperation," Neumann lit a cigar, "but they have more testosterone than both of you put together. Tanya probably shaves more than you do."

They all laughed like it was a meeting of the good ol' boys at a sales convention in Atlantic City.

"Besides, men, we need deniability, even though the big

boys have sanctioned this project with the devil himself."

❧

"I was to be married. He was supposed to clear me with the Nazis and their racial purity rules," cried out Sandrine. "Instead we were sent to Auschwitz. My fiancé never knew what happened to me. He moved to New York and got married there. Me! I was beaten, tortured, probed, cut, and raped. And yes, to answer your question, because I was an identical twin."

There was a shriek from Matilda as she covered her mouth as if she was about to vomit.

The dog growled.

"Amen, *still!*" shouted Sandrine to her dog.

"*¡Madre de Dios!* Johann, please tell me this is not the truth," Matilda glared into the eyes of the skeletal figure lying on top of the hay.

Schmidt stared back at her without saying a word.

"It is true. The same thing happened to me and my brother at a different concentration camp," Nan jumped in hypnotically. "We were twins too, but not identical. Fraternal twins were not as useful as the Zwillinge, the identical twins. They only performed minor experiments on us," she laughed sardonically, unconsciously rolling up her sleeve. "And we got black and white angel tattoos. Not the double black ones."

"Johann, how in heaven's name could you have done such an evil thing?" admonished Matilda in a piercing voice, fighting back her angry tears. "What did you do to my sister?"

There was a slight breeze that broke into the stagnant air. Two flashlights suddenly blinded the three women surrounding Schmidt.

"Hands in the air where we can see them," commanded the voice. "Any sudden moves and I will shoot."

Sandrine slowly raised an open hand from the side of her body over her head like she was in a classroom ready to answer a question. Nan and Matilda also raised both arms in the air.

The two flashlights walked slowly toward them. One fixed on them while the other swept the area from side to side.

"Okay, where is he?" Tanya bellowed, waving the Mauser P38 by her ear.

The three instinctively looked over to the pathetic figure handcuffed in the stall. Tanya walked over to the women who were as quiet as stones and jerked the candle out of Matilda's hand.

"Who's this?" Tanya pulled the hood down from Matilda's head. "This is not the daughter! I think someone did not keep her promise. Naughty! Naughty!"

"It really doesn't matter," Vera turned and approached the tethered prisoner. She also carried a Mauser. "Okay, tell us where the information is and we'll let these nice people go."

The subjugated being looked up and slowly shook his head no.

"You said that you would release my brother if I brought you to Schmidt," called out Nan. "I kept Schmidt alive for you!"

"You know, you are right. He is alive," Tanya's left hand pointed her pistol toward Schmidt. Nan's head automatically turned toward the prisoner.

Blood splattered over everyone as a bullet passed through Nan's head with a sound that startled everyone. The smell of sulfur permeated the space.

"And I promised you that you would be able to join your

brother," sneered the shooter. "And I kept my promise."

Matilda sank down to her knees and started to pray. Now Vera dropped her knapsack onto the ground next to Schmidt.

"Why don't you let us go?" said Sandrine boldly. "I don't care what you do with this worthless piece of crap. In fact, I prefer that he die for his sins."

"That might work if he gives us the information we want," growled Vera leaning over Schmidt. "What about it? Would you tell us what we want if we spare your sister-in-law and this old JI agent?"

The poor soul's body started to shake. He opened his mouth, but words failed to come out.

"We can't hear you!" shouted Tanya who now stood between Sandrine and Matilda.

There was a fetid smell that emanated from the manacled person as his head fell backward onto the straw.

"Do you know what? I don't think I'm going to kill these two. In fact, I'm going to let them live," Tanya growled fiercely. "But I will burn every inch of their skin off! Tell me now!"

The beaten body tried to right itself up, but could not.

"It's really unfortunate," Tanya threatened icily, waving the candle in her right hand, "because after these two suffer, we will kidnap your daughter."

Tanya switched the gun from her left hand to her right and raised it toward Sandrine's head. She held the candle out to her left. "Tell me . . ."

A bolt of lightning flew from a stall toward the threat. Amen lunged onto Tanya and sank his fangs into the throat of the perpetrator. The candle was knocked over onto the dry hay.

Instinctively, Vera fired toward the dark beast that had

attacked her co-conspirator. Amen growled as he fiercely twisted and turned Tanya's brawny neck. One shot after another flew toward the entangled pair. Finally, there was a whimper and the dog's body went limp. Tanya lay on the bloodied floor convulsing.

Greyish black smoke began to rise from the little fire that had sprung up next to Schmidt's stall. Vera ran over to Tanya to assess the injuries. As she did so, Sandrine jumped on top of her. They struggled on the hay-laden floor. They rolled over and over on each other.

The fire started to edge toward Schmidt. The smoke was getting thicker and sparks were flying through the air.

Vera was younger and stronger. Finally, she easily flipped the exhausted Sandrine over on her back and started to pummel the older woman with her fist. Blood spurted from Sandrine's face that was starting to swell up like a watermelon. Then Vera grabbed the victim by the neck and started to strangle her, pounding her head against the ground.

Ashes now flew everywhere, starting little fires throughout the stable. The flames were licking Schmidt's feet as he tried desperately to withdraw them. He was whimpering.

The crack of a pistol sounded. There was a cry. Sandrine remained motionless. Matilda was choking. She had Tanya's fallen gun aimed at the shorthaired blonde's form. Matilda inched forward and struggled to push the limp body off of Sandrine.

"Come on, ¡Santa María!" she was gasping as she tried to help Sandrine to her feet. "Let's go! Hurry!"

No one checked Tanya's condition as she lay motionless on the stable floor.

There was desperate whimpering emanating from the stall where Schmidt was. He was now being slowly engulfed in flames. The grey smoke was permeating the whole stable. The air was hot with sooty ash.

Suddenly, he howled, "God forgive me! Don't let them get it!" This was Schmidt's last cry as his wretched frame formed a fireball.

Matilda pulled her cloak over both Sandrine and herself as they blindly inched their way toward the entrance of the stable. There was a large crash. The back part of the stable had collapsed and sent a conflagration toward the roof.

They were twenty feet from the white van when the stable exploded, sending pieces of old planks a hundred feet into the air. The concussion threw the two women forward.

CHAPTER 52

SMOKE AND MIRRORS

Monday, July 29, 1974, Early Morning, Half Moon Bay/ San Francisco

When the explosion occurred, Matilda found herself and Sandrine airborne. She landed on her hands and chest with her face hitting the ground hard. Her cape had sheltered them from most of the debris and fire, but her hands were pitted with tiny pebbles and her chin was scraped. The bleeding was minimal.

"Are you all right?" she asked the older woman who still lay facedown. Matilda tried to pull her up.

Sandrine nodded affirmatively. She seemed to be dazed.

"I think they are all dead," said Matilda crossing herself.

Slowly but surely, they made their way to the white van. Matilda escorted the injured woman to the driver's side and opened the door.

"You can drive," Sandrine said in a weak voice.

"I can't," apologized the other. "I don't know how."

Sandrine muttered something under her breath, and gingerly climbed into the driver's seat. She grunted with pain every time she moved. It took her several minutes to get her awareness back. She started the van and drove cautiously down the gravel road swerving from one side to another. Matilda watched Sandrine carefully to see if the old woman was able to drive.

They turned north on Pacific Coast Highway. It was a half hour past midnight. Sandrine pulled over twice when she started to get dizzy. Matilda was praying in a low voice.

After an arduous hour of driving, Sandrine was fully conscious again. Matilda feared that Sandrine was in shock and would pass out at any moment.

"I miss my Amen," cried the old woman. "He saved our lives."

Matilda directed her toward the residence in the Presidio. Matilda invited her to stay the night, but Sandrine refused.

About a hundred yards from the house, Matilda got out of the car, but not before Sandrine told her to leave the cape and shoes in the car. Matilda did not ask why, but proceeded barefoot to the house and entered through the downstairs back door. Although the air smelled of pine, her clothes and body reeked of smoke and gun powder.

☪

The air was thick with smoke and ash. It was around one o'clock in the morning when the dark blue van started to slow down. A California Highway Patrol car with its lights flashing and its police radio squawking incessantly was parked behind a black utility vehicle on the shoulder of Highway 1.

The passenger of the van saw the outline of a fire about a mile away.

"Don't stop! Keep on going!"

The two men continued southward to the downtown area of Half Moon Bay. They finally found a pay phone outside a convenience store.

"Project is aborted," the passenger advised his JI contact succinctly. "Unable to make the pickup."

"Okay. Come on in," responded the recipient. "We'll monitor things from this side."

೮೪

Campos was shaving when his wife knocked on the bathroom door.

"*¡Mi amor!*" the black-haired, brown-eyed woman hollered. She was still dressed in a long purple sleeping tee shirt with white irises. "There is a lady on the phone!"

The detective, still looking at the mirror, wiped the shaving cream off of this face. He emerged from the bathroom in just his boxer shorts.

"Who is it?" he asked as he dried his hands with a small white towel.

"I think she said her name was Gracie. Breakfast in ten!"

His wife handed him the phone from the bed stand and left the room. She knew that it was police business after many years of untimely interruptions into their private life. The kids were still in bed. She grabbed a cup of coffee and added artificial creamer and fake sugar. She was bracing herself for the complaints from her children who were bored with summer vacation because there was nothing to do.

"Sorry to call you at home, David," the FBI agent apologized, "but I think we caught a break in the Schmidt case."

"No problem," the detective grabbed a pen from the nightstand. "What do you have?"

Gracie explained that an FBI bulletin had come in early that morning and it looked like the crime scene of the Schmidt kidnapping had been found. The San Mateo County Fire Department had responded to a blaze reported by a passing motorist. The county sheriffs were then called in. They found several bodies or parts of bodies strewn throughout the premises. And one dog, she added parenthetically.

The county authorities then called the FBI because they

were not equipped to do such a comprehensive CSI.

The sheriffs had traced the Valiant to a rental agency under a Sellarebu Pharmaceutical Laboratories account. They also found an abandoned black utility vehicle parked next to the turnoff road to the fire's location. It was traced to a U.S. Department of Defense purchasing department.

Only one body was tentatively identifiable. Nan Hill's driver's license was found inside a charred leather wallet, mostly intact. They also found a severed right skeletal hand that was still manacled to a splintered wooden post. The body of a large animal, presumed to be a dog, was also charred beyond recognition and its breed could not be immediately determined.

Gracie narrated more details for at least ten minutes.

After they hung up, Campos called Leong.

"Hey, Leland, Gracie just called," the detective was struggling to pull up his trousers and juggle a cup of black coffee at the same time. "Meet you in 45."

There were dozens of messages on Campos' desk when he arrived at the office forty-five minutes later that morning. Two were from his captain who ordered David to see him immediately. Campos put them at the bottom of the pile. The next one seemed important and he dialed the number.

"Hola, lover boy," there was heat at the other end of the line. "You really do owe me."

Campos' face flushed as he conversed with Fátima. She had found out some intel on Jerzy Kulongoski and Justice International. Unfortunately for the detective, he had to almost engage in phone sex in order to get the information.

"We heard that JDL did not participate in the Schmidt abduction because he was no longer an asset to them," Fátima's voice was throaty. "That corresponds with the official JI version. JI went at it alone. However, my sources said that Justice International botched the whole kidnapping and everybody was killed. Good guys and bad guys."

"Where does Schmidt fit in?" Campos pressed her. "And how about Sellarebu Pharmaceutical Laboratories and the U.S. Department of Defense?"

"I don't know," replied the vamp. "But I'll check it. Then you'll really owe me."

"Thanks," he said, weak at the knees.

"And I plan to collect, *mi amor*. There is a juicy papaya waiting just for you."

☙

Matilda found two old pillowcases that under most conditions would have been considered almost new.

She drew a bath and poured in some Epsom salts. She wiped alcohol onto to her hands, wincing with each swipe. She looked at the bloody mess in the mirror. The application of alcohol to the bottom of her chin brought tears to her eyes. Matilda disrobed and brought the dirty clothes up to her nose. They reeked. She stuffed all her discarded garments into the cases. She climbed into the tub and closed her eyes. She was exhausted, but could not sleep.

Matilda recalled that she had told Andrés that she was leaving for a short period that night on an errand with Nan. She extracted a promise from him to keep it a secret. Matilda did not want to worry her niece. Andrés naively agreed. He told her that he was trying to act as guardian for the family as long as Schmidt was absent. She had smiled at his innocence.

What could she share with him now? And with Astrid? She pondered.

She washed her hair several times. After she got out of the tub, she dried herself off and looked at herself in the mirror.

This will never do! She cogitated. She put on her bathrobe and slippers and snuck over to Nan's room that was located on the other side of the double building. There she rummaged through Nan's toiletries, retrieving tweezers, bath powder, several types of cover-up makeup, and other feminine beauty products.

 C҂

Doña Matilda arrived at the church at five-thirty dressed from head to toe in black, with a black veil concealing her face. She had called a taxi to pick her up after she had scribbled some instructions to Astrid and to the new cook in Spanish. The cab had dropped her off at the McDonalds, a block away from the church. The night was still pitch black and the amber streetlights provided little illumination. There she furtively left two brown paper bags near a trash container. She smelled her leather gloves. They had a slight scent of smoke so she discarded them also. She had other ones in her small black leather purse. A white goateed African-American pushing a grocery cart passed her on the sidewalk. She could smell alcohol emanating from him.

She had rehearsed what she was going to say in the confessional. She would not lie. Matilda knew that under God's Fifth Commandment, it was a mortal sin to kill another person. She would tell the confessor that it was self-defense. *How could he refute that?* She had saved another person's life.

"Bless me, father," she began as she heard the screen of the confessional slide open, "for I have sinned . . ."

Afterwards, as she said her penance and prayed during the mass, she was very disappointed that the priest had been so parochial in his admonition to her. He advised her to report the incident to the police.

She had just arrived back at the house when Andrés was

walking down the stairs for breakfast. He stared at her coal-colored outfit without saying a word.

"Good morning, Andrés," she broke the ice. "I've just come back from church."

The cook had set out some coffee, cream, and sugar on the table. There were a few pastries for Andrés to munch on while everyone waited for Astrid.

The windows of the house were all open and the new housekeeper was busy washing the windows and mirrors. After Bert's disappearance, a new cook and housekeeper had been brought in to help Nan with the household chores. There was a strong aroma of ammonia and vinegar curling throughout.

The phone rang and the cook answered it.

"*Doña Matilda*," the cook gave the message to the matron of the house. "*La policía llamó. Ellos vendrán esta tarde.*" The police called and they are coming by this afternoon.

∞

Detectives Campos and Leong arrived at the Schmidt house after their quick fast food fix at a Vietnamese eatery in the inner Richmond area. Astrid escorted them into the library. The cook brought in coffee, blueberry scones, lemon curd, and almond tarts for the guests. A few minutes later, Andrés and Matilda walked into the room together. Matilda took the seat furthest away from the detectives. Before greeting the detectives, she had washed her face and hands again and had tried to repair her makeup. Matilda then changed clothes trying to surreptitiously cover as much of her body as possible so as not to arouse suspicion over her wounds.

"We regret to inform you that Mister Schmidt was found deceased earlier this morning," Campos began in a sterile, narrative fashion, "as well as your maid, Miss Hill. We are sorry for your loss."

Astrid screamed and rushed into her aunt's arms. "No! No! It can't be!"

"There, there, my child," the matron stroked the girl's hair. "It is God's will. We will need to pray for them."

"Did he suffer?" blurted out Astrid sobbing. Her nose was running. "How did he die? Was he murdered?'

Campos looked over at Leong for a split second. "We don't know yet. They are still investigating."

Andrés slowly moved over to Astrid and Matilda and stood behind them. Nobody had touched the coffee.

"If you don't mind, we need to ask a few more questions," Campos automatically continued. He had investigated over a hundred homicides. He had become seemingly immune to the emotional side of the tragedies.

"When was the last time any of you saw Miss Hill?" the detective began.

"I heard the car start sometime between nine and ten last night," jumped in Andrés immediately. He moved to a different chair, away from Astrid and her aunt. "I assumed that it was Nan because Doña Matilda doesn't drive."

Matilda continued to hold her niece, veiling her appearance to the police and not saying anything. Doña Matilda and Andrés had talked alone after breakfast and agreed that they would try to keep her involvement a secret. They would not lie, but neither would they necessarily offer up any information not specifically asked for.

"Are we talking about the Plymouth Valiant?" Campos wanted to be more specific.

Andrés pretended to be helpful. "It must have been because you guys still have the Mercedes."

The seemingly casual, but formal questioning went on for at least an hour. Matilda kept rocking Astrid in her arms as the child kept sobbing. Finally, the matron was forced to interact with the officers when they asked about the backgrounds of Nan and Bert. She told them that she had arrived several weeks prior to Schmidt's arrival to San Francisco in order to set up a household for him and his daughter. She had hired Nan and Bert through the referral service from the Presidio administration office. She surmised that they were both European. They were pleasant, efficient, and good workers.

Leong kept sniffing the air and rubbing his eyes as if he noticed something strange, but did not say anything. He finally yielded to a sticky, sliced almond topped tart.

The conversation came back to Schmidt and his employment. They wanted to know more about Sellarebu Pharmaceutical Laboratories.

"My recollection is that he began as a Production Manager for Sellarebu Pharmaceutical Laboratories in Buenos Aires," Matilda stated. She was relieved that she was not being pressed on the prior night's events, but she remained alert for that topic being reopened.

"Do you know when that was?"

"I think in the late 40's. I am not sure. I know that he came to Chile in 1950 or 1951 to run the Santiago operations."

Campos grabbed a cup of coffee as they moved on to questions about Schmidt's personal history. He found out about Schmidt's marriage to Matilda's sister and her subsequent death, and the stroke that left him partially immobile in 1966.

The cook with her Salvadoreña accent inquired if anyone needed anything else as she replenished the coffee.

The other part of the tag team, Detective Leong, who normally just listened and took notes, jumped in.

"Why did Mister Schmidt move to San Francisco?"

"His company, the one he works for, Sellarebu Pharmaceutical Laboratories, has a consultant job for him at Letterman Hospital," she inadvertently used the present tense.

"Do you know what kind of a consultant he was?"

"No, not really," she had been lulled into the rhythm of answering questions. "It had something to do with a special project. He was the only person that was qualified to manage the project. I think it had to do with something that your Department of Defense was working on."

Campos' head swiveled toward his partner who returned the look.

"And do you guys want to know something freaky," interrupted Andrés. "His company is not really in the hospital. It is like behind it. Kind of hidden away."

"How do you know that?" frowned Campos.

"Because Astrid and I were booted out of there one day when we tried to check out her dad's office."

Campos gave his partner the look. Leong nodded.

CHAPTER 53

OFF THE CASE

Monday, July 29, 1974, Afternoon, San Francisco

"Those f__king bitches!" Neumann had been dodging angry phone calls all day from the Pentagon. "How in the hell could they have f__ked this up so badly?"

"I don't know, sir," Polk said sycophantly, "but Drew and I can snatch the daughter."

"What for, you idiot?" he lashed out. "Schmidt is dead. He's the one that had the information."

The two DOD henchmen leaned back in their chairs.

If there is a silver lining, Neumann thought, *it's that I can retrieve the money that I wired the Stasi girls and have it transferred to my Swiss bank account without any problems.*

"Hold on a sec," Neumann started to dial. "I need to make this call."

It was around five o'clock when the phone rang at the Schmidt residence. Matilda had been lying on her bed trying to take a nap when she was summoned to the phone.

"Miss Grossman, this is Arnold Neumann from Sellarebu," he said unctuously. "We just wanted to express our condolences for your loss."

"Thank you," she replied in a stoic tone. Her instincts told her not to trust this man.

"Since he worked for us, we want to assure you that we will continue our obligations to you and the family until you can get things straightened out."

"That would be nice," she replied, not letting down her guard.

"We also heard that Miss Hill is no longer with us," he stated this more as a question rather than as an assertion."

"We haven't seen her since last night," Matilda countered. "And the car is missing. We'll need another car as soon as possible please."

"Why, of course, may we send over a car tonight?" he didn't seem surprised at her response.

"Tomorrow morning by 7 o'clock will be good enough, thank you."

They continued with the conciliatory conversation, sounding quite pleasant with one another, over the dismal tragedy. Neumann told her that he would personally take responsibility for arranging a memorial service at her church on Friday. He would also arrange for assistance with the packing and moving of their household.

CB

"Tell me what you have so far," directed the captain to the two police detectives.

Campos and Leong went into a long and drawn out discourse with their superior about the recent homicides.

"So what do you think?"

"Most of the facts and evidence seem to center around Johann Schmidt," stated Campos. "Just how, we don't know for sure."

He went on about the difficulty of trying to trace the identity of anyone connected to the case. The preliminary crime scene investigative reports found that the bodies of everyone at the stable had been burned, including the dog's. This had compromised the ability to extract fingerprints.

Additionally, the initial indications suggested that the dental work on all of the corpses had been European, most probably Central or Eastern. No one would have easy access to these types of dental records.

"Can we even be sure that one of the bodies was Schmidt's?" probed the captain.

"Not one hundred percent," admitted Campos, "but with the death of the chauffeur and the kidnappings of Schmidt and his valet, everything leads back to him being a vic."

"But what's the motive?" persisted their superior.

"We think that different people wanted Schmidt for different reasons," opined Campos.

"In other words, we have diddly squat," huffed the captain. "But, gentlemen, today is your lucky day."

The two officers looked at each other, squirming in their hard wooden chairs.

Maybe he is going to buy us a beer after work, Campos thought, knowing that hell hadn't frozen over judging by the recent heat wave in the City.

"The San Mateo District Attorney says that his office doesn't have the expertise or resources to pursue this case, thanks to Governor Moonbeam. And our wonderful District Attorney doesn't want to handle the case because it is not sexy enough. She also says that there may be jurisdictional problem vis-à-vis the feds. She suggests that we defer to the FBI. They have all the resources. Let's get the feds to find out what's what. Any problems with that?"

Campos and Leong knew that they shouldn't contradict the chief when he had already made up his mind.

"No problem. Can we finish up on a couple of loose ends before we submit our final report?" Campos was trying to finesse a few more bites of the apple before the transfer. "We have been working closely with Special Agent in Charge, Grace O'Malley, of the FBI. May we turn over our files to her?"

"Sure. Sure," grumbled the captain. "You have until I finish the damn paperwork."

Shortly afterwards, Campos and his partner bellied up to the bar at a local cop watering hole.

"I think we probably have a week before the transfer," grinned Campos.

ભ

After dinner, Andrés was alone in the library with Doña Matilda.

Astrid was upstairs. She was distraught about the recent horrific events. She endeavored to keep distracted by lying on top of her bed and writing letters to her family and friends about her father's passing. She did not give the details of his death.

"Thank you for this morning," Matilda said in an unusually soft tone with him. "And for last night."

She had spent most of the day in her bedroom praying and weeping. She was torn with emotion. She did not know what to do. The priest that morning had been less than helpful.

When Matilda had come downstairs for dinner, she had willed herself to be impassive and not show any signs of emotion to Astrid and Andres. The subject matter of the recent deaths was not mentioned.

"We will have the memorial service on Friday at the church." she announced to him. "I will need you to drive me to church every morning this week in time for eight o'clock mass."

"By car?"

"They are supposed to give us a car tomorrow morning. By seven. I will be going back to Santiago as soon as things are straightened out," she gave him a sad look. Her brave front started to fold. She was getting weary. She anticipated his next question and said apologetically, "I don't know what I'm going to do about Astrid. I am worried about her being here alone. She has family and friends back in Chile."

Andrés remained silent. He was ambivalent in his feelings toward Astrid. She was nice and fun to be around, but he did not want to be tied down. In a few weeks he would have to start school for real and couldn't afford any distractions. Besides, commuting to Mills College over in the East Bay in order to see her would be a drag.

"We are going to start packing up the house tomorrow," she informed him. "You won't have to do anything . . . Maybe just a few little things. Johann's company will move us."

The cook came in and inquired in Spanish if they needed anything. They didn't.

Matilda further explained to Andrés that she had to return to Santiago as soon as possible to meet with the attorneys. She had to cancel several contracts now that Schmidt was dead and reestablish the household down there. She noted that Sellarebu would be responsible for the disposal of Boehner's property and for clearing out the garage area and the servants' quarters.

Matilda would take charge of her own modest wardrobe and possessions. She would label the furniture, paintings, and other possessions that would be shipped back to Chile.

"I have borrowed a few books from the library," confessed Andrés.

"Keep them," she graciously said. "In fact, take as many of them as you want. The remaining will be donated to a college in Santiago. That reminds me. Excuse me for a minute."

Doña Matilda exited the room and came back with a small parcel wrapped in wrinkled brown paper and tied with a hempish twine. There was no inscription on the outside of the bundle.

"Johann wanted you to have this at the completion of your service with us. Now is as good a time as any."

"Thank you. Thank you very much," he stuttered in a surprised tone.

"And this too," she handed him a white envelope.

CHAPTER 54

TIES

Tuesday, July 30, 1974, San Francisco

In many ways Detective Campos was relieved that the Schmidt case was being handed over to the feds. He disliked all hate groups like the Neo-Nazis. He also recalled former President Dwight D. Eisenhower's mistrust of the federal government's military-industrial complex and its motto that "Might Makes Right."

When he had arrived at the office earlier that morning, he initially resisted calling Fátima and letting her know that they no longer had the case. He rearranged his desk and got a cup of lukewarm coffee. He heard Leong conversing on the phone about a transvestite being arresting for using the wrong bathroom at a public restaurant. It turned out that the poor person was hermaphroditic and was allowed to use either facility under the law. The arresting officer was now the center of relentless hazing.

"Oh, hot cakes!" Fátima immediately threw him into a fluster when he finally called her. "You are making my day. Wish I could do you right now."

He quickly tried to explain that the Schmidt case had been transferred to the FBI. He found himself playing with his paisley tie as he rattled along.

"Well, that's messed up," she empathized. "And we had even found some good stuff for you.

"The rumor mill around D.C. is that Sellarebu has been tinkering with genetic reengineering to create super human soldiers. The feds are all hot and bothered to get their secret formulas."

"Sellarebu is the company Schmidt was working for, isn't it," queried Campos.

"Oh, yes, binga pinga Sellarebu Pharmaceutical Laboratories was started by some Nazis who escaped from Germany after the war. They have been investigated for years for experimenting on indigenous people in Brazil, Argentina, Uruguay, and Chile. Every time a criminal prosecution became imminent, the case was suddenly dropped. A lot of money has passed hands, if you catch my drift."

"Yeah," Campos was now leaning back in his chair softly biting his lower lip contemplating. "You know, Fátima, we couldn't find any records for Schmidt before 1946 or '47. And he is supposed to be from Chile."

"Not really, sweetie," Fátima checked him. "There is strong evidence to suggest that his real identity is Teufl. Augustin Teufl from Austria."

She went on to read the dossier about the horrific crimes that Teufl was responsible for committing.

"But why is this Schmidt or Teufl so important to everyone involved?" queried Campos.

"From what we have been able to gather . . ." Fátima paused. "This, of course, is unofficial and partially speculative, but Teufl was working on some sort of top secret project when he was in Germany. He may have actually directed it. It had to do with military androids."

"What it the heck are those?"

"I think that they're a cross between Frankenstein and zombies," she laughed.

"You have to be kidding!"

"Not really, *mi amor*. Nixon and his boys are taking a lot of heat from the heavy body count in Nam," she explained. "These military androids are not really human."

"What do you mean not human?"

"I don't know the details," she was backtracking. "I don't know if they are bred to be this way or given some sort of injection or irradiated."

"You've been reading too many Spiderman comics."

"Anyway, Teufl supposedly has the Seele Project report which contains the secret formulas and protocols. Nobody knew that he had them and he never shared them with Sellarebu Pharmaceuticals. But somehow the U.S. government found out about the report and they put pressure on Sellarebu to get the info."

"I can't believe it."

"Neither can I."

"But haven't other countries tried to create some sort of military robots?"

"Yeah, probably. But supposedly, Schmidt had a better scheme for doing it. They say that he found the genetic coding for the human soul. Unfortunately, he was the only one that had the info and research. I couldn't tell you much more, *mi corazon*."

"Holy shit! This is stranger than '*War of the Worlds*' times two!" Campos took a deep breath. "Thanks, Fátima. I owe you."

"Actually, you're safe for the moment. I have this cute Puerto Rican who is rocking my *chalupa*."

೮೩

At promptly seven o'clock that morning, there had been a loud tapping at the front door. Doña Matilda had instructed the cook to answer it. A young man with a butch haircut and a pocked face left a set of keys with her.

The marine layer was keeping the air temperature cool. It was expected to heat up in the afternoon. Andrés liked the red Chevy Vega. It looked awesome and was fast. He dropped Matilda off at church. She told him to come back in an hour. He drove off to his apartment and picked up his mail. It was mostly junk mail plus his phone bill and a two-for-one coupon to a new Burmese restaurant (use it with Judy?) in the neighborhood. Andrés entered the stuffy apartment and unloaded his backpack. From it, he pulled out the books that he had retrieved from Schmidt's library and the parcel.

He walked around the apartment. His few plants were dead from lack of watering. Andrés disposed of half of the penicillin-infested food in his refrigerator. He grabbed two clean tee shirts and two pairs of socks and stashed them into his backpack.

Finally, Andrés succumbed to temptation and opened up the envelope that Matilda had given him the night before. It contained a thick stack of twenty-dollar bills. He counted them. The sum added up to $500. He pumped both fists into the air and shouted.

He left his apartment and walked upstairs and knocked on the door. He encountered Maurice who was already dressed to go to work and who invited him to come in.

"We don't see you around here much anymore," remarked Maurice not really making eye contact. He was preoccupied with making the final adjustments to his pinstriped Brooks Brothers suit. "Hope you are doing well."

Andrés nodded and handed him an envelope with $300 for his rent. John appeared and motioned him into their living room. There were two lavender finches singing in their cage in the far corner.

Without prompting, John brought him a cup of coffee and a wonderfully smelling piece of ham and cheese quiche leftover from their breakfast. The boy never said no to food. It was delicious. They made small chitchat and Andrés departed when Maurice had to leave to catch his ride.

ᚙ

A bus honked at him as Andrés parked in the white-curbed passenger-loading zone in front of the church. Matilda was patiently waiting for him.

"We're going to start the packing process today," Matilda went into her compulsive planning mode. "Have Astrid take you to Johann's closet. Take whatever ties you want. The more, the better. You might also want to check the drawers. See if there are any belts. I don't know if there are any sweaters that will fit you . . ."

The sun was now breaking through and the streets were filled with people moving about. Andrés took the turns a little fast and nearly hit a pedestrian who was jaywalking.

"And maybe, you should look in his jewelry box for some cufflinks or whatever . . ."

Andrés was stunned by Doña Matilda's generosity. He had never had much clothing and for sure no jewelry (except for his few singlet earrings). In fact, his current watch was made out of rubber. It had been cheap and he liked it.

ᚙ

Astrid, who was wearing a black skirt and sweater, sadly greeted Doña Matilda and Andrés as they arrived. Her eyes were red from all the crying. Matilda and Andrés had stopped at the grocery store where Andrés purchased milk, orange juice, fruit, and cottage cheese for the household.

Matilda beckoned them into the study and motioned for

them to sit.

"I have been thinking, children," she said in a gentle tone. "Now that Johann is gone, we have no justification for staying in this house. I have prayed for guidance on what is to be done. I must leave within the next ten days."

"What about me?" interjected Astrid, alarmed. "What about school?"

"I haven't made up my mind yet," she stared at one of the paintings on the wall. "My primary concern is that you are safe and secure."

"What about Andrés?" she leaned toward her aunt with pitiful eyes. "He can take care of me."

"My dear," she was trying to be gentle but firm. "Andrés needs to finish his own studies. We have imposed upon him all summer. Also, Mills is too far away for him to watch over you."

Andrés was ambivalent. He had been generously paid, but he had to graduate. He couldn't babysit Astrid, even though she was nice.

"But what would I do in Chile?" she argued.

"You could go to the University of Chile. Or you could go where Andrés spent this last year, the University of Valparaiso," the aunt turned toward him and gave him a Dracula-like stare into his eyes. "You liked it there, didn't you, Andrés?"

"Yes," he muttered mesmerized.

"Father would have let me go to Mills."

That remark was a painful blow to Matilda's heart, but she assumed a somber posture and diverted the topic.

"Anyway, my dears, we have a lot of things to do before the memorial service on Friday." She recited a litany of tasks and responsibilities. She was clearly using the mundane tasks to block out the horror she still felt about Johann's real identity. She noted that the moving company that was being hired by Sellarebu would start packing the following day. Matilda also told them that whatever was not going to be transported back to Chile, would be given to the local Catholic charity.

Astrid and her aunt went to examine Schmidt's private files in his office and the papers in his bedroom safe. Andrés had the job of going through Schmidt's clothing and accessories. He went through the closets, dressers, and armoire and pulled out anything that he wanted personally. He carefully separated out those things he thought the family might want to keep.

They had a late lunch and reported what they had accomplished. Andrés had selected at least ten ties. Unfortunately, they were old and out of style. He found a nice brown leather belt and a few other things. He saved out Schmidt's photos. Astrid had begun packing her jewelry and other personal belongings. She would let the movers do the rest.

The aunt had found some interesting files that Johann had kept in the safe.

"Andrés, please deliver these to Detective Campos when you have an opportunity," she said as she handed him a black leather portfolio.

CHAPTER 55

THE MEMORIAL SERVICE

Friday, August 2, 1974, San Francisco

The priest eulogized Schmidt as though the two had been best friends. Unfortunately, Schmidt had never gone to mass. He had always maintained that he had a special understanding with God. The memorial service mass was only attended by the immediate family, Andrés, SPL staff, and a few federal governmental types. Detective Campos and FBI agent O'Grady were in the last pew observing the proceedings.

There was a funeral urn on a table bordered by two burning candles. Doña Matilda had requested special permission for Schmidt's ashen remains to be present in church during the funeral liturgy. She had explained to the priest that she had been a nun and that her brother-in-law's body had been charred beyond recognition. The pastor had then contacted the archbishop who readily granted the request.

The aunt and niece were dressed from head to toe in black. They were shrouded in black lace veils. Andrés was wearing a grey herringbone sport coat with one of Schmidt's old ties, silver silk with red and blue diagonal stripes.

At the Schmidt house, several of the rooms had already been packed up, including those of Andrés and Schmidt. Starting tonight, Andrés would be spending his evenings back at his apartment.

After the service, everyone scrambled over to the parish hall. Sellarebu had provided an assortment of cold dishes and non-alcoholic beverages. Antipasto, Brie cheese and crackers, grapes, chips, and everything else Andrés might care to munch on.

"Like I said on the phone the other day," Neumann positioned himself between Matilda and the youths, "we are sorry for your loss."

"Thank you," Matilda bowed her head. "This is very nice. Johann would have appreciated your gesture."

"How is the packing coming along? Do you need any other assistance?" Neumann fawned. "There is no rush for you to move."

An older man in a military officer's uniform and crew cut arrived and flanked Neumann. He addressed Doña Matilda. "If you could do us a big favor, ma'am, and set out separately any documents or reports that he was working on for us, we would appreciate it," he said, his gravelly voice lacking tact.

Neumann turned and gave the military man a dirty look. He looked back at Matilda and grinned politely. "Is there anything I may bring you to drink or eat?"

☙

"Aren't those the DOD jerk-offs?" Campos pointed with his chin to O'Grady. "Those guys will make trouble for you. Be careful."

Detective Campos and FBI agent O'Grady walked up to Matilda and expressed their condolences.

"By the way, we are transferring the case to the FBI," the detective informed her. "Special Agent O'Grady will be the lead. She is very good."

Matilda was a bit surprised. But she was from Chile. People never asked questions. It was too dangerous to be labeled a subversive; and when that happened, the consequences were extreme with no redress.

Campos casually strolled over to one of the food tables while Grace spoke with Matilda.

"Thanks," he said cautiously to Andrés who was piling his plate with seconds, "what you dropped off the other day was dynamite."

∞

On the prior Wednesday morning while Doña Matilda was at mass, Andrés had dropped off the materials that she had given him that were for Campos. The police detective was not in, but Andrés had handwritten a note that the documents were for the detective.

Campos came in around 8:30. He had several other active cases that he was working on and did not get to the Schmidt materials until Thursday.

"Holy crap!" Campos waved Leland over. "Look at this!"

For the next hour, they scrutinized Schmidt's private files. Some of documents were in German. There were executive summaries of various projects; reports on medical experiments done in South America; and correspondence between Sellarebu Pharmaceutical Laboratories and the U.S. Department of Defense.

"Can you translate the ones in German, Leland?" asked Campos in all seriousness. "You did go to Cal."

Leong gave him an unimpressed grimace. "I took Spanish for three years," he smirked. "Probably speak it better than you, coconut."

Campos raised his hands in surrender.

"I'll call Grace right now," he was getting energized. "We can meet her for lunch and turn these papers over to her. She is going to shit."

"Don't forget to ask her if she speaks German," cracked his partner.

∞

Doña Matilda was emotionally and physically drained as they drove back to the house after the memorial mass. She had dark circles under her eyes. Her hands were shaking. The reception seemed more like a political event than a celebration of life for Johann. Astrid did not handle it well. She would constantly break down and sob.

As Andrés drove up the incline toward the Schmidt home, he could see fire engines, Presidio park police cars, and black utility vehicles. Several had their lights flashing. Men in black garb, masks, and helmets were going in and out of house from all of the entrances. The whole area was cordoned off with yellow tape. As he approached, a large figure with a badge, dark sunglasses, and a big gut extended his right arm.

"Sorry, this road is closed," he announced.

"But we live here," protested Andrés as he rolled down the window. He could smell smoke that smelled like gunpowder. He didn't observe any flames from the house.

"Sorry, son," continued the traffic cop, "there has been an explosion in the home. You can't go in."

"What type of explosion?" chimed in Astrid leaning over to Andrés' side of the vehicle.

"Don't know. Can't say," mechanically spoke the officer. "Let me call this in. I'll try to find someone who can assist you."

Andrés thought he observed Polk, the DOD agent, entering the garage from where blackish curls of smoke were emanating. Andrés turned the engine off. They just waited.

"I wonder if anyone was injured?" Astrid threw out, nervously running her fingers through her hair.

Matilda studied the scene pensively without uttering a word.

ᘓ

Earlier that day, before the funeral service, Neumann and the Department of Defense police commander had briefed a team of Special Forces to simulate a bomb explosion at the Schmidt house and secure the premises for at least twelve hours while the house was searched from top to bottom.

"We have been doing onsite inspections as part of the packing and moving detail," explained Neumann to the commander. "Once we get everything packed and in boxes, we'll re-inspect everything over at the lab. We just needed this in case someone is trying to hide something. If the report exists, we'll find it."

"Make sure to remove the wire taps on the phones," reminded the DOD commander.

CHAPTER 56

DELIVERY

Friday - Saturday, August 2-3, 1974, San Francisco

On Friday afternoon, Neumann arrived at the Schmidt residence fifteen minutes after being notified by the traffic control officer.

"Oh, Miss Grossman," he had said unctuously. "I can't believe what happened."

Within the hour Matilda, Astrid, and Andrés were driving the Vega to the Fairmont Hotel on Nob Hill, following a black utility vehicle provided by SPL. Andrés had noticed that the grill of the escort vehicle had an eagle symbol emblem. He couldn't recall why that looked familiar.

Andres had never valet parked before and was surprised when a bellman asked for the Vega's keys as he stopped at the entrance of the hotel. He had wanted to go home that day, but after the situation at the Schmidts' residence, he had decided to stay close to Astrid and Doña Matilda.

∞

Andrés dropped Matilda and her niece back at their house Saturday morning. The police and firefighters had dispersed. There still were the odors of the explosion. The house was in fairly good order considering the number of people who had trampled through the place. There did not seem to be any smoke damage.

The cook and the temp maid were not there and there

was no indication as to where they had gone. There was a large bouquet of fragrant flowers on the dining room table with a little note attached.

"Sorry for the inconvenience. I told the packers not to disturb you over the weekend. There may be some SPL staff coming over to inspect for damage. If you wish, you may spend a few more nights at the hotel. We will make all of the arrangements. Please contact me if you need anything." It was signed Arnold Neumann.

∞

Andrés went to his apartment to finish up some work. His place seemed so cramped and tiny compared to the last few days that he had been in the Schmidt home and at the Fairmont Hotel. He opened the window and lit a scented apple-cinnamon candle to try to freshen the air. He would no longer have his laundry done at the Schmidt house or his meals prepared. *Bummer!*

He puttered around the apartment, discarding yet another dead plant. Andrés grabbed the mail, but only found more pizza ads and solicitations to buy insurance or apply for a credit card. He made room on his makeshift brick and board bookshelves for some books that he had recently taken from the Schmidt library. He noticed that the parcel that Matilda had given him was still lying on the sofa unopened. He brought it to the table.

The teakettle whistled. Andrés sat down to eat a peanut butter and jelly sandwich on nearly moldy white bread.

He grabbed a small kitchen knife and cut the twine on the package. He ripped open the parcel and found a handwritten letter, a book, and some sort of booklet.

The note had been written by a shaky hand and was tough to decipher. It was from Schmidt to Andrés.

"My son, thank you for all that you have done for my family these last few weeks. We live in difficult times. In my life I have made certain misguided decisions. Some are now threatening my family. I am most concerned that my daughter be protected. Astrid is still young and naïve. I wish you happiness and success."

He poured some more hot water for his red zinger tea.

The accompanying book had a darkened leathered spine and speckled edged pages. The volume was written in old German script. Andrés deciphered the title and author. It was Goethe's *Faust*. Andrés had never read it, but he knew the thematic metaphors. Inscribed on the inside of the front cover were the words "*Gott verzeih mir*" [God, forgive me] written in the same handwriting as Schmidt's note, but much sharper. Andrés did not know what this meant. He wrote it down on the back of piece of scratch paper. He would show it to Astrid and ask her to translate it for him.

He leafed to the title page and read another inscription in faded blue ink. He copied this down also. "*Liebe Keichelle, Wir werden für immer zusammen sein. Augustin.*" [To Keichelle, We will be together always. Augustin]. This handwriting looked the same as the other two exemplars.

Andrés continued to flip through the pages. He loved old books. Maybe one of these days he would read the story in English.

The third and last item in the parcel was a thinly bound booklet that had scores of illustrations of human body parts, cells, and molecules accompanied by mathematical formulae. This was also in German and seemed more like some kind of scientific report. At the beginning of the manuscript, the words "*Streng Geheim*" [Top Secret] were stamped in red ink. Andrés was about to read the title "Die Zwillinge – Teil

2 – Zusammenfassung." ["The Twins – Part 2" Executive Summary] when he was interrupted by a knock at the front door.

Andrés closed the booklet and slid Schmidt's note into the *Faust* book. As he arose, he mechanically scooped up and slotted the German novel and the report into his bookshelf to the right of his books by Zola. He went to open the door.

"Hey, John," Andrés cheerily greeted his landlord. "What's going on?"

"I just stopped by to drop this off," John was holding a special delivery envelope with dozens of foreign stamps, seals, and imprints.

"Thanks," Andrés took the envelope. "Do you want to come in?"

"Sorry, don't have time," John backed away, but handed Andrés a white bag. "I'm cooking Maurice something special for dinner. Enjoy."

Moments later, Andrés found that the bag was filled with lemon squares. He sat back down and started munching. He could see that this delivery was from Chile. He cut open the envelope and pulled out a large manuscript. It was a three-hole punched, fastener-bound copy of a dissertation on British piracy in the Caribbean. There was no note. His roommate during his year at the Universidad de Valparaiso was Mirón Forlán, who was now an intern at the Santiago daily newspaper, *El Mercurio*.

Andrés had recently called him from the Schmidts' residence and enlisted him to find out some information about the Schmidt household. He wanted to know what made Schmidt so special that people had kidnapped him. Mirón was a bit hesitant at first because of the chaotic political climate in Chile. He knew that most correspondence was intercepted by the Chilean authorities and could be suppressed and the author brought in for interrogation by the local police or military.

Andrés undid the fasteners and scanned through the pages individually, having two stacks in front of him. About two-thirds the way through, he found a five-page copy of an old newspaper article from 1956 recapping the death of Carmen Grossman, the wife of Johann Schmidt. There was a photo of the deceased at an early age. Andrés observed that she bore no resemblance to her daughter, Astrid.

There was also a typewritten note in a different font size that stated that the coroner had ruled Carmen had died in childbirth. But Mirón noted that the local hospital had no record of any birth from Schmidt's wife. The death certificate also stated that there was no next of kin besides Johann. Matilda's name was nowhere to be found.

There was also a two-page copy of a Ministry of Justice's investigative report on Sellarebu Pharmaceutical Laboratories. It mentioned a secret project involving the development of a serum named the Faust Cocktail and the feasibility of genetic engineering of human embryos for military purposes.

Andrés picked up his phone, "I would like to speak to Detective Campos please."

CHAPTER 57

SANDRINE

Sunday, August 4, 1974, San Francisco

The cooler weather had returned. The morning had been overcast. There was the normal hustle and bustle at the church when the trio of Doña Matilda and the two youngsters attended mass. Little children wore tiny knit sweaters and caps. After the service, the congregation poured out of the church. Some people stood around and conversed with others. A salt and pepper couple passed out leaflets for a rally in Oakland that afternoon. Others whisked away their families in order to return home or go out for breakfast.

Today Doña Matilda made an unusual request of Andrés and Astrid. She didn't want to be driven home. She was going to talk to the pastor and then run some errands. She would take a taxi back.

Andrés offered to come back and pick her up at a time certain but she graciously declined.

After they drove off, Doña Matilda went to see the priest in the rectory. She told him of her dilemma about leaving her niece alone in a foreign country when she returned to Chile. He tried to comfort her advising her that God would give her an answer. While she felt a little better, she thought, *I don't need an answer . . . I need the right answer.*

☙

At the back of a Middle Eastern eatery, the silver grey

haired woman stood up as Matilda approached her. The older woman had one eye half closed and had scabs on her disfigured face. They gave each other a heartfelt hug. The wonderful smells of Arabian spices were dissipating into the dining room from the small kitchen.

"Well, Matilda, we have so much to discuss," said the throaty voice, "At least this time it is under better circumstances."

"I am so puzzled with everything that happened," Matilda shared. "Who was Schmidt really?"

"Let me order some hot tea and shawarma for us. Hummus?"

Matilda nodded her head politely. She had no idea what Sandrine was talking about.

"A long time ago, before the Second World War, I was a happy young girl working in a bookstore with my fiancé in Vienna," Sandrine began.

Sandrine narrated a tale about her and her sister being betrayed by a young doctor named Augustin Teufl. He had been responsible for them being sent to Auschwitz where they were experimented on, tortured, raped, and subjected to all types of crimes against humanity. She also explained about the Doctors Trials where Teufl was a key witness against the Nazi hierarchy, for which he was granted immunity.

Sandrine said that she had been working for Justice International, the organization that tried to bring these criminals to justice.

"What happened to your fiancé when you suddenly disappeared?"

"He had tried to find me, but Teufl deceived him," continued Sandrine in a passionless monotone. "He was told we had gone to Italy."

The food came and was placed on the white resin table. Sandrine did not stop her narration. Eventually, after the Russians liberated her from the concentration camp, she had tried to find her fiancé, Delčevç. He had gone to New York City. She returned to Vienna and found out more about the cruel medical experiments by the Nazis. She testified against the German doctors at the War Crimes trials. Afterwards, Kulongoski recruited her into Justice International as a secret agent. Her cover was working as a nurse in a hospital for several years. In 1972, she came to New York only to find out that Delčevç had married. He broke down when he found out that she was still alive. He was forlorn and he cried, but said he could not divorce his wife because he had four children. Sandrine pretended to empathize, but realized that the Nazis had ruined her life.

She started working for the Justice International office in New York City. She was assigned to investigate the Nazi fugitives who had started Sellarebu Pharmaceutical Laboratories in Argentina. After months of investigative research, she had surmised that when Augustin Teufl disappeared from the planet, he had assumed a new identity, namely that of Johann Schmidt.

When Schmidt came to San Francisco, Hubert Gniewosz and his sister Nan Hill, who were both JI operatives, had positively identified him as a Nazi concentration camp doctor. "Bert" and "Nan" posed as domestic help in order to monitor Schmidt. Sandrine had been assigned to assist in transferring Schmidt to the Jewish Defense League who had him on its wanted list.

"You know the rest," Sandrine had not touched her meal. It had gotten cold.

"I am so sorry for you," empathized Matilda. "How are

you feeling? Did you ever see a doctor?"

Sandrine nodded her head no. "So you are going back to Chile, Matilda. Will you try to rejoin the convent there?"

"I can't," she sighed. "I have blood on my hands. I killed somebody."

"I had to kill somebody too because of that monster," Sandrine became unnerved. "That is why I wanted him dead. My sister died because of him! Remember that God helps those who help themselves!"

Matilda had heard what Sandrine said. Was she justified in killing the attacker? Was it God's will? She needed to meditate on it. But not now. Later. She decided to shift the direction of the conversation.

"What are you going to do now, Sandrine?" Matilda gently put her hand on the shoddy, moth-eaten shawl that covered her companion. "You can live with me in Santiago. You can have a decent life. Are you still working for Justice International?"

"I haven't reported in yet," Sandrine was starting to calm down. "I am probably terminated anyway for what happened the other night. They probably think that I'm dead. I need to stay off everyone's radar for a while. But thank you anyway for the offer."

"In many ways, we are sisters," Matilda said in a soft tone. "I have a proposition for you."

Matilda explained the dilemma with her niece. She asked Sandrine if she would keep an eye on Astrid while she attended college without her niece knowing. She added that Sandrine would be handsomely compensated for the favor.

"I don't know if I would be any good at it," admitted Sandrine, "but I can give it a try."

"Thank you."

"You're not going to thank me after you read this," Sandrine handed her a file in a manila envelope. "My JI contact in Chile tracked it down."

ଔ

Astrid wanted to go to Andrés apartment after they had dropped her aunt off at church.

"I just want to enjoy my last few days of freedom," she suggested. "Let's go to your place."

What the heck? He thought. *I have a few things I have to do at home.*

When they arrived at his place, he retrieved a couple of soft drinks from the refrigerator.

He pulled out the piece of scrap paper with the German phrases written on it and sat on the sofa.

Astrid jumped down next to him before he had an opportunity to say anything. "Are you going to miss me when I'm gone?"

"No," he said with a straight face.

"Why, you brat!" she jumped on top of him and started to lightly pound him.

He wrapped his arms around her to stop the pummeling. She quit the barrage and tried to hug Andrés. She reached up to kiss him.

"Astrid, please don't"

"Why not?" she attacked his neck.

He pulled back. "I know that I must be a jerk to say 'no' to you," he was looking seriously at her. "But, I made a promise to your father. I have to keep it. I have to be righteous."

"But what about before?" she pouted.

"I think that I am beginning to understand what being a grownup is all about," Andrés replied.

ଔ

Andrés and Astrid had barely made it back to the Schmidt house before the taxi dropped Matilda off.

The matron walked up the stairs to her bedroom and closed the door. *Why had Sandrine acted so strangely when she gave me this manila envelope?*

She tore open the thick packet and found a copy of a PAGE folder. She saw a sticky label adhered to its back and discovered that the acronym stood for Physicians Against Genetic Engineering. This file puzzled Matilda. She was proficient in German and with ease began to peruse the document.

The name of Carmen Grossman appeared in the tab of the folder. *That was her sister! What was this all about?*

Matilda's hands started to press together as she read each section of the file. Her stomach began to feel acidy. According to the medical documentation, Carmen had been artificially inseminated with a genetically mutated embryo without her knowledge. There was a daily log of readings, medications, and other information on the expectant mother.

The folder also had several photos of Carmen Grossman and strands of hair in a clear plastic bag. The last page was a DNA report.

Sad tears slid down Matilda's cheeks. It had been a horrific experience reading the surrogate pregnancy of her sister that ended in her death.

೦೪

Andrés was sleepy as he entered the police station late Sunday night before going home. Detective Campos had instructed him to drop off the new materials with the watch commander because he would not be in the office until Monday morning. Andrés initially had been carrying only the information from Chile for the detective. Now an hour ago Doña Matilda had given Andrés the medical reports from Sandrine that Campos had to see.

Doña Matilda appeared to be despondent so he didn't ask her any questions. Andrés was scared that she had found out about his afternoon rendezvous with Astrid. He was fearful about peeking at the new documents, but knew something was amiss.

03

"What do you mean you found zilch?" barked the flat-topped solidly built dark suit. "What in the f__k happened?"

"We looked all through the house. We searched all the possessions and the entire premises several times," Neumann was nervously recoiling. "We looked here and in Chile. We didn't find anything."

"We saw the executive summary of the Schmidt report at that Next Generation cabinet meeting," stated the blue-eyed military veteran. "You had one of your minions read the English translation, so please don't tell me the research never existed."

"No, but maybe he destroyed it," feebly offered Neumann.

"We have spent millions of dollars to get a military advantage and you f__ked it up!" screamed the old warhorse.

Neumann knew that the human military drone industry would be worth billions, but he didn't care. He had already bought a one-way plane ticket to Miami. He was leaving within the next few hours. From there he didn't know if he was going to return to Chile, Uruguay, or Germany. Maybe he would transfer his money to the Cayman Islands and chill out in the Caribbean for a year. He would lose his U.S. visa soon enough anyway. He just didn't want to "disappear" at the hands of the U.S. military.

CHAPTER 58

EXODUS

Friday, August 9, 1974, San Francisco

Campos sat down in the booth at the back of the Kopper Kettle as Grace was dropping two sugars into her coffee. She had called the detective at home the night before and set up this breakfast tête-à-tête. The breakfast place was filled with the neighborhood regulars who would sit at the counter nursing a coffee, smoking cigarettes, talking loudly, and then leaving a meager tip after two hours.

"What's going on, Grace?"

"Shit has been hitting the fan all week within the agency," the FBI agent remarked. "But let me tell you about the Schmidt case first."

Gretchen, the waitress, came over and poured Campos a cup of coffee. Grace and Campos were now reviewing the menu, even though they ordered the same item every time.

"You were lucky that they transferred the case away from you guys," she shook her head. "That company that Schmidt worked for, Sellarebu Pharmaceutical Laboratories, is really bad news. Several of our international sources have it on their watch lists. It seems that this company has been involved in some sort of crazy ass shit research with Brazilian native tribes."

"What kind of research are we talking about?" Campos was now awake.

"The intel that I received from Doctors Without Borders said that they were conducting eugenic experiments on mothers that resulted in the delivery of mutant children. Genetic mutations. Radiation. Chemicals. All sorts of bad stuff."

"Ick!" Campos shook his head in disgust. "Did any of the tests deal with twins? Especially identical twins?"

"I don't know. It wasn't specifically mentioned," she put catsup on the hash browns that Gretchen had served her and now she was salting the over-easy eggs. "They also think that the Nazis had done some more elementary experiments on Namibian slaves during the Second World War."

"Who in the heck are the Namibians?" Campos asked, forking a piece of maple-flavored, syrup-covered pancake into his mouth.

"South Africans."

They ate and discussed the information for another half hour. Patrons were never in a hurry to leave the place, much to the Gretchen's chagrin.

☷

The flight to Santiago was being called for boarding. There was crying and people saying their goodbyes in Spanish. The passengers started to line up in a queue.

Doña Matilda was dressed in somber black garb with her head wrapped with a dark colored rebozo.

"Andrés, thank you for everything," she leaned over and gave him a tender embrace.

Astrid looked at her aunt, grabbed her hand, and held it to her chest.

☷

Neumann claimed his two brown leather suitcases and exited the baggage area of the Miami Airport. His eyes carefully perused the queue of chauffeur drivers waiting for their clients.

He spotted a tall, well-built driver holding a small white sign with the name of "Alfred Nuss." He went straight to him and dropped his two bags in front of him.

The driver tipped his cap and said, "*Willkommen, mein Herr.*"

Neumann nodded. He was using an alias on his transcontinental journey.

The chauffeur carried the luggage to a black Mercedes limousine. He opened the back door for Neumann before loading the two suitcases into the hold.

"*Das Fountainebleau, bitte,*" Neumann directed the driver to the hotel.

He would stay a few days in Miami and then decide where to go and spend his money. All is fair in love and war, he thought as he grinned to himself. The U.S. could never have even gotten this far with their human military drone project without his assistance. What a bunch of *Scheisseköpfe!*

α

Matilda had been totally overwhelmed by the file that Sandrine had given her. It was a terrible secret that had been revealed to her.

Her sister Carmen had been a young secretary working for Sellarebu Pharmaceutical Laboratories when she married Johann Schmidt. Guilelessly, Carmen had undergone several medical procedures under the pretense that the doctors told her that she had an inverted uterus. The medical people were, of course, SPL people. A mutated embryo that had been manufactured with the cloned cells from Keichelle's lock of hair was inserted into her womb without her knowledge. The special doctors convinced her that she had a very risky pregnancy and required her to come in for checkups on a weekly basis.

The delivery led to a healthy baby girl. At the same time, the mother had been euthanized with an injection of sodium thiopental, potassium chloride, and pancuronium bromide. The autopsy report listed it as a death in childbirth. They did not want to leave any evidence of the artificial insemination.

Astrid was initially raised by Johann in his home until it was discovered that Carmen had a surviving twin sister who one day showed up at his doorstep unannounced.

CS

There was a subsequent boarding call for her flight. Andrés handed over Matilda's brown leather satchel that he had been toting for her.

All week Matilda had debated in her mind about what she was going to do with Astrid and what she was going to tell her about her parentage. Was Astrid even really her niece?

During one of her last confessions, she had again asked the priest for advice, but he naturally demurred to the Will of God lecture. On Tuesday night Matilda announced to Astrid that she was allowing her niece to attend Mills College. Matilda had made arrangements with the college for Astrid to move into student housing starting that weekend.

The next day, the movers had transported Astrid's possessions that were mostly comprised of all types of clothing, cutesy toys and souvenirs, and some of her father's books. The rest of the Schmidts' belongings filled the large moving van. The house was now empty.

Astrid and her aunt had been residing in a hotel for the last few days. Matilda was still pondering on when would be the appropriate time to share with Astrid the mystery surrounding her birth.

ℭ

"Where in heck is your partner?" Grace was finishing up the last piece of buttered toast.

"Who knows?" Campos was on his third cup of coffee. "Am I my brother's keeper?"

Grace looked at her watch impatiently.

"Hey, I drew a blank with the inquiry down in Chile," she recited without any emotion as she pushed her plate away. "I contacted the authorities down there. There was a formal request to exhume the body and run toxicological and other tests. Unfortunately, the body of Carmen Grossman was cremated."

"It figures."

ℭ

Matilda walked down the jet way. She was heartbroken that she was leaving Astrid behind. She didn't have the heart to tell Astrid about her background.

She sat down in her seat next to a middle-aged woman and pulled out her rosary. She began to pray.

What difference would it make? She loved Astrid. She had raised her. Blood was overrated. Astrid had been given to her as a gift from God. She began to pray. God helps those who help themselves, she thought.

ℭ

Neumann had poured himself a stiff drink from the bar in the back of the limousine. He started to doze off.

The outline of the city started to fade. The beaches were lit up with thousands of lights.

People were out in the streets at all hours of the day and night dancing and making noise.

A half hour later the road veered to the right and the way became darker. The number of cars became fewer and fewer.

Without warning, the limousine pulled in behind an abandoned gasoline station. The driver turned the engine off.

Four men wearing black masks over their faces rushed over and opened the back door of the limo. Two of them roughly grabbed the drugged passenger and dragged him toward a light green telephone company van.

The chauffeur knew that high rollers and pretenders to the throne always imbibed. However, this time the liquor had been spiked with a powerful sedative, compliments of the Israelis.

The pair gagged Neumann's mouth with duct tape and tied his hands and feet. He was tossed into the back of the van.

The third man had retrieved both of Neumann's suitcases and the chauffeur's little white sign. These items were thrown into the van also.

The last and seemingly oldest of the kidnappers went over to the chauffeur and handed him an envelope.

"*Toda lecha*" [Thank you, friend.]

ଓଃ

Andrés escorted Astrid to the taxi stand outside the San Francisco Airport terminal. Jet fuel adulterated the air. They stood in line behind business travelers.

The niece had been emotional about her aunt's departure. Her face was wet with tears.

On the other hand, Astrid had been elated that she was being allowed to attend college. This weekend Andrés would accompany her to her new lodging in the East Bay. Matilda had slipped him a white envelope. The thousand dollars would help him survive the upcoming school year. He was eternally grateful.

There was also a handwritten note in the envelope. It

was from Astrid. His eyes read through the note that said: "*Friendship is an ocean of which you can not see bottom.*"

"I've never been separated from my aunt," Astrid gave a sigh as she gave him a tempting look. "Who is going to be my guardian angel?"

Andrés just smiled. He was reluctant to take the bait. He had thought that Astrid might still be mad at him, but the note indicated otherwise. The taxi coordinator motioned for them to enter the yellow cab.

"Where to?" asked the Middle Eastern driver.

"We can go to my hotel room or your apartment," the young vixen put her hand on his thigh. "Afternoon delight?"

Andrés was awe stricken. He was speechless, but his head nodded negatively.

"Chill!" she laughed, "I just want you as my friend."

ೞ

Detective Leland Leong finally arrived at the Kopper Kettle. The dishes had been cleared and the check had been set on the table.

"Sorry, I'm late," he sat down next to Campos and threw the morning paper onto the table.

"I guess you'll be staying a little longer," Gretchen poured out a fresh cup of coffee for the new arrival. "Are you going to order something else?"

"The usual for me," casually stated Leong. "Hey, did you guys know about this?" He picked up the newspaper and held it up for his colleagues to read.

The bagel with cream cheese and jelly was placed next to Leong.

"NIXON RESIGNS" headlined the paper. Several stories reported that facing near-certain impeachment in the House of Representatives and a strong possibility of a conviction in the Senate, Nixon resigned the presidency effective August 9, 1974.

"I need to be going," Grace suddenly got up to leave. "There is a rumor that I'm getting a promotion or demotion because of this Schmidt disaster.

"And, yeah, like I said, all hell's breaking out at the agency. There have been several unsubstantiated rumors the last few days that some sort of top secret reports were anonymously sent to former Attorney General Richardson, Deputy AG Ruckelhaus, Senate pro temp Eastland, and General Haig."

"What type of reports?" Campos asked with an innocent look.

"Some bizarre shit," Grace threw up her hands in the air. "A clandestine operation by the Defense Department working with neo-Nazis to create human military drones. Something called the Seele Project."

"I wonder who leaked the info, David?" Leong asked his partner.

ABOUT THE AUTHOR

Rocky Barilla lives in the San Francisco Bay Area with his wife, Dolores, and the dozens of feathered friends who visit the bird feeder daily. He was formally educated at the University of Southern California and at Stanford University. He spent two academic quarters in Vienna, Austria.

His passions are 19th Century French literary fiction, Mexican history, global traveling, and cooking. He is a bad golfer.

Rocky has been actively involved in human rights issues, especially involving Latinos and other people of color.

He is the author of "A Taste of Honey" (Second Place Winner in the category of Fantasy/Science Fiction in the 2015 International Latino Book Awards) and "Ay to Zi" (anticipated date of publication 2016).

His mantra is "Life is Good."

Made in the USA
San Bernardino, CA
19 August 2018